THE BIRTH OF A MONSTER

"It was on a dreary night of November that I beheld the accomplishments of my toils. With an anxiety that almost amounted to agony, I collected the instruments of life around me, that I might infuse a spark of being into the lifeless thing that lay at my feet. It was already one in the morning; the rain pattered dismally against the panes, and my candle was nearly burnt out, when by the glimmer of the half-extinguished light I saw the dull yellow eye of the creature open; it breathed hard, and a convulsive motion agitated its limbs . . ."

That is Mary Shelley's version of what happened on that dark and stormy night. Now learn the awful truth . . .

THE
FRANKENSTEIN
PAPERS

FRED SABERHAGEN
THE
FRANKENSTEIN PAPERS

BAEN
SCIENCE FICTION
BOOKS

THE FRANKENSTEIN PAPERS

This is a work of fiction. All the characters and events portrayed in this book are fictional, and any resemblance to real people or incidents is purely coincidental.

A Baen Books Original

Baen Publishing Enterprises
260 Fifth Avenue
New York, N.Y. 10001

First printing, February 1986

ISBN: 0-671-65550-7

Cover art by Steve Hickson

Printed in the United States of America

Distributed by
SIMON & SCHUSTER
MASS MERCHANDISE SALES COMPANY
1230 Avenue of the Americas
New York, N.Y. 10020

Of Medical Electricity

The firft application of electricity to the cure of diseafes was made by M. Jallabert, profeffor of philofophy at Geneva, on a lockfmith whofe right arm had been paralytic fifteen years ... He was brought to M. Jallabert on the 26th of December 1747, and was compleatly cured by the 28th of February 1748. In this interval he was frequently electrified, fparks being taken from the arm, and fometimes the electrical fhock fent through it.

Dr. Franklin and others mention fome paralytic cafes, in which electricity feemed rather to make the patient worfe than better.

Mr. Wilfon cured a woman of a deafnefs of feventeen years ftanding—and Mr. Lovet confiders electricity as a fpecific in all cafes of violent pains, obftinate headachs, the fiatica, and the cramp. The toothach, he fays, is generally cured by it in an inftant. He relates a cafe, from Mr. Floyer furgeon at Dorchester, of a compleat cure of a gutta ferena; and another of obftinate obftructions in two young women.

Hitherto electricity has been generally applied to the human body either in the method of drawing fparks, as it is called, or of giving fhocks. But thefe operations are both violent, and though the ftrong concuffion may fuit fome cafes, it may be of differvice in others, where a moderate fimple electrification might have been of ufe.

The great objection to this method is the tedioufnefs and expence of the application. But an electrical machine might be contrived to go by wind or water, and a convenient room might be annexed to it, in which a floor might be raifed upon electrics, a perfon might fit down, read, fleep, or even walk about during the electrification.

It were to be willed, that fome phyfician of underftanding and fpirit would provide himfelf with fuch a machine and room. No harm could poffibly be apprehended from electricity, applied in this gentle and intenfible manner, and good effects are at leaft poffible, if not highly probable.

Chapter 1

May? 1782?

I bite the bear.

I bit the bear.

I have bitten the white bear, and the taste of its blood has given me strength. Not physical strength—that I have never lacked—but the confidence to manage my own destiny as best I can.

With this confidence, my life begins anew. That I may think anew, and act anew, from this time on I will write in English, here on this English ship. My command of that language is more than adequate, though how that ever came to be God alone can know.

How *I* have come to be, God perhaps does not know. It may be that that knowledge is, or was, reserved to one other, who has—or had—more right than God to be called my Creator.

My first object in beginning this journal is to cling to the fierce sense of purpose that has been reborn in me. My second is to try to keep myself sane. Or to restore myself to sanity, if, as sometimes seems to me likely, madness is indeed the true explanation of the situation, or condition, in which I find myself—in which I believe myself to be.

But I verge on babbling. If I am to write at all—and I must—let me do so coherently.

I have bitten the white bear, and the blood of the bear has given me life. True enough. But if anyone who reads is to understand then I must write of other matters first.

Yes, if I am to assume this task—or therapy—of journal-keeping, then let me at least be methodical about it. A good way to make a beginning, I must believe, would be to give an objective, calm description of myself, my condition, and my surroundings. All else, I believe—I must hope—can be built from that.

My surroundings: I am writing this aboard a ship, using the captain's notebook and his pencils. He was wise not to trust that ink would remain unfrozen.

I am quite alone, and on such a voyage as I am sure was never contemplated by the captain, or the owners, or the builders of this stout vessel, *Mary Goode.* (The bows are crusted a foot thick with ice, an accumulation perhaps of decades; but the name is plain on many of the papers in this cabin.)

A fire burns in the captain's little stove, warms my fingers as I write, but I see by a small sullen glow of sunlight emanating from the south—a direction that here encompasses most of the horizon.

Little enough of that sunlight finds its way in through the cabin windows, though one of the windows is now free of glass, sealed only with a thin panel of clear ice.

In every direction lie fields of ice, a world of white unmarked by any work of man except this frozen hulk. What fate may have befallen the particular man on the floor of whose cabin I now sleep—the berth is hopelessly small—or the rest of the crew of the *Mary Goode*, I can only guess. There is no clue, or if a clue exists I am too concerned with my own condition and my own fate to look for it or recognize it. I can imagine them all bound in by ice aboard this ship, until they chose, over the certainty of starvation, the desperate alternative of committing themselves to the ice.

Patience. Write calmly.

I have lost count of how many timeless days I have been aboard this otherwise forsaken hulk. There is, of course, almost no night here at present. And there are times when my memory is confused. I have written above that it is May, because the daylight is still waxing steadily—and perhaps because I am afraid it is already June, with the beginning of the months of darkness soon to come.

I have triumphed over the white bear. What, then, do I need to fear?

The truth, perhaps?

I said that I should begin with a description of myself, but now I see that so far I have avoided that unpleasant task. Forward, then. There is a small mirror in this cabin, frost-glued to the wall, but I have not crouched before it. No matter. I

know quite well what I should see. A shape man-
like but gigantic, an integument unlike that of any
other being, animal or human, that I can remember seeing. Neither Asiatic, African, nor European,
mine is a yellow skin that, though thick and tough,
seems to lack its proper base, revealing in outline
the networked veins and nerves and muscles underneath. White teeth, that in another face would
be thought beautiful, in mine, surrounded by thin
blackish lips, are hideous. Hair, straight, black,
and luxuriant; a scanty beard.

My physical proportions are in general those of
the race of men. My size, alas, is not. Victor
Frankenstein, half proud and half horrified at the
work of his own hands, has more than once told
me that I am eight feet tall. Not that I have ever
measured. Certainly this cabin's overhead is much
too low for me to stand erect. Nor, I think, has my
weight ever been accurately determined—not since
I rose from my creator's work table—but it must
approximate that of two ordinary men. No human's clothing that I have ever tried has been big
enough, nor has any human's chair or bed. Fortunately I still have my own boots, handmade for me
at my creator's—I had almost said my master's—
order, and I have such furs and wraps, gathered
here and there across Europe, as can be wrapped
and tied around my body to protect me from the
cold.

Sometimes, naked here in the heated cabin, washing myself and my wrappings as best I can in
melted snow, I take a closer inventory. What I see
forces me to respect my maker's handiwork; his
skill, however hideous its product, left no scars, no

visible joinings anywhere. Such skill as he was unable or unwilling to exert again, when the time came— but I anticipate.

My navel might once indeed have been the terminal of the cord of birth—but I know that it was not. My two arms, both huge and muscular, seem, like my two legs, a matched pair—did each limb once live and grow upon a different body? And what of my brain? Could it conceivably be compound too, with all the languages that it contains? And the strange, fleeting memories, that sometimes come and go, and puzzle me. *He* would never tell me whence it came.

And, surely, no single human individual was ever cursed with this face I bear. Oh my creator, whose handiwork in other details approaches wizardry, if not Deity, why did you curse me so?

And why did you not give me a name?

Was hatred for me growing in you even then?

The earliest memories of my present life are not yet three years old. But in trying to sound even such shallow depths, I must part clouds more thick than any polar darkness. It seems to me that the first language that I ever spoke was German. But I cannot be sure. It may have been French, for I have spoken and can speak that too, and quite well. In whatever body my brain first grew, it leaned much there; and some of what it learned, for good or ill, has come to me.

The first remembrance I can call up is of a tiny room. It is high up under someone's roof, because it has a slanted ceiling. Though the window is partially open, within closed shutters, the atmosphere is tainted with the smell of rotten meat, and acrid with chemicals and electricity. Logic—and perhaps other things as well—assure me that this is the room at the top of the house where the student Victor Frankenstein then lodged, in an old and quiet quarter of the Bavarian university town of Ingolstadt,—where he lodged, and where he did his secret work.

I am standing beside an empty table—there is just height enough for me to stand upright under the pitched roof—and feeling overwhelmed with the narrow meanness of this cramped and noisome room, that forms the only world that I as yet have known. Fitful flashes from a thunderstorm provide the only real illumination. The shelves that occupy most of the walls of the room, and the two other tables besides the empty one, are filled with jars, bottles, electrical apparatus, whose meaning I but dimly comprehend.

I am alone, and it is night, rain beating on the single window and dripping on the sill, thunder grumbling not far away. A sleepy human voice or two, in other, distant rooms of the big house, are murmuring about the *donner*. A bolt has just struck somewhere in the near vicinity.

Though as far as I can tell this is the very beginning of my consciousness, I am not an infant mentally. I can walk. I do not foul myself with my own wastes. My hands are fumbling with something around my collar—somehow I have already acquired clothing, real clothing, much better than the rude wrappings that I am wearing now.

I know what a door is, and how to open one. And

this door, anyway, is already standing very slightly ajar.

Moments later I am in another room, this one on the next level of the house down from the top. This is a small bedchamber; I draw back the curtain of the bed, and by the light of a guttering bedside candle I behold a young man lying there, fully dressed in good but neglected clothing, fitfully asleep. It was, of course, none other than Victor Frankenstein who lay before me, though I did not yet know his name. In some senses I recognized him. I think I understood even then, somehow, that he was someone of great importance to me.

The young man stirred as I gazed at him, and opened bloodshot eyes. He stared back at me with the horrified gaze of one who awakens to find that what he had thought a nightmare is indeed reality. His movement in the bed, edging away, wafted toward me a wave of fumes, strange to me then, but now, in memory, identifiable as those of brandy.

I stretched out a hand toward him, and uttered an inarticulate sound. What purpose was behind my gesture I do not know, but I intended no harm. He uttered a choked cry and rolled out of the bed on the side away from me. A moment later he had sprung past me and was out the door, and I heard the quick sounds of his booted feet descending stairs.

Exactly what I did immediately after that, what I thought, what I felt, I am not sure. I know only that I must have fled the house.

I find I must pause now in this effort. Those early memories are too strong for me.

*   *   *

Later— I must keep on with this journal for the sake of my sanity. And soon I must search the ship again, and more thoroughly, for provisions. Though if, as I suppose, her crew abandoned her when threatened by starvation, there seems little chance that any substantial stores remain.

For now, back to the fierce chore of remembering.

The next scene to come clearly out of the mist is set out of doors, in a gloomy November forest that must have been near Ingolstadt. It is early morning, shortly after dawn, some days after my first clear memory.

I have been sleeping, and today is my turn to be awakened. Someone, using a hound, has tracked me down. I emerge from chaotic dreams and stick my head out of my shelter, a half-fallen tree, to see two human beings and one hound staring down at me.

The young men are much too well dressed to be peasants. I need a moment to realize that one of them, dark-haired and slender, is the same man I saw lying in bed amid brandy fumes a few days earlier, terrified of me. Now, in daylight, the expression on his face is different, more complex, harder to describe or to understand. Fear has not vanished from his countenance, but it has been joined there by elation, shame, disgust, and pride, all struggling to dominate. His breathing is heavy, I think more because of this emotional turmoil than with the exertions of his trot through the woods behind his hound. The animal, not liking me—dogs seldom do—backs a little way into a thicket, grumbling.

"There you are," the young man said to me,

confronting me, fists on hips. I have not the words, in English or any other tongue, to describe the mixture of feelings evident in his tone.

The other young man has hair of a lighter brown, and a frame not really much bigger. But somehow he seems hardier and sturdier than slender Frankenstein. He is so far exhibiting little except sheer astonishment. From the way his jaw works he would like to say something pertinent as he gapes at me, but thus far he is speechless. I will come to know him later as Henry Clerval.

Frightened, I too am wordless as I crawl forth and stand erect. As I leave the tree my movement pulls out with me the nest of leaves and grass that had kept me warm enough to sleep. I was on the point of running away, even as last time he, now my discoverer, had fled from me.

"Stay!" he said to me sharply. "I am Victor Frankenstein. I am your creator."

"Creator." Dazed by the idea, I mouthed the word back at him numbly. Standing, towering above him, I took an uncertain step toward him, once more reaching out a hand.

Frankenstein took a quick step back, and his hand went near the curve of a short wooden handle at his belt. I took no more steps forward. I understood the meaning of a pistol even then. Beside him, Clerval stood as if paralyzed.

"The power of speech is yours, then,"the youth who had already spoken muttered in a strange, almost feverish tone. "Repeat my name!" he commanded briskly.

"Victor Frankenstein."

"Ah. Good. And some degree of understanding."

He turned to his companion. "The cerebrum is not decayed after all, Henry, or at least . . . residual memory in the fibers. As I had hoped." He spoke confidently but gestured vaguely; his companion gaped at him, hoping intently for enlightenment, not getting much.

Regaining his assurance, Frankenstein stepped forward. For the moment pride and wonder were uppermost in him, his fear and loathing put aside.

"I made you," he murmured to me, and in his voice were tones I have since heard in the prayers of the devout. "I really did."

And was it French that the three of us were speaking together on that day? But no, I think that it was German.

Whatever the language, I could not at first believe that statement when he made it, that simple claim to be the author of my being. And yet I think that, on some deep contradictory level of my being, I already was convinced.

The hound, after circling me uneasily a time or two, had lain down, while Victor paced back and forth under the dripping trees, hands clasped behind his back. Clerval had gradually overcome his paralysis; I could see that he was thinking now, staring at me as he stroked his chin. I stared back, trying to comprehend the marvel that I had just been told.

Frankenstein stopped his pacing suddenly and said: "I am going to write about him to Priestley in London, and to Franklin in Philadelphia. To others as well. Cavendish, I suppose, though he'll never answer. Let me see. Mesmer. Lavoisier. And to Edinburgh, the medical school there . . ."

"I think that Franklin is not in Philadelphia," said Clerval softly. He was preparing some kind of additional objection, I thought, when I interrupted him.

"What is my name?" I asked. My voice is strong and deep, but I have been told that it is not unpleasant.

Frankenstein appeared surprised at the question, almost as if it had come from one of his laboratory animals.

"I do not know," he replied at length. "I never gave you a name. I suppose that now you are at liberty to choose one for yourself, should you feel the need." Awe grew in his voice as he was speaking, and as he uttered the last words he was staring at me again in simple wonder.

I did feel the need for a name, or I should not have asked the question. For that moment at least it had seemed of immense importance. Yet I had no idea of what name I ought to have.

As I stood dumbly by, my creator was starting to make plans with Clerval. "He cannot stay here. Obviously. There's no telling what trouble he might get into. And I cannot bring him back to the house . . ."

"No, hardly," Henry cautiously agreed.

"Nor, I think, anywhere in Ingolstadt. I think he must be taken to Geneva . . . or somewhere near there." In ecstasy and agony, he stared at me again. "I must have time to think. To plan."

"I'll help you," Henry Clerval assured him. Then Henry addressed me boldly, while holding one hand, perhaps unconsciously, near his own pistol. He demanded: "How do you live here? Are you troubling the local peasants? What do you eat?"

"I sleep here." I pointed to the hollow tree from which my dried leaves had spilled. "I eat—what I can find. Sometimes the people—the peasants—see me, but they always cry out and run away when that happens. I don't try to follow them. Victor, I am—"

"You are not to call me 'Victor'." Frankenstein said quickly. I believe he shuddered. "By rights it should be 'master', I suppose."

"Master." I tried the word out on my tongue; French, German, English—in whatever language, I like it not, and did not like it then. Though it is hard now for me to remember just what I was thinking then. Perhaps I was scarcely capable of thought at all, but only dealt with things as they happened in the world around me, and grasped at memories—odd things, mostly fragments that came and went before they could be seized and examined closely. My mind, perhaps, had not yet cleared from the electric trauma of my birth.

The two young men began to take food from their wallets and put it before me, setting some of it on the ground, as if I were an animal—or some minor deity being offered sacrifice. I was hungry, as always—I fell to and began to eat. Bread, cheese, sausage. The food they provided was better than anything I had yet been able to find in the forest.

Victor—it was not long before he changed his mind and gave his tacit consent that I should call him that; what closer relationship could two beings have?—Victor, I say, went on pacing and thinking aloud. Soon they had the rudiments of a plan; between them they were starting to work something out.

I was commanded to stay where I was, by which they meant near the spot where we were presently standing. In a few days they would return, bringing more food, and meet me on a disused road nearby. They would be driving an old carriage, a wagon, some kind of inconspicuous vehicle which they would obtain in the meantime.

Clerval insisted that someone named Roger would have to be consulted on the scheme—Roger was spoken of, by both of them, with uncertainty and respect. Frankenstein was uncertain about everything, and plainly relieved to have the support of his friends in dealing with his so passionately sought responsibility—that is to say, myself.

When they had brought the wagon, I would ride concealed in the vehicle while they drove. Somehow I would be taken to Geneva, the city where Victor's family lived and where he could be sure of additional help. Somewhere in the vicinity of Geneva I would lie concealed, while my creator-master and his friend Henry—presumably still in conference with the mysterious Roger—pondered what to do with me next.

I listened to it all, bemused, uncertain, not knowing what part of the strange world around me I ought to trust, unless it should be this man who said he had created me, and his companions. Rather than listening to the planning so intently, I should have watched their faces, and tried to gauge the depths within their souls. But how could I have done that then?

In any event, their plan, as I shall relate, was altered drastically.

*   *   *

Again I find that I must pause in my struggle with these memories. At the same time I must continue writing, to retain a hold on sanity, and on my newly-restored determination to deal with the world around me. I have conquered the white bear . . .

Let me relate more of what has happened since I came to be the sole voyager upon this ice-bound ship. Oh yes, it is indeed a voyage that I now endure, and not sheer immobility. The ice is moving. The sounds it makes are proof enough of that, even if it were not possible to see the great cakes sliding and crumbling along the *Mary Goode's* stout timbered sides. Toward what destiny the ship may be drifting, and how rapidly, are questions I cannot hope to answer while there are no real landmarks to be seen. Only rarely in the midst of this months-long day, darkened only by brief periods of twilight can I even glimpse the stars or moon. And the sun, never moving far from the horizon, is of but little help in determining my location. I can make a rough judgment of south and north, and that is all.

Have I not already mentioned the circumstances of my first arrival at the ship? It came at the end of a flight of nearly a year, that had begun in Paris when I realized that Franklin was unable to help me, and that my enemies, Frankenstein among them, were closing in on me again.

From Paris I traveled ever north and east, thinking to lead my pursuers ever farther from the lands with which they were familiar, and in which their wealth and power had their roots. Month after month I fled from them, by coach, on foot, and at last, from the vicinity of Archangel, by dogsled.

When I came upon the *Mary Goode* I was staggering on foot over the ice, my dogs long since eaten or drowned. I had abandoned the last platform-portion of my sled when most of my supplies were gone and it would no longer serve me as a raft. In such a plight I came sliding and scrambling toward the ship, because in all the vast white emptiness there was no other goal in sight.

Exhausted by my long flight, I dragged my hungry, weary body aboard the hulk. Here in this cabin I found lamps, oil, a stove, and wood aplenty. I contrived to start a fire. That done, I pulled the bedding from the captain's bunk and, wrapped in what had once been the captain's blankets, fell into a slumber so intense that it was akin to a swoon.

How much time I have been asleep since reaching the ship I cannot say, only that most of my time aboard has been spent in that condition. There have been intervals of full wakefulness, in each of which I have been increasingly aware of hunger. Each time I awoke I fed the stove, and melted ice and snow on it to drink. Then I fell into oblivion again, wrapped in furs and blankets. Sometimes on awakening I ate sparingly from the small stock of provisions I still had. Later, somewhat rested, and increasingly aware of my plight, I began to search the ship more or less methodically. I found only frozen crumbs.

So things stood when the bear came.

I was sleeping, as usual, on the cabin floor beside the berth, when sleep was broken by an awakening sharper, more sudden, and more complete than any that had preceded it. Hunger was my first thought—that the beginning of starvation had again tipped the balance against exhaustion. For a moment, still wrapped in fur, I lay in the endless twilight, staring up into the gloom of dark planks above my head. The ship creaked around me, with the ponderous, glacial movement of the ice shifting its grip.

A moment later I was sitting bolt upright, throwing off my furs and blankets. Another moment and I was on my feet. A rhythmic component of the sound had separated itself from the inanimate noises of ice and water—a heavy, padded shuffle on the deck above.

I was not the only inhabitant of that frozen gloom, nor the only one who hungered fiercely. But that sound emanated from no human agency. Thus I first heard the tread of the white bear.

Moving swiftly to the cabin door, I made shift to close and block it with such poor materials as were at hand. My effort came none too soon; a hungry snuffling and a heavy scraping soon began outside the door. The keen senses of the beast had led it unerringly to warmth, motion, and potential food.

On my first arrival, I had noticed a musket leaning in the corner of the cabin, as if it had been set down there by some careless or distracted hand, and then forgotten. I could picture the captain, tormented by the fear of some mad mutiny, and then abandoning his precaution when another danger became more real and pressing. I had supposed, without giving it much thought, that the weapon must be loaded. Whether the powder in the pan might still be dry and ready was something I might have ascertained earlier, but now had no time to try; my slight barricade at the door was already about to fall.

Gripping the weapon in one hand, I smashed out

one of the ice-covered windows in the stern, and made shift to clamber out and up, quickly gaining the poop deck.

When I reached the deck I realized that my escape from the cabin had availed me only momentary respite. As always, the eternal icefields stretched away in all directions to an indeterminate horizon. Out there lay only death and desolation. My only chance for life was here aboard the *Mary Goode*, and I suddenly discovered that life was, in spite of all, all-precious to me.

The bear, on discovering the cabin empty, and hearing my movements on the deck above, was not long in coming after me. The only delay was the few seconds required for the bulky animal to turn itself around in the cramped quarters below. Then as I had expected, it reappeared on deck. But to my consternation it came up by a different companionway than the one where I had aimed my musket.

I swung my aim quickly toward the animal, and pulled the trigger. Almost to my surprise, the musket fired. But I had not aimed accurately enough. The musket-ball, that at point-blank range could have slain the beast instantly, instead tore into the furry neck and shoulder, producing as its only immediate effect a most savage roar. A moment later, the bear had lurched free of the companionway onto the open deck, and with a blow of its paw had knocked my now-useless weapon from my grasp.

With all my agility I sprang away, just in time to avoid the next sweep of that deadly arm. Leaping to grab the frozen shrouds, I swung myself from line to line, across the ship and back again. I might have climbed one of the masts and got my-

self well above the monster's reach; but I perceived at once that such a maneuver would only
leave me hopelessly trapped, in a place from whence
I must eventually climb down, or fall, or freeze in
place if I did not.

There was nowhere to flee, nor did I wish to. A
mad rage was upon me, and I roared as fiercely as
did the bear.

I maneuvered myself above the wheel, and certain crates and other obstacles upon the deck, more
quickly than the bear could dance around them,
and thus attained the position of advantage that I
wanted. Then, giving a howl compounded half of
rage and half of despair, I sprang upon the monster from behind. Locking my right forearm under
its throat, I gripped my hands together with all
my strength, while my legs clamped the great body
of the beast between them. With eyes closed I sank
my teeth into my adversary's hairy ear, adding the
strength of my jaws to that of my arms and legs in
the effort to keep my position as the huge body
thrashed and rolled and bellowed beneath me.

The horizon of ice and snow and sky spun round
me, and the masts seemed to be toppling together
upon my head. Indeed, when the beast rolled over
in an effort to dislodge me, I thought that they had
done so. Yet still, with the strength of rage and
fear combined, I persisted in maintaining my grip.

The slavering, roaring jaws of the bear were
only inches from my face, yet he could not turn
the inches necessary to fasten those great teeth
into my skull. The four mighty limbs of my enemy
worked with pile-driving force, yet almost helplessly, for I remained out of their reach while the
claws tore splinters from the mast and deck. I

tasted the blood torn by my own teeth from my enemy's flesh, and I gripped the furred body ever harder with both arms and both legs. Again and again I was battered and bruised as the massive weight rolled over me, pounding me against the deck, the rails, I know not what. Fighting for breath, certain at each moment that in the next I must be torn off and devoured, yet I clung on, my whole being concentrated on maintaining my grip, and even tightening it.

A moment came when the bear roared no longer, because it no longer had the breath to roar. How long the grim contest continued after that I could not tell, only that it was a long time before the struggles of my opponent ceased. A long time later still I dared release my hold. Quivering, gasping, bruised in every fiber of my body, I dragged myself away, and lay for long hazy minutes on the verge of fainting before I could regain my feet.

Probing the dead carcass with a knife has confirmed my first impression about the musket-ball: The damage done by it was hardly more than superficial. With my teeth, my hands, my arms, the strength of my body, I have slain the white bear.

No human being could possibly do such a thing. My creator, in some ways, wrought exceedingly well.

That was the day on which I began this journal. Since then I have feasted on the bear's meat, scorched over the fire in my stove. I have fitted a sheet of clear ice over the cabin window from which I broke the glass in my escape.

And since my fight with the bear I have looked long into the captain's frozen little mirror. The face that gazes back at me is still smeared with traces of the bear's blood, and is undoubtedly inhuman. But it is no less alive and worthy for all that.

Whatever the mirror may tell me, whatever answer the universe may hold to the riddle of my existence, I am determined now to remain alive. So much has the bear accomplished for me.

Chapter 2

June? 1782?

I have been ill for I know not how many days, and very weak. Tried eating some of the bear's liver, which sickened me.

Will write more later. It seems to me essential that I keep on with this journal.

Some time later— Much better today. It appears that I am going to survive the poisoning. The rest of the bear's carcass, which of course is well-preserved by cold, still nourishes me.

As nearly as I can determine, daylight is still waxing with every cycle which the sun makes round the horizon. My best guess now, as I have written above, is that the present month is June.

The ship is still moving, drifting, I know not where. Now and again I glimpse patches of open water, clear and dark, amid the shifting hills and cakes of ice. It would seem that my long flight continues, whether I would have it so or not.

Alas, Frankenstein, are you now really dead? And should I swear vengeance upon Saville and Walton and their men for killing you?—you, who out of all the men and gods on Earth I must call father.

Is Earth herself my mother, then? No other parents have I, certainly.

There was a time when I thought my creator might indeed be something like a father to me. A few days after that first daylight meeting between us in the forest near Ingolstadt, he came back to meet me with a covered wagon as promised—though the plan was no longer to drive me to Geneva.

Clerval again accompanied him, and this time another young man, a few years older than Clerval and Frankenstein, was with them.

It was my first meeting with Roger Saville. Not that what happened between us can be described as a meeting in any ordinary social sense. Sitting on his horse, his head in that position not a great deal higher than mine as I stood erect before him, Saville took his first good look at me and said something unpleasant. But still, as he studied me for the first time, it was obvious that he was intrigued, deeply interested.

He was blond and looked British, indolent, and arrogant; and I was sure that when he was forty he would be fat. I am still sure of that, if he should live so long.

Saville exchanged a few words with the other two men. He did not actually speak to me—I think he spoke not ten words directly to me in all the long weeks of the journey that began that day for both of us.

I quickly climbed into the back of the wagon, as my creator bade me, and huddled there, more comfortable physically than I had ever been out in the cold and leafless woods. There I rested, under canvas, very nearly out of sight of the world, while the three men sat in a row on the front seat, driving the wagon and talking among themselves. There were spare horses—perhaps they were even English horses, the best available—hitched to the rear of the wagon, and weighty supplies of provisions stacked around me. It was obvious that an extended journey of some kind was contemplated.

I began to open containers, and to sample some of those foodstuffs as we rode. Meanwhile, up front, oblivious to my actions, Saville wanted the others to make sure that I understood I was forbidden the more expensive viands; I think he was a little disappointed that Frankenstein could not assure him that I would be content to share the horses rations. English horses or not, I did not think that I could go that far to accommodate him.

We were headed west—I had a good idea of directions—and soon I had heard enough to know that we were not going to Geneva. The first destination I heard mentioned, as one that my proprietors had firmly in mind, was Strasbourg. Once there we would get a boat and descend the Rhine. But why descend the Rhine? It remained for some time, like almost everything else, mysterious to me.

I knew somehow, in a general way, where Strasbourg was. Had I ever been there? But the mists of memory, or rather the mists that shrouded memory, were even thicker then than they are now.

From scraps of overheard conversation I began to learn of my origins. Victor Frankenstein had not created me from nothing, or from the dust of the earth. He had employed graverobbers to bring him his materials.

". . . and still no word of Karl," Clerval was saying to Frankenstein, "since the night of your success."

"Got the wind up, I suppose." Saville was more at ease talking English, and the others generally accommodated him. "Back in his village with a blanket pulled over his head, or whatever they use for blankets."

They talked a little longer on the subject, and I soon gathered that Karl had been Victor's assistant, or one of his assistants, responsible, along with another man called Metzger, for supplying the philosopher with the material he had needed for his experiments. Dead flesh. Corpses. I looked down at the skin of my arms. Me.

I soon lost count of the days as we went driving across Germany, on one road and then another, keeping mostly to the lesser-traveled ways. All their waking hours the men talked and argued. It was almost as if I were not present, as far as their conversation was concerned.

As a rule I emerged from my hiding-place in the rear of the wagon only after darkness fell, and we frequented out-of-the-way stopping places rather than inns or hostels. The men saw to their own cooking and to mine. This was not a measure of economy; already I had heard enough of this and that to realize that Saville at least must be immensely wealthy. Rather, the goal was secrecy; no menials were to know of my existence.

Indifferently I accepted the role of servant. The coarser chores of cleaning up were almost invariably left to me, and I discovered that in a rough general way I was aware of how they should be performed. Might I have been a servant in my previous life, or lives? If so, why such evidence of education as I display? I had no idea then, and have little now.

When it came time to sleep, I was relegated to the out-of-doors, while the men snored under canvas.

In a privately chartered riverboat we went down the Rhine to the sea, and it was in the port of Rotterdam that I first met Captain Walton. There it was that I first boarded his ship, the *Argo* of evil memory. But I will write of that anon.

This good ship, the *Mary Goode*, continues drifting. She is moving fairly rapidly, I think, a mere chip caught up in the massive migration of the ice. At times I can hear the ocean murmuring beneath the hull, and by certain prominent features in the distant icefields I am able to determine that the hulk is turning amid the floes and cakes that alternately grip and scrape against its sides. If I were able to see the stars I might learn more about my motion; but to catch more than the merest glimpse of celestial objects is impossible, what with the frequent cloudiness and the nearly continuous daylight.

Two days later (by estimation)— Still drifting. There is still a vast reserve of bear meat left, though I have grown heartily tired of the taste. This, more than any need, led me to search again, and this time my efforts were rewarded by the discovery of a hidden cache of food, well preserved by cold. I conjecture that some member of the vanished crew established this small secret store, then somehow perished before he could enjoy it. Or, perhaps more likely, he was forced to leave it behind when he joined in the general evacuation of the ship.

The cache contained:

Two or three pounds of ship's biscuit, not at all wormy.

An approximately equal weight of dried beans, wrapped in a paper packet.

Twice as much of salt pork, wrapped in paper and oilskin.

An equal weight of bacon.

I have sampled some of each item already, a welcome relief from scorched bear.

One day later— My search of the ship for food continues, but without any further success. As I had thought, imminent starvation was the reason why this stout vessel was abandoned.

In my investigations I have turned up a considerable variety of clothing—none of it, naturally enough, big enough to fit me.

Two days later— Much to tell. Company has arrived, and I am no longer alone. Six human beings have joined me, two men, two women, and two small children. I suppose that these are the folk known to us as Esquimeaux, though the name seems to mean nothing to them when I pronounce it. All arrived in a group—*from where?*—traversing the shifting fields of ice by dogsled and on foot without apparent difficulty.

Neither French, German, nor English make any impression on them, nor does my smattering of Russian. Their language does not sound to me like any that I have ever heard before.

The two men, armed with short spears for hunting—any people less warlike it would be hard to imagine—came clambering onto my ship before I had reason to suspect the presence of any human beings within five hundred miles. On hearing the sounds of movement, I emerged from belowdecks with my reloaded musket at the ready, more than half believing that the presence of four more unfamiliar feet upon my deck signalled the arrival of another bear.

Naturally enough, my visitors recoiled at first from such an apparition as myself. But then they quickly, though with an obvious effort, mastered their initial fright, and by words and signs endeavored earnestly to convey to me that I had nothing to fear from them. I put down my weapon and responded in kind, as well as I was able. Finding language of no use, I employed what sounds and gestures I could think of to make my guests understand that they were welcome to feed themselves, their wives and children, and their dogs, from the carcass of my bear, which trophy I think much impressed them. From that beginning our sociability has progressed, I think to a remarkable degree. Indeed, I already find myself more at ease in their company than in any other that my admittedly imperfect memory can bring to mind.

Later— The women are, if anything, friendlier than the men. They all intend, if I understand them correctly, to make camp—somehow—on the ice hard by the ship, rather than accept my invitation to move aboard. I have done my best to indicate that they are welcome.

These folk are not natives of Lapland, or at least they do not respond to the few words of that tongue that I have lately recollected and tried on them. My only reward was looks as blank, if as pleasant, as before.

Later— My friends the *Inoot*—that is as nearly as I can try to spell the word by which they seem to call themselves—are much taken with my writing, the captain's notebook which I use, the graphite pencils, and the small knife with which I carry out the occasional ritual of sharpening.

I am excited. One of the men has made the sign of the cross, from which I infer the presence of missionaries. Now I can hope that some outpost of civilization may exist, at a reachable distance from where I am.

European civilization—is that indeed what I now yearn for? But my origins, the answers to the riddle of my life, must lie in Europe. And Walton and

Saville are there, most probably, if vengeance on Saville and Walton is what I really seek.

My life—from whatever cause, and even though the whole world find it hateful—flows strongly in my veins. I am determined to survive, and to seek out the secrets of my self.

When the *Inoot* move on, I shall go with them.

Chapter 3

June? 1782?

I write this by clear sunlight, though the time is near midnight—the sun has dipped its closest to the horizon. Between me and this sun there are no cabin windows. The ship, the cabin, all ships and all cabins, are far behind me now.

The aperture through which the sun must pass to fall upon my paper is the narrow doorway of a small house made of ice. This strange structure my companions, with some trifling help from me, have erected in less than an hour's time, cutting and placing the blocks with a sureness and rapidity that must be born of long practice. Inside the house is a single chamber, with room for seven travelers to huddle in their furs. Directly in the center of the floor of ice there burns a small oil-lamp, with a small chimney-hole directly over it, at the apex of the ice-dome. The single curved surface of the interior wall gleams with melted and re-frozen water. The air inside the dwelling is grown surprisingly warm; any warmer and soon I shall find my fur robes oppressive.

The *Inoot* and I are headed into the south—where else? But I have doubts that I am still in the longitude of Europe. If not, then it is to be North America; my own flight from Europe, my last nightmarish encounter with my tormentors aboard the *Argo*, and the drifting of the *Mary Goode*, have carried me farther west than I at first thought possible. But the truth of the matter is that I can scarcely guess at my location.

So, with my new friends—undoubtedly my only friends in all the world—I go south. When we have managed to reach something other than ice and snow, then I may grow more particular as to my destination. The remnants of the frozen bear travel with us, and now with other food supplies are walled away from the dogs in a small ice-closet constructed for that purpose.

The dogs do not like me, any more than did the ones I drove in Russia. But then sled dogs do not like anyone or anything, except when it appears as food.

Next morning— or, at any rate, after some hours of sleep. And after much else.

For as far back as I can remember I had been firmly convinced that no human female would ever, conceivably—at least without great financial inducement—be willing to join herself to me in the manner of a woman with a man, not even in a fashion devoid of all the finer sentiments, and purely animal or brutal. This assumption—I was persuaded

of it by many things that my creator said, and by
other evidence as well—has now been proven
wrong.

My thoughts are humble ones, and yet in a way
proud, as I write of the experience. Even as my
encounter with the white bear marked a point of
sharp division between one epoch of my life and
another, so did last night's encounter with Kunuk
signal another end, and a beginning.

I marvel at the suddenness and naturalness with
which it came about. In the confined space of the
ice-shelter there was no question of privacy. As we
all made such preparations as were possible before retiring, I observed that my companions, male
and female, young and old alike, divested themselves of all clothing before entering their beds of
sleeping furs. Years of experience as a traveler
have taught me that when about to embark upon
some unfamiliar activity, it is wise to imitate the
actions of the natives when they perform the act in
question; and I considered that sleeping in a house
made of ice was new and strange enough to bring
this rule into full force. I removed my clothes
entirely.

The women made not the least effort to conceal
themselves from me, and I, following the lead of
my hosts, was equally frank in my behavior. The
older woman was indifferent to what she saw; but
the younger gave evidence in her facial expressions and her manner that what she beheld amused
and perhaps amazed her; and with unmistakable
gestures she beckoned me to share her furs. Here,
it seems that morals and customs that are well-
nigh universal in other lands must give way before

the sheer animal need to conserve warmth, and, I suppose, to avoid conflict among members of a party when all are confronted at every hour with the challenge of survival in a most savage and unforgiving environment.

No one else in the group, not even the man I had supposed to be Kunuk's husband, appeared to be in the least surprised by her invitation, nor offered the least objection to it. And verily I had none.

This morning, in my eyes, even the world of ice has a certain warmth about it. The very sun is brighter. Ye have been wrong, ye gods who attempt to control my destiny, whoever ye may be— who from my creation have despised and detested me! I have put behind me the curse of death ye would have fastened on me from my creation, and I go on to life!

I babble foolishly. But it does not matter. We go south. I shall probably write no more today. Or tonight.

Next day— Last night with Kunuk again. My appetites, long denied, seem insatiable. And yet. There is already an undercurrent of dissatisfaction. The woman is good, and kind, and gives me much— and yet she is not of *my* kind. And there is much— something—I would have, that she cannot give.

The hunters this morning killed a seal, spearing it through a hole in the ice, and we have fresh meat again. Entrails and all are devoured, as with the bear. When we left the frozen ship, my friends insisted on bringing with them the bear's liver, along with the other meat, despite my gestures of warning, meant to describe sickness. Now I see

that they feed some of the liver to the dogs, and
eat of it themselves without harm, by mixing small
morsels with large amounts of other meat. I dared
to taste a mouthful of the mixture, and have suffered no ill effect; I suppose that what is poisonous
in large quantities may be of benefit in small. And
memory comes and goes, fleetingly; memory from
some life before this one, gone again before I can
even try to fix its shape or substance.

As always, I hoard up bits of knowledge of this
mysterious world in which I find myself. The time
will no doubt soon come again when I must confront its mysteries alone.

Kunuk, who will never be able to read these
words, you have been all to me that you can be. I
already realize that I will miss you keenly when
that hour of our parting comes. And whether my
life be long or short thereafter, I shall remember
you until its end.

Later— I believe that we are still proceeding almost directly south. Still I do not know whether I
am north of Iceland, Greenland, or even Labrador.
There has been no chance for me to get my bear-
ings from the sky. My companions however seem
to know where they are going; at least they evince
no sign of uncertainty or uneasiness about their
route.

Kunuk has rejoined her husband in his sleeping-
furs, though not without a look or two at me, as if
she were concerned over what I might think of this
change. In truth I did not like it much; yet how
could I object?

The older woman, whose name I am still uncertain of, smiled at me tentatively; but I only smiled back, and closed my eyes, and fell asleep.

Next day— I am alone again. It is a strange, almost a frightening situation after so many days of unaccustomed companionship. But I have thrived on loneliness before, and shall again.

The end of fellowship—and of more intimate gratifications—came before I was well prepared for it, yet hardly as a surprise. I had known from the start that my path and that of my companions might diverge at any moment. Land, solid and undeniable, had come into view, hills no taller than I am but looming like the Alps in this eternal flatness.

No sooner had we climbed onto the land, than my party showed their intention of turning west among the snowy, barren hills.

I, however, rightly or wrongly, persisted stubbornly in my determination to continue south; and I no longer had the least doubt as to which way that was. My most weighty reason was that I had already satisfied myself, by dint of long and patient gesturing, that whoever had taught these people the sign of the cross was to be found in that direction.

My friends, when they saw I was determined, wasted no further time or strength in argument. They insisted on going west from the point of our landfall, and so we amicably, and somewhat sadly, separated.

I have some food, some fishing hooks and lines, and a seal-hunter's spear, the last traded to me for a large share of my supply of fish-hooks and some other trade goods that were on the hulk. After what I have survived already, I do not fear to face the miles ahead. So far, since our separation, the weather has been favorable, and I see no sign of immediate change. And hardihood against the elements is mine, greater than that of any human being.

On to the south alone!

Chapter 4

Early August? 1782?—At any rate much later than my last entry

Twenty days (if my reckoning of time is accurate) of nearly continuous travel have at last brought me free of the perpetual ice. I now traverse a land of mosses and stinging insects, wild flowers and dwarf birches. In some ways—the rocks and grass, the uninhabited distances, the dearth of trees—this territory reminds me of that other sea-girt land of evil memory, to which I was brought by Frankenstein and by his mentor Saville, a man more evil than himself, to be their slave, their accomplice, their companion—it would take a long list of words to exhaust all the possibilities of what I was to them at one time and another. Now I am fairly certain that my creator is dead. And toward that other, and the human creatures who serve him, I can know only enmity.

The resemblance between this land where I now

find myself, and those isles in the north of Britain
has been rendered all the more acute by a deterio-
ration in the weather. Since leaving my friends I
have endured three or four storms, or squalls; one
of them a veritable tempest of snow and freezing
rain—I am sure that no human, unsheltered as I
am, could have survived it.

At the moment the rain has ceased. I am writing
this overdue entry in my journal whilst seated on
a granite outcropping in what is almost a verdant
meadow. I believe the month now to be August;
and I am now virtually certain that, despite the
similarities of landscape mentioned above, I am
now in America and not in any part of northern
Europe. The differences in terrain, and in flora
and fauna, are too great to admit of any other
conclusion. This, of course, will mean another long
and arduous journey, a crossing of the sea, before I
can confront those who hold the secrets of my
being—if those secrets did not die with Frankenstein—but still, in my heart, I am relieved not to
be on those desolate Scottish isles now.

The *Argo*, sailing from Rotterdam, did not bear
us directly to that northern land. I had heard
enough from the men who thought themselves my
owners, to understand that our first destination
was London, but not enough to explain to me why
it must be so. I was already beginning to distrust
those men; but I had no one and nothing else to
trust. It was for me a hideous voyage; I suffered
somewhat from seasickness, and of course, at the
command of my creator, remained below decks

almost continuously. Few or none of the crew even knew that I was on board.

It seemed to me even then that I had not always been confined out of sight lest I terrify anyone who caught a glimpse of me—but when and where could that have been?

My chief occupation on the voyage from Rotterdam to London, then, was thought—and so much thought can be dangerous. Not only did I think, but I made every effort to listen to more conversations among my masters as to what they were planning to do with me, and for me.

I was able to gather that the ship either had already, when we came aboard, some cargo deliverable to London; or that some had been taken on when Saville informed Captain Walton of his new destination. I was no expert on maritime affairs; and yet such concepts as cargo and profit were in some way familiar to me.

Who was I?

Who had I been—before?

Why had I still no name? I ought to have one—in fact I did have one. I grew increasingly certain of that, but I could not remember what my name was.

The fact of my actual presence on board remained a secret. But from mutterings I overheard among the crew I understood that they were aware, as sailors will be aware, that something or someone strange was on board—they heard or smelled or dreamt enough to suggest to them a strange and invisible presence—but they never got a good look at me.

There were days when what tormented me more

than anything else was that there was no place below decks where I could stand up straight.

Later— So far, during my present journey, feeding myself has presented no real problem. The walrus and the whale are beyond my powers as a hunter, but fish, birds, wild hare, and berries are not.

Only once since leaving my friends have I encountered other human beings, and on that occasion I made no effort to approach or speak with them. They were a small group of hunters, at least half a mile away, and headed in a direction I had no wish to go. Whatever human contact I might have achieved with them would almost certainly have been brief, and I saw no reason to think that it would be satisfactory; indeed, having some sense that I must be nearer to civilization now, I felt virtually certain that my appearance would once more excite disgust and suspicion.

Later, the same day— Much has happened, and quickly. Another small group of men came into my sight, and at the same time, beyond them to the east, a large body of water, too broad for the farther shore to be visible at any point.

These men were not embarking upon a hunting expedition, but were busy with something on the shore. This time I did approach my fellow beings, in hopes of establishing some contact with civilization. I experienced a familiar sight as I drew near them—how, as my exceptional stature became apparent, their attitudes were changed; and how, when my face was near enough for them to see it clearly, a still greater change came over theirs. These men were much warier than the *Inoot* had been, confirming my idea that civilization in some form might not be far distant now.

I smiled gently and spoke softly, as I have learned to do. One of those before me had a few words of English, and from him I learned that I have now reached the shore of Hudson Bay, though I cannot yet determine at what point on that immense length of coastline I have arrived. Dealing with this man and his fellows through gestures, I have now bargained away all of my remaining trade goods for a well-used *kayak*, with which I now mean to continue my journey southward along the shore. Today the sea in front of me is calm, free, or almost free, of floating ice, and the wind mild and favorable.

A day later— I write this by the light of a small fire, as I attempt to dry my clothing. The *kayak*, though as I thought purchased cheaply, proved to be no bargain. After an hour's use it began to leak so badly that, though I was no more than a hundred yards from shore at any time, I had all I could do to get back within wading distance of the shoreline before the craft sank. I endured a partial wetting, but retained everything I had of value, and was able to light a fire of twigs and driftwood.

Thoughts of revenge afflict me. But to pursue the man who sold me the cursed boat would be pointless, and achieve nothing but to take me farther from my true goal. Think of it no more. Or, if I am to dream of vengeance, let my wrath be directed against those who have done me far greater harm.

Onto the south, once more on foot. In some curious way I am glad that the boat is gone, glad to be traveling on my legs again.

Chapter 5

August 14, 1782— At last, a date to be written down almost with certainty. And a pair of eyes, other than my own, to read these words

After the incident of the sunken boat, I traveled south along the shore on foot, seeing now and then traces of human passage or occupation, but no living man or woman. The third morning brought me to a small cove, and, on the low cliff at its head, a permanent human habitation. The largest of the two or three buildings—ambitiously larger than necessary, as I soon realized—was obviously a church or chapel. I had reached the home of Father Jacques-Marie Alibard.

As I slowly approached the door of the small central cabin, wondering how to present myself with a minimum of shock to whoever might be within, the door opened and the priest came out, a slender figure in a fur jacket, the wind off the Bay ruffling his iron-gray hair. If what he saw in my countenance engendered horror, or if my size had terrified him when he beheld me through his window, he had mastered those emotions before allowing me to see him. He spoke in kind tones, using what must have been one of the languages of the inhabitants of this land, and was surprised when I answered him in quite passable French. I was made to feel welcome at once; it is plain that the poor man has been suffering intensely from isolation. He has been here—in this territory at least—for more than ten years as a missionary.

I write this evening's entry in this journal seated on a wooden floor—there are chairs available, but I distrust them—within a furnished room, by lamplight. My host's cabin is high enough inside for me to stand erect, if I take care to keep under the ridgepole log. The good father is, I am sure, bursting to hear my story, but he will not allow the least bit of curiosity to show regarding what I might be writing in my book—and I am not anxious to tell more than I must.

He said, a little while ago: "You are European, then."

"I am."

"French by birth?"

"No."

"I did not think so, though you speak the language well. You did not tell me your name."

"Alas, Father, I have none."

He considered that for a moment before replying: "You mean that it has been—lost?" I do not know precisely what he had in mind—perhaps that I had been somehow disgraced, and my family had disowned me.

"No. To my knowledge, I have never had one."

"Ah." If he was very much surprised at this claim he did not show it. "If you do not mind my asking, how old are you?"

"Not yet three years, to the best of my knowledge."

He said "Ah" again, and looked at me carefully, and fell silent. He has yet to resume his questioning. In a way I wish he would.

It has become plain to me in the hours I have been here with him that the priest is not a well man. He is quite alone here at present; had he been healthy he would not have been at home when I arrived, but on the trail somewhere among the tiny, far-flung settlements whose inhabitants he is pleased to think of as his parishioners. I have not seen any of them as yet, and do not know what they think of him.

His color is bad and he coughs a great deal. He is about fifty years of age, I estimate, and spare of frame. He was a Jesuit, I have learned, until the suppression of that Order some eight years ago. What exactly his ecclesiastical (if that is the right word) status may be now is not yet clear to me, but apparently he remains a missionary of some kind, in good—or at least tolerable—standing with his superiors, who are far to the south of here, in Montreal.

It is obvious that tonight we are going to talk. I will let him read of this book if he should ask directly—but I think he is not likely to do that.

August 15— The Father and I have come to know each other a little better now. He has declined to respond to my hints that I thought he must be curious about my journal. Instead he is curious about me. Naturally enough. But he is not impatient. As I look back on my arrival now, it is almost as if I had been expected here.

We have had another little session of questions and answers. Dutifully the good priest has made his first inquiries upon the state of my immortal soul.

"*You* may well possess such an appendage, Father," I told him. "Just as you have a name. But there is no reason to believe that I do."

I suppose he was shocked, but if so it was evident from his continued calm that he had heard many things more shocking still. Shocked or not, he was certainly intrigued. Perhaps no penitent had ever presented him with exactly this theory before.

"Are you not a man, my son? Even if you are nameless as you say, are you not one of Adam's children?"

I laughed; I cannot remember having done such a thing before. "I have—more or less—a man's form, as you see. But have you ever known a man who was eight feet tall?" I had switched to English, and used the English form of measurement—even as my creator had sometimes switched, for some reason, when he lectured me. Perhaps it was because the English-speaking Franklin had suddenly popped into Victor's thoughts; he thought and spoke of Franklin frequently.

The priest loked me up and down. "I see that God has given you enormous strength. But surely you are not *eight* feet tall."

"It is perhaps hard to believe."

"Yes, it is very difficult indeed. Oh, yes. It was an Englishman who helped me build this cabin, years ago, and the measurements were done in feet and inches. The central log sustaining the roof beams is itself not so much as eight feet from the floor—I remember well, all of the measurements and calculation. I was so methodical then. No more than seven feet and a half. And your head does not touch it."

"I tell you I—" I sighed. "But what does it matter? Yes, I have great strength. And great, more than human, ugliness as well. Surely you cannot fail to see that. One of Adam's children? No. I think not."

He looked at me carefully. Violent madmen are not unknown here in the far north, I am sure, where a man may be imprisoned by the elements for months or years at a time, and my priest has learned to be careful. But my demeanor and speech remained calm, and eventually he was reassured. Then nothing would do but that he must rummage around until he had found a ruler, and conduct a measurement of his ridgepole's height. While measuring up the wall he said: "Beauty in the eyes of God is not measured in the configuration of the face." And when I did not answer, he went on: "You will pardon me, but about your not being one of Adam's children—that I do not, I cannot, understand. I fear you are laboring under some tremendous error."

"It is a long story, Father. Best told, I think, a little at a time."

"Ah. There—you see?" Standing on a chair, he had reached the top of the wall, triumphantly.

"No more than seven and a half feet, as I said. As for your story, I am ready to listen when you are ready to speak."

But I was distracted—he was perfectly right, I had watched his progress with the ruler. Seven and a half feet up to the ridgepole from the floor—unless there was something wrong about his ruler—but that was foolish. Seven feet and a half to the ridgepole, and I fit under it, standing erect, with perhaps an inch or two to spare. It was unlike Frankenstein to be so imprecise in matters of measurement, and I was sure that he had told me several times that he had formed me with a height of eight feet exactly.

This trifle worried me unduly. There even occurred to me the absurd idea that I might be slowly shrinking. With the bulk of my clothing mere wrappings, a change in size might not be easy to determine. But no, my boots had been made to fit me, and they fitted as well as ever; my feet at least were unchanging. And surely I would have noticed any change in my own bodily proportions.

For some time after the measuring of the walls we spoke merely of housekeeping matters. Then suddenly the priest said: "I must continue to believe, my friend, that we are both sons of the same God."

"Ah. But you see, Father, *my* creator was not God. If I owe prayer, it is to someone else."

He avoided asking the obvious question—perhaps he feared what answer I might give. He only said: "What you say sounds like blasphemy, yet I do not believe that you intend it so."

* * *

Later— I have learned one more important fact about my host. Some months ago the good Father received orders from Montreal—they had heard that his health was failing—to abandon his post here, and return to that city as soon as practicable.

He explained to me: "Until you arrived, I had convinced myself that I should stay until spring, and not attempt the journey to Montreal alone. But now you are here, and you say you are determined at all costs to go south before the winter. To me it seems that God has sent you to accompany me. If you are willing, we can leave tomorrow. I have a large canoe, in good condition, and little enough to do to get ready. And if we are going south ahead of winter, we must press on quickly."

"You are ready, then," I asked in some surprise, "to leave all your parishioners?"

"I am ordered to go." He hesitated. "Besides . . ." He could not find a way to say it.

I thought I knew what he wanted to say. "There are not that many of them who come here, and you cannot go to help them when you are ill."

He nodded gratefully. In the morning, then, we are departing.

September 18— Aided by a fortunate spell of fair weather, we have set a good pace now for many days. Because I have devoted all my energy to the needs of the voyage, I have failed to make entries in this journal. Father Jacques says that he remembers the route to Montreal well, and I believe him, though years have passed since he has traveled it. He is a fearless canoeist, though no longer a strong one, and we are able, now and then, to save time by cutting across a broad inlet in the shore of the Bay to a dim point of land that I might otherwise have supposed to be an island.

My companion is impressed with my strength, which is the universal reaction, and also by my endurance as a paddler. Canoes were strange to me when I began—how could they be otherwise? —but the art is simple, my sense of balance sure, and I learn quickly. His own strength, I fear, is fading rapidly.

I feel an impulse to suggest, more strongly this time, that he should read my journal. But though he has said nothing, I feel that he is somehow reluctant to do so, as though he feared to find out that, after all, I am only mad. Mad I may well be, I suppose, but hardly *only* mad. Events more terrible than madness have made me what I am.

As our acquaintance lengthens, the good priest will, I think, become more likely to believe a greater portion of the truth, however much of it I eventually tell him. Great God! I think that no one could believe it all.

I want to write of Scotland. But I cannot. I am not yet ready.

September 19— Last night the subject of my origins came up again, rather suddenly. We were lying in our robes under the stars and the false dawn of the *aurora borealis*, with our small fire between us. I had thought my companion was asleep, when suddenly he rolled to face me and said: "You told me on the first day that we met, my friend, that God was not your creator. Forgive me if I press you for an answer, but how is it possible that that honor belongs to someone else?"

"Honor indeed." I sat up, still wrapped in fur, to stir the fire. We were out of the wind, camped against a low mount of land that broke the monotony of the even lower shore.

Still waiting for a real answer, he prompted: "The 'someone else' you mentioned is no doubt a parent?"

"As much of a parent as I have. But I am sorry that I said anything at all to you about it. You are a good man and need no nightmares. I trouble you to no purpose. Good night. Go back to sleep."

"I am a priest, my friend. It is my business to hear the nightmares of the troubled. I am only sorry that I cannot be of help, in return for all the help that you are giving me."

Father Jacques is now indeed weakening rapidly, under the stresses of the journey. I write more boldly now, in the growing belief that he will never read these words.

Today I raised aloud the possibility that we might turn back, and winter in his cabin, for I have begun to doubt that he will ever reach Montreal alive if we press on. But he refused at once, and to tell the truth I do not much like the idea myself, and did not press him on it. That he would survive the winter in the cabin, and be stronger in the spring, is to my mind doubtful also. Nor am I anxious to delay my own quest for almost a year.

Or am I? If I knew exactly what my quest is, I would doubtless refuse to delay it for even an hour. Is it vengeance that I seek, or only truth?

Or not even truth, perhaps, but only consolation.

*   *   *

September 26— Today Father is no longer able to rise and walk. I carry him to the canoe, and paddle quickly south. Thick snow is already falling, and I want to get him as far as possible beyond the worst of the advancing winter. We rest tonight in a tiny shelter of pine boughs and logs, and I write in part because he has urged me to do so.

But I must keep writing. And set down what happened in London. And in the north of Scotland, when we attempted to revive the dead. But I cannot write of that tonight.

Chapter 6

September 28— My heart is heavy. My companion is dead.

It was a long and difficult dying, of more than four-and-twenty hours. When the breathing of Father Jacques became harsh and uneven, and he looked at me without recognition, I began to feel certain that the end was near. Yet life clung to him tenaciously. He sank by slow degrees into a stupor, then into total unconsciousness.

Only toward the end did the good priest rally briefly. Turning his eyes on me, he recognized me once more, and in a feeble voice gave me his blessing; he would have raised his hand, to sign me with the cross, but he could not. A minute later he had breathed his last.

To mark his passing, snow squalls churned their way across the Bay, while to the south, above both land and water, lightning and thunder wept and raged. There are times when I feel a kinship with these forces greater than with any man or woman. Is it perhaps because I know that these powers of the atmosphere assisted at my birth?

My friend's death has affected me, more than I had anticipated. I have tried to pray—but no. That is not strictly true. It would be more accurate to say that I wanted to make an attempt at prayer, but could not. In the end I heard myself muttering some foolish vow, based on no more than the sanctity of my own nature. A vow to do what? I do not even know that. I am not sure now where those words came from, or even what they meant. As I now remember and write down the fact, it appears incomprehensible; and yet at the moment it seemed to me that there was meaning in the words I muttered.

There is rock nearby, a rare sight along this low shore, and an outcrop shattered by weathering has afforded material for the mound under which my friend now lies buried—it is impossible, particularly without more tools than I possess, to dig in this frozen ground, and there are wolves. They are howling not very far outside the shelter as I write this, and I feel very much alone.

The lonely isles at the north of Scotland are not perpetually frozen, as most of this ground must be, but their soil is cold and very rocky. Still, in that soil we dug graves. It was the second grave for most who were put into the ground there, and the rude burial service—if it can be called a burial service; I do remember seeing Clerval's lips moving with muttered prayers—must have been the second for those poor dismembered beings also.

Not that there had been, between their burials, anything that could have been called a second life—but I am anticipating the order of my tale.

I must take great pains to make sure that it is all set down, as coherently as I can do so. Then if I do not survive, there will still be some hope that someone may read it one day and be warned.

Now, I have procrastinated quite long enough, and I must write of London. The *Argo* made port there in early February of 1780. with Robert Walton captain, and Roger Saville, her owner, on board along with Victor Frankenstein, Henry Clerval, and myself. We had sailed eagerly up the Thames, glad to be out of reach of the Channel storms that had tormented us, and arrived in sight of the metropolis at sunset.

At that time, judging by such of their conversations as I had been able to hear, my human masters (as they continued to believe themselves) still had not determined by what plan they should be most likely to profit from my existence. One of their problems in coming to an agreement among themselves was that their different natures compelled them to seek different goals. Saville craved power and wealth, even beyond the great amounts of each he had already. Walton wanted adventure, and, some day, fame. Clerval—I think he was one of those whose greatest desire is to know secrets that are denied to others. Also he was truly Victor's friend.

And as for my creator . . . but it is not so easy to set down the goals of Victor Frankenstein. He shared to some degree in the yearnings of each of the other men. And yet in his case there was something more.

However varied their final objectives might be, the four gentlemen had agreed, well before we reached London, that the next step in any successful plan must be for Victor to provide me with a mate. In some of their debates (to which I was a silent listener, more often than they knew) they even favored the scheme of supplying me with more than one female, for breeding purposes; the larger my harem, as Saville frequently remarked, the better the chance of quickly producing a population of willing slaves and workers.

Saville in particular was convinced that none of my progeny would, or could possibly, ever nurse any higher ambition than to serve in one of his burgeoning Birmingham factories, or perhaps labor on one of his Jamaican plantations—he owned several—under conditions where the blacks of Africa tended to die off unprofitably. He strove to implant this vision in the minds of Frankenstein and the others, and kept coming back again and again to the specification that all the workers ultimately produced must not only be docile, strong, and enduring, but should be able to subsist, like swine or goats, on acorns and other inexpensive roughage, with now and then a handful of berries as reward for some particularly difficult labor.

My own feelings were mixed as I listened to these discussions. Had I taken Saville's plans seriously, I would have been outraged. I realized *he* took such schemes very seriously indeed, and that the other men were at best indifferent to them, at worst his eager followers. But before any such design for breeding slaves could be put into effect, it was necessary that my mate, or mates, should be created. Somehow I could not, or did not wish to, look beyond that point. Let that be done, successfully, I thought. Let me be granted another like myself, mate and companion, and then we shall see what we shall see. Looking back now, I have a hard time understanding what my state of mind was then. But it was centered on an utter loneliness, an estrangement from the world, from which I have only lately started to emerge.

Clerval from the start took me more seriously than did any of the others, even my creator. To Henry it was never totally inconceivable that I might have some legitimate thoughts and aspirations of my own. In conferences with the other gentlemen he frequently expressed his opinion that they would be doing a great wrong in making me a slave, without first determining beyond doubt that my nature was fitted for nothing better. By raising this point he usually managed to awaken a twinge of conscience in Frankenstein, and got at least soothing agreement from the others. But then five minutes later the discussion would have returned to the question of whether plantations or mines would offer the most profitable use for my multitude of potential brothers, sisters, and descendants.

As for Walton, he was, as I have said, an adventurer; and what we were engaged in was for him a superb adventure, whatever it might turn out to mean to others. From the moment we came aboard his ship, and he heard from her owner some of Frankenstein's story and mine, Walton began taking notes in preparation for its telling. Saville, after giving the matter some thought and cautioning the captain on certain matters, allowed him to proceed with his plan for eventual publication, in some form. I wonder now if anything will ever come of that.

What of Victor himself? If he failed to regard me as a person, he had at all times a proprietary interest, and sometimes protested jealously that the others were, in attempting to decide my fate, robbing him of what was rightfully his. But Saville could always placate him with offers of a superb laboratory in which to work, almost unlimited funds, assistants, most of all a powerful friend to stand between him and the obtrusive world—and Victor would be soothed.

As soon as the *Argo* was moored to a London wharf, all of the crew who could be spared were set free, and wasted no time in descending upon the taverns and brothels ashore. I was allowed to stretch my limbs by being freed from my tiny closet of a cabin, granted the rare privilege of emergence into the barely larger chamber wherein Clerval and my creator had been quartered, and which formed the only means of egress from my own closet to the world.

"What is happening now?" I whispered. There were times during those days of confinement and enforced silence when I felt that I was losing, through disuse, the power of speech. Oh, I might have rebelled, physically, and with temporary success. Knocked out of my way the men who thought themselves my masters, risen to the deck, terrifying some sailors who had not dreamt that anything like me was aboard ... but what would I have done after that? Remember that the world out of sight of my gentleman–captors was utterly unknown to me, and what little evidence I had of it looked strange and frightening indeed.

The plan, or that part of it of which I was condescendingly informed, called for Clerval to remain on board to keep an eye on me, whilst Frankenstein and Saville were escorted ashore by Captain Walton, who claimed to be able to conduct them promptly to certain men with whom they would be able to do business. He had already sent a message ashore, and those men would be waiting. Exactly what sort of business was to be conducted in London first was not explained to me, but I thought that I could guess. To duplicate his feat of creation, Frankenstein would need laboratory equipment—he had brought very little with him from Bavaria. Also the raw materials would be required—human bodies, or the component parts of them, that had once been living but now were not. The dead of night, I somehow understood, would not be the proper time to set out to purchase laboratory equipment.

I did not argue with my orders to stay aboard, but neither had I any intention of obeying them. I knew that the mission that took the men ashore was vitally connected with my own future, and I meant to discover what decisions were being made on that subject, and what was actually accomplished.

Less than a minute after the departure of Walton, Saville, and Frankenstein, I had managed to get over the ship's side by unorthodox means, acting decisively as soon as my remaining guardian's back was turned. Swinging on lines, leaping with an agility more than human, I needed only a moment to gain the dock.

It was a substantial relief to have my feet planted again on solid land. Listening carefully to the sounds of the city, the docks, the river, as I stood there swathed in night and fog, I was barely able to pick up the murmuring of the three familiar voices in time to hurry after them.

The streets at this hour were dark as coal mines. The occasional hurrying passerby with his lantern was unaware of me except as a pair of soft footsteps, a dim and sizeless presence in the night.

The three men I was following carried no lantern, and I had some difficulty—more than once I almost lost them in the fog. At length they turned into a mews, traversed it for a hundred yards, and then emerged upon another street. Presently I at last heard one of them tapping at a door. I was only a few yards behind them when the door opened, and I could confirm the presence of their three shadows, outlined in a faint wash of light against the fog.

Even before the door had closed behind them I was moving close to the small building they had entered, which was not much more than a large shed. The one small window that faced the street side had been blocked off, and I had heard the street door being locked after the gentlemen went in. Trying my ear first against the door and then at the window, I was unable to hear more than a faint unintelligible murmur of voices from within.

Stealthily—I can move softly and lightly when I choose—I made my way around to the rear of the building. There, to my satisfaction, I found it possible, my great height being an advantage, to position myself outside a high dirty window in such a way that I could obtain a very satisfactory view of the interior of a rear room, and also hear most of what was being said within.

By the light of a cheap tallow candle, I could see two landsmen, both rather scruffy-looking, seated at a table with Frankenstein and Saville, while Walton stood by with folded arms. There was a bottle of rum on the table, along with some chipped and dirty crockery, and the two Londoners were helping themselves to drink, though the gentlemen had evidently disdained to do so under these conditions.

On another table nearby, a trestle construction even rougher than that at which the men sat talking, there lay a shape as of a human body. It was very small, motionless and covered by a dirty canvass. I saw at once that my surmise as to the nature of the business to be conducted at this meeting had been correct.

If any further confirmation had been needed, it was provided by the first words I heard. They came from one of the strangers and were to the effect that though in London there existed a thriving trade in the bodies of the newly dead, as in any other trade, reliability and devotion to quality work were by no means universal among Resurrections.

Frankenstein, whose English was accented and somewhat limited, asked in puzzlement about the meaning of a word. "Resurrectionist? I take it that is—?"

The more heavily-built one of the resurrectionists answered with an expansive gesture. "Why, it's no more and no less than it sounds like, sir. It's quite a good solid trade here in London, as I 'ad the honor to inform you, and my partner here and me are as well-established in it as anyone you could hope to find." He gave a self-satisfied nod, including Saville and Walton in his glance. "Should any of you gentlemen 'ave your doubts, you could look in at Doctor Hunter's anatomy school in Windmill Street, and ask 'em there."

Frankenstein turned aside to Saville, and explained that such conditions must represent a new factor in his calculations. Where he had been working before, on the Continent, medical schools and other researchers who were considered legitimate had a fairly easy time obtaining bodies .

"But here—I had not realized, but now I see—if even the anatomy schools here must steal their materials, no doubt for us things will be even more difficult. Here I suppose it will be a serious criminal matter to possess a stolen body?"

The other landsman, whose general air was that of a man who has come down in the world, now spoke up, in a voice considerably more cultured than that of his business associate. "Now there, gentlemen, just there, if I may say so, is where the gentleman is wrong. Possession of a dead body, any dead body, in England is not criminal. Oh, there are certain times and places when, for those engaged in our trade, caution is certainly needed. Some of the cemeteries have augmented their fences with dogs and guards. But by the laws of England, no one can have property rights in a corpse. It is not possible, therefore, for mortal remains to be considered stolen property. The medical schools, you see, have no other dependable source of supply besides our trade, and really none at all within the law, which says that the veriest pauper must be buried. God rest their souls in peace. By the way, will you be needing the teeth?"

Frankenstein blinked at him. "Yes—some of them at least—one good set, certainly—why do you ask?"

"There is another market. The dentists use them sometimes, to implant in living jaws."

"Dentists?" Saville sniffed at the word. "Oh, yes, Frenchified tooth-drawers, I suppose you mean."

"I shall need at least one good complete set of teeth," said Victor. "Probably the largest sound specimens available. I care not what you do with the rest." I ran my tongue around inside my mouth; good solid work, like most of the rest of the construction.

My creator was now expressing his anxiety lest there should be any difficulty in getting just the kind of fresh young female specimens that he wanted. While considering this question, the group rose from the table, and went to the other table, where the canvas was drawn back. With the men's backs to me I could see little of the body now revealed to their inspection. It was described by its proprietors as a "large small," it being somewhat over three feet long. A child, from what I could observe of one puny marble leg.

"A bargain, gentlemen, I assure you." The elegant graverobber waved a hand in a dismissive gesture. "Only three guineas."

Saville drawled: "That is certainly excessive." He treated himself to a pinch of snuff.

Victor said firmly that in any case this particular body would be much too small, even if it had been fresh enough. He announced, with the air of one having to repeat something far too often, that his needs were special. He pulled the sheet up again, shrouding the trestle's burden, and turned away from it.

The two Londoners exchanged glances with each other. "Very fresh is sometimes difficult, sir," said the coarser one, "but not impossible. There's no problem in laying hands on any special kind of corse a gentleman might want." He looked with a certain expression, meaningful and leering, at his companion.

The other nodded sagely, and remarked in elegant tones that he had heard before of gentlemen who put in orders for young girls freshly dead—he recalled, tolerantly, knowing someone in his own business who thought along quite similar lines.

"And what is that supposed to mean?" Victor inquired sharply. I had thought the meaning was quite plain.

The languid ruffian turned over a hand, palm up; an elegant gesture of a wrist that had doubtless once worn lace. In his pallid face the hatred was quite plain.

A dispute quickly flared up, and as rapidly turned violent. At first it appeared that no one was armed, and the gentlemen were giving a good account of themselves in the game of fisticuffs, though Frankenstein did nothing but retreat dazedly into a corner. Presently, however, in response to an outcry from one of the professional graverobbers, the door leading to the adjoining room burst open and three more men rushed in, one of whom could have been described as a giant—in human terms at least. The other two were armed with wooden cudgels.

Captain Walton had at first been rather obviously enjoying the fight, but this change in the odds was a little too much for him. He drew and fired a pistol, but his shot missed.

My own immediate and overwhelming concern was that my creator must be protected at all costs— else my own future appeared bleak indeed. The danger to Frankenstein now appeared too great to be tolerated. I crouched and sprang up, bursting in through the window, to the great astonishment of all inside.

I had landed in a crouch on the floor of the shed; my first act after springing to my feet again was to reach the side of Frankenstein, and shove him protectively beneath a table. Then, bellowing like a beast, and hurling about furniture and bodies, living and dead, with a strength and violence quite sufficient to impress the enemy, I had in a matter of seconds routed them completely. The men with the cudgels had been given little chance to use them, and the giant had been lucky to escape.

Frankenstein, unharmed but trembling, was slow to emerge from his concealment, and appeared stunned when he came out into the candlelight again. Walton, for the first and only time, behaved toward me as to a fellow man, offering me congratulations and even his hand to shake. Saville did not extend himself that far, but I got a nod of approval from him, and a word or two, such as he might have bestowed upon a favorite dog or horse.

The field was ours. We were left in possession of a small stock of dead women and children, four or five bodies in all. Some of them, which I had not observed till now, were on another trestle table even deeper in the shadows of the room. All were ours now by right of possession, and even legally, if what the resurrectionists had said on that subject was true—I learned later that it was.

But a cursory examination by Frankenstein showed that none of the remains were at all suitable for his purposes. He was a different man, authoritative again, as he looked the bodies over.

I was not even chided for my disobedience in having left the ship and followed my supposed masters; and I was allowed to stand by, listening openly to the discussion. After all, the enemy might conceivably return, and I might once more be needed.

In the end we abandoned the field, not desiring to retain any of the spoils. The only practically useful thing to come out of the episode was a suggestion by Walton, that struck him while looking at the corpses. It was that hogsheads of brine might be just the thing in which to keep our merchandise when it was finally obtained. Such containers could be loaded aboard his ship and transported to our final destination without alarming the sailors who did the work; there would be no need to inform them of the true nature of the cargo.

But on that night we returned empty-handed to

the ship. Whatever scheme was decided upon would have to be put into practice later, with the help of another and more tractable crew of resurrectionists.

Such was my first night in London.

I am pushing on to the south. But first I shall take the time to bid a last solemn *au revoir* to Father Jacques.

LETTER 1

October 17, 1782
To: The Honorable Benjamin Franklin
Hôtel de Valentinois, Passy, France

Honored Sir and Parent—

Let me begin by adding my own small congratulations to those that must be pouring in upon you from all corners of Europe and America, on your success in representing the cause of our fledgling nation (for I believe we must eventually be no less than that) with the French. Since Yorktown a year ago there has been no doubt that King George must eventually come to serious negotiations; and I have no doubt that when that time arrives you will represent us admirably in dealings with the English Crown.

I have read with care your instructions regarding the investigation you wish carried out of the strange events involving the Frankenstein family of Geneva. I appreciate the fact of your personal acquaintance with the family, and your resulting interest. Naturally I shall do my best.

Indeed, if it were not for your personal knowledge of some of the participants, and the assurances you give me regarding them, I would be inclined to regard the whole matter—the supposed facts, as you state them—as a hoax. But you are my employer as well as my begetter, and I am sure you do not mean to waste my time or your own upon a chimera.

When your message reached me, I was already in a convenient location (yes, upon another matter, in which you have an interest; no need to mention it here) and so I proceeded directly to the university town of Ingolstadt. I am writing this in a small rented room in the very house in which the then-student, Victor Frankenstein, conducted his mysterious experiments up until three years ago; and where his supposed monster was created. (I say "supposed" advisedly, Sir; you will no doubt appreciate why, as you read on).

The town of Ingolstadt is interesting to American eyes, and no doubt worthy of description; but I shall not try your patience much in that regard. Suffice it to say that the old church is as picturesque as claimed for it, and there is here a printing press of the fifteenth century, which you, in memory of your original profession, would no doubt find worthy a visit on some more peaceful and leisurely occasion.

As the seat of a university of some reputation, Ingolstadt is accustomed to entertaining wandering youths of diverse nationalities, and my presence here has evoked a second look from no one. A few preliminary questions, asked in a tavern or two, gained me sufficient information about the location of the house. When I arrived at her door, the landlady, a Frau Bauer, assumed without asking that I was a student. One of the vacant rooms she showed me was, I was sure, the very chamber where he lodged, near the top of the house. (I will give, presently, more on the reasons for my certainty.) Naturally I engaged the room at once.

From the landing outside its door a small, narrow stair goes up even higher; despite a firm prohibition from Frau Bauer, I have managed to get a look at the single room up there, and am convinced that it is the very chamber where the Frankenstein experiments took place. It contains no real bed, only a long, low table, stained and marble-topped, with drain and sink attached, reminding me of something out of a dissecting-room at medical school—save only that this example is nine feet long. A couple of other tables and some shelves, all empty, and most of them stained as if with powerful chemicals, complete the furnishings. There are certain metal fittings screwed into the woodwork on the walls and at the window, that I found curiously reminiscent, Sir, of some of your own electrical equipment; it was almost as if one of your lightning-conductors had been installed in the room and then partially removed.

There are marks on the door and frame, suggesting that several locks and bolts once there have also been removed. One lock remains, and it is ordinarily kept secured.

Once settled into my rented room, I began to ask questions about the young man, Victor Frankenstein, who lived here only a few short years ago. Frau Bauer gave me suspicious looks at that point, and no real information. I did not press the matter with her, but walked out to see what I could learn among the academics themselves.

I have heard much conversation from these gentlemen in a brief time, but as to what I have learned . . . I understood from your letter, Sir, who met the young man once and have long known his father, that this young Frankenstein, if his claims were true, was not only the foremost electrical experimenter in Europe, but absolutely the first in the entire world. From what I have been able to learn so far here at the university, from the men who knew him, he is either one of the world's greatest philosophers, as you suggest—or one of its greatest frauds and humbugs.

M. Waldman, the first professor that I spoke to, claims to have once met you (I sometimes think that almost every educated man in Europe has done so), and on reading my letter of introduction was at pains to welcome "the son of the distinguished Franklin." His English is far better than my German, and perhaps superior to my French, and so we conversed mostly in English.

Perhaps you will remember M. Waldman. He is now in his fifties, a man of quiet dignity with an air of sadness about him; short and straight of build, with a pleasant, convincing voice. He has read the Walton account of the Frankenstein affair (which is the same version, I trust, as that which came to your attention in Paris and caused you to write to me). M. Waldman seems to find it difficult to believe that such fantastic events—the reanimation of corpses, etc.—could really have taken place; but evidently he can see no alternative to belief. Or rather, perhaps, he will consider none.

Matters are quite different with M. Krempe, professor of natural philosophy, who also held that post during the years when Victor Frankenstein was a student here. Krempe also counseled the young man, and says that he remembers him quite well. Krempe like Waldman is short in physical stature, but beyond that it would be hard to find two men who are more different. Krempe's voice is gruff and forbidding, his face—not to mince words—ugly, and his whole personal appearance slovenly to an unusual degree.

Krempe's first reaction to the name of Frankenstein was a cold stare. "Have you really, young man," were his first words to me, "spent much time and effort in pursuing this story? I advise you strongly to give it up. Victor Frankenstein's work was ——!"

The concluding word was spoken in some dialect, an obscure one I think, of German. I heard it but imperfectly at the time, partly because of the explosive violence with which it reached my ears; and I would hesitate to try to set down its orthography; but I fear the precise meaning was unmistakable from the great expression of contempt with which it was uttered.

From my student days I am well aware that disagreements among learned professors are no rarity in universities, and I suppose that Ingolstadt is no exception. But this conflict seems unusually fierce. The one thing all parties are in agreement on is that Frankenstein should not be much talked about at all; and this accord, combined with their evident strong divergence of opinion about the experiments themselves, makes me think that the truth, if I can uncover it, ought to be interesting indeed.

Now, as to the Walton papers—what Waldman has shown me is an English-language copy of a thick pamphlet, really a book, entitled *Frankenstein; or, the Modern Prometheus*, that was published in London this summer and seems to be identical to the one you mentioned to me: the production of an English Captain Robert Walton, purporting to contain Victor Frankenstein's true story, as told to Walton aboard his ship. The story is couched in the form of letters from Walton to his sister, a Mrs. Saville, in London.

Frankly, Sir, I find it, on first reading, an incredible relation. Captain Walton would have us believe that Frankenstein, who had been traveling alone by dogsled, came aboard the captain's ship, the *Argo*, while she was on the verge of being locked into the Arctic ice last summer. The young philosopher, emaciated and weakened by great hardship, gasped out—at considerable length, and with many digressions—his tale of monsters, murder, and revenge, and then died in the captain's arms.

Walton also reports a brief visit to his ship by the monster, following the death of Frankenstein, after which the creature was last seen driving another dogsled in the general direction of the Pole. There the nameless "demon" (as his creator often calls him in the book) vowed to die, in some such words as these: "I shall ascend my funeral pile triumphantly, and exult in the agony of the torturing flames . . . my ashes will be swept into the sea by the winds."

Yes Sir, all in all, I certainly have my doubts. If there were no other obstacle to arouse them, the improbability of anyone planning to arrange a "funeral pile" in that wasteland of ice and water would be enough.

I would send you a copy of the whole Walton relation as it exists here, so that you could be sure it is identical to the version you have already seen; but I have at the moment only M. Waldman's own copy, which he has been kind enough to let me borrow—your name, Father, is one to conjure with, here in Ingolstadt as elsewhere. In any case, my own first hurried look at the story assures me that it rambles and wanders into many digressions. It will be easier for both of us, I think, if I assume your familiarity with the general matter of it. I will copy directly for you only those passages that seem to bear most directly on that central topic in which you are interested—the existence or nonexistence of the monster—and his true origins, nature, and behavior if he does exist. Thus we may be sure we are considering the same supposed events.

In this publication of letters from the pen of Walton, then, Victor Frankenstein is quoted as describing briefly his childhood and early youth in Geneva, as a member of that prominent family with whom you, Sir, are acquainted.

The book says that Victor's interest in natural philosophy, and in electrical phenomena in particular, was sharply awakened at age fifteen, when a giant tree was "shattered in a singular manner" before his eyes during a thunderstorm.

> On this occasion (his journal continues) a man of great research in natural philosophy was with us, and excited by this catastrophe, he entered on the explanation of a theory which he had formed on the subject of electricity and galvanism, which was at once new and astonishing to me . . .

I suppose, Sir, you have no difficulty in recognizing yourself in this, as the "man of great research." I had none, having heard, years ago and from your own lips, the anecdote of the riven tree and the fascinated Genovese youth. Might it be that you now feel some responsibility for young Victor's later philosophical endeavors? If so I hope that you do not concern yourself unnecessarily.

To this extent, then, the Walton relation is confirmed. But we have barely started.

It was two years after the incident of the riven tree that young Frankenstein went off to the university, having wasted much of the intervening time in studying, for some reason, such ancient and long superseded authorities on nature as Paracelsus, Cornelius Agrippa, and Albertus Magnus. As to why he then chose the university at Ingolstadt, or why, perhaps, his father chose it for him, I can discover no clue in the Walton papers. Perhaps the reason can be unearthed elsewhere.

At Ingolstadt the young student "attended the lectures and cultivated the acquaintance of the men of science," who soon disabused him of the ideas he had gained from Albertus Magnus and other half-wizards of the past. M. Waldman and M. Krempe are the only two faculty members mentioned by name in Walton's letters, both rather favorably. But as you may know, Sir, there is also at Ingolstadt a medical school of no little reputation. Frankenstein does not mention enrolling in that school, and there is no record that he did so. Still he may have attended certain classes . It may have been then that he found his attention "peculiarly attracted" to "the structure of the human frame."

> Whence, I often asked myself, did the principle of human life proceed? It was a bold question, and one which had never been considered as a mystery; yet with how many things are we upon the brink of becoming acquainted, if cowardice or carelessness did not restrain our inquiries.

He was not long at the university before determining to "apply himself more particularly to those branches of natural philosophy which relate to physiology."

> To examine the causes of life, we must first have recourse to death. I became acquainted with the science of anatomy, but this was not sufficient; I must also observe the natural decay and corruption of the human body. In my education my father had taken the greatest precautions that my mind should not be

impressed with supernatural horrors. I do not remember ever to have trembled at a tale of superstition or to have feared the apparition of a spirit. Darkness had no effect upon my fancy, and a churchyard was to me merely the receptacle of bodies deprived of life, which, from being the seat of beauty and strength, had become food for the worm. Now I was led to examine the cause and progress of this decay, and forced to spend days and nights in vaults and charnel houses. My attention was fixed upon every object the most insupportable to the delicacy of human feelings . . .

His studies continued until:

After days and nights of incredible labor and fatigue, I succeeded in discovering the cause of generation and life; nay, more, I became myself capable of bestowing animation upon lifeless matter.

How he managed to perform this feat, he never says. There are only a few scattered hints throughout the book.

I have quoted all this, so far, Sir, without comment. But now let me state my own opinion more bluntly than before. It is that M. Krempe's evaluation of Frankenstein's work may well be right.

In your letter to me you say you "have good reason" to believe there is some truth in even "the strangest of these events," though you do not disclose the reason. So you will not agree, at least unconditionally, with my first assessment; and you may of course rest assured that I shall continue to do my best, whatever my personal opinion, to find out the exact truth.

One point, that continues to add fuel to my suspicions, is my failure so far to discover any witness in Ingolstadt who will admit to actually having seen the monster with his own eyes, though several, like Professor Waldman, are convinced of the truth of its existence. One witness in particular whom I have so far sought in vain is a peasant known only as Karl, or Big Karl, who frequented the lower quarters of the town, and is said by some of the townsfolk to have been employed as a laborer by Frankenstein, and sometimes seen in his company. Big Karl apparently left Ingolstadt at about the same time—three years ago—as Frankenstein himself.

To return to the Frankenstein (or at least the Walton) account. Here is the young philosopher's description of his own reactions when he realized he had discovered how to create life:

> When I found so astonishing a power placed within my hands, I hesitated for a long time concerning the manner in which I should employ it. Although I possessed the capacity of bestowing animation, yet to prepare a frame for the reception of it, with all its intricacies of fibres, muscles, and veins, still remained a work of inconceivable difficulty and labor. I doubted at first whether I should attempt the creation of a being like myself, or one of simpler organization; but my imagination was too much exalted by my first success to per-

mit me to doubt of my ability to give life to
an animal as complex and wonderful as man
... as the minuteness of the parts formed a
great hindrance to my speed, I resolved, contrary to my first intention, to make the being
of a gigantic stature, that is to say, about
eight feet in height, and proportionately large.

After arriving at this decision, Frankenstein
"spent some months in successfully collecting and
arranging his materials." The proximity of the medical school and its suppliers, who must have a
stock of bodies constantly available for dissection,
would, I suppose, have been of some help to him
at this point. So might the sturdy Big Karl, whose
comings and goings were sometimes noticed, though
only when they took place in daylight.

Who shall conceive the horrors of my secret
toil as I dabbled among the unhallowed damps
of the grave or tortured the living animal to
animate the lifeless clay?

This, sir—if we are determined to take the matter seriously—I believe to be the most direct hint
in the entire relation, as to exactly what means
Frankenstein used to achieve animation—somehow
the "torture," by some means, of a living animal,
was essential. But not sufficient.

I collected bones from charnel-houses and disturbed, with profane fingers, the tremendous
secrets of the human frame. In a solitary chamber or rather cell, at the top of the house, and

separated from all the other apartments by a
gallery and staircase, I kept my workshop of
filthy creation; my eyeballs were starting from
their sockets in attending to the details of my
employment.

And so were mine, dear Sir, I assure you, when I
first glanced over this horrific record. But then I
soon grew doubtful.

Fortunately for our purposes—and no doubt for
Frankenstein's as well—Frau Bauer is somewhat
deaf, and suffers a stiffness in the joints that makes
her unable to climb to the small topmost room
within her tall old house. She is a touch near-
sighted too, I think. The small handful of other
lodgers are as elderly and harmless as herself. So
it is perhaps possible that such researchers as those
described by Frankenstein could have been carried
out inside her house without her knowing it. I
ought to mention that the house, and the rear
stairway, are easily accessible from an alleyway in
the rear. For Big Karl or anyone else to come and
go unseen by night would have been perfectly
easy.

The job of "filthy creation," according to Walton's quotation of Frankenstein, took him at least
an entire year.

It was on a dreary night of November that I
beheld the accomplishment of my toils. With
an anxiety that almost amounted to agony, I
collected the instruments of life around me,
that I might infuse a spark of being into the
lifeless thing that lay at my feet. It was al-

ready one in the morning; the rain pattered
dismally against the panes, and my candle
was nearly burnt out, when, by the glimmer
of the half-extinguished light, I saw the dull
yellow eye of the creature open; it breathed
hard, and a conclusive motion agitated its
limbs.

But success, so long sought and long delayed,
brought only "horror and disgust" to the experimenter.

Unable to endure the aspect of the being I
had created, I rushed out of the room and
continued for a long time traversing my bedchamber, unable to compose my mind to sleep.
At length lassitude succeeded to the tumult
I had before endured, and I threw myself on
my bed in my clothes . . .

And slept. But not for long.

I started from my sleep with horror . . . a cold
dew covered my forehead, my teeth chattered,
and every limb became convulsed; when, by
the dim and yellow light of the moon, as it
forced its way through the window—shutters,
I beheld the wretch—the miserable monster
whom I had created. He held up the curtain
of the bed; and his eyes, if eyes they may be
called, were fixed on me. His jaws opened,
and he muttered some inarticulate sounds,
while a grin wrinkled his cheeks. He might
have spoken, but I did not hear; one hand

was stretched out, seemingly to detain me, but I escaped and rushed downstairs.

And out of doors, where he spent the night, as he says, "catching and fearing each sound" in terror of "the approach of the demoniacal corpse" to which he had given life.

Strange behavior, Sir, I think, for a man who brags of being utterly free of all superstitious terror.

In the morning Frankenstein, accompanied by a friend of his named Henry Clerval (who is now, unfortunately, also reported dead) re-entered the house and ascended to the upper rooms. The creature, to Frankenstein's joy and amazement, had completely disappeared. Clerval, who had no idea of what sort of experiments had been going on, or of their result, was "frightened and astonished" to see how the philosopher in his relief "jumped over the chairs," clapped his hands, and laughed aloud.

Frankenstein then very promptly—on the same day—fell ill, with an acute attack of brain fever, from which it took him months to recover. During these months no appearances of the "monster" are recorded anywhere.

Frau Bauer says she remembers no such extended period of illness afflicting her lodger. She does, I think, remember the night of the experiment, almost three years ago—some peculiarity then occurred—it is hard to get her to say anything that might allow me to deduce what it was. But according to her, only a few days after that night, Victor Frankenstein, appearing agitated but healthy, left her house and the town, never to return. The university records support this. Frau Bauer says she thought the young man was going back to his home in Geneva.

I fear, Sir, that this epistle has already grown far too long, and I am uncertain whether you, having read this far in it, may not already have concluded that the information that prompted you to write me was mistaken, this whole matter is all silliness, and that neither of us should waste more time upon it. That is—I am almost sure—my own opinion. It would be so without qualification, were it not for the grimly silent attitudes of some of the people here. There is a certain looking over the shoulder that I detect—though it is hard to put one's finger on—and what might be a tremulous secret listening.

I fear that I am not conveying my impressions well. They are that *something* quite out of the ordinary happened here three years ago, something startling which has not yet become common knowledge. And I am quite sure that the truth of it has not yet been told, in Walton's pamphlet or anywhere else.

Yr Obdt Srvt
Benjamin Freeman

LETTER 2

November 3, 1782

My esteemed Parent—

My life here at the university, or rather on its fringes, goes on apace. Most of the folk whom I encounter in Ingolstadt, I am sure, take it for granted that I am but another student—I am only a handful of years older than most of those in attendance. Still I flatter myself that were I to put on a solemn mien, I could convince many that I am a youngish master.

To my American eyes and ears this university is something of a strange place, filled with rumors of a secret society called Illuminaries, or Illuminists, and including in the student body, as it does, a number of young men whose favorite recreation, beyond drinking beer and wenching, seems to be duelling one another with swords.

And, perhaps rather more to our present purpose, there is the medical school.

I have learned that a certain medical student, enrolled here until four years ago, was named Saville—it is of course to a Mrs. Saville, in London, that the Walton letters are supposedly addressed. Whether this coincidence of names be more than a mere result of chance, is certainly one of the questions that ought to be answered in the course of my investigation. Quite possibly, if there is a real Mrs. Saville in London, it was she who arranged for their widespread publication.

The story here is that the student Saville, having attained the age of five-and-twenty years, came into a very considerable inheritance. At about that time he ceased to be a student, the former circumstance no doubt contributing materially to the latter. However, he continued in residence in Ingolstadt for some time, probably a month or two, after ceasing to attend the university. Alas, the well-to-do Ingolstadt Saville is no longer here, though in his case I have heard no report of death.

M. Krempe has been kind enough to let me audit one or two of his classes, and I am coming to think that his tirade against Frankenstein should not be taken too seriously. While I was in his presence the good professor delivered at least two more similar outbursts, one against lazy students in general, and the other targeted (sorry, Father, I know you dislike the cobbling of good nouns into verbs; perhaps it is my recent efforts to speak German that derange my English) against some unnamed colleagues on the faculty, for precisely what crime I am not sure.

I do have the feeling, however, that the professor's feelings against Frankenstein are especially bitter, as if there had been at one time some real affection, now betrayed.

As for M. Waldman, the speech I have heard him deliver to a group of beginning chemistry students was but little different, I think, from one that is recorded in the Walton papers:

> The ancient teachers of this science promised impossibilities and performed nothing. The modern masters promise very little; they know that metals cannot be transformed, and that the elixir of life is a chimera. But these philosophers, whose hands seem made only to dabble in dirt, and their eyes to pore over microscope or crucible, have indeed performed miracles. They ascend into the heavens; they have discovered how the blood circulates, and the nature of the air we breathe. They have acquired new and almost unlimited powers; they can command the thunders of heaven, mimic the earthquake, and even mock the invisible world with its own shadows.

Stirring words, but I think that the old man's heart is no longer in them when he delivers his set speech of inspiration to each new crop of students. Something, I think, has happened to discourage him.

And I do *not* think that any philosopher has yet ascended very far into the heavens, nor begun to command the thunders thereof; but you, Father, are more advanced in these matters than I, and must correct me if I am wrong.

My talks with both professors again today confirmed the difference in their views of Frankenstein and his experiments. Waldman still has almost reverent feelings toward his former student, whom he considers a great genius; nor does he believe that the terrible events that followed, in Geneva and perhaps elsewhere, were Frankenstein's fault. But Waldman persists in his reluctance to speak of the subject, and only my repeated mention of your interest induced him to say as much to me as he did.

Later—a small flirtation with a maidservant here in Frau Bauer's house has enabled me to take another look at certain parts of the establishment where the good landlady does not wish anyone to trespass. I am perfectly sure now that the little room at the top was Frankenstein's laboratory, and that secret, or at least inconspicuous, access to it is perfectly possible by means of the stair at the rear of the house and the alley behind it.

And you will be pleased to know, Father—I may have mentioned it before—that the iron points of your most famed invention are in use here, as I suppose they are in every more or less civilized region of the globe. This house wears two of them upon its uppermost extremities; yet I can see where it has sustained some damage, almost certainly from lightning, upon a chimney near the high room in which the experiments took place. Perhaps the young philosopher who used these rooms, in his eagerness to sample the electric fluid from the clouds, took liberties with the arrangement of conducting rods to the detriment of the good Frau Bauer's property.

I continue to pursue my inquiries as best I can. Failing to receive any instructions to the contrary from you within the next fortnight, I purpose to travel on to Geneva, there to investigate the next chapter in the story.

Yr Obdt Son

Benjamin Freeman

P.S. I shall not forget to look further into the matter of "Saville" before I go.

Chapter 7

November 9, 1782—
I have arrived at long last in Montreal. The final days of my journey were accomplished over the surface of a river covered with several feet of ice, upon which snow of equal thickness has already fallen. More snow is descending now. If I have not outraced the winter to this latitude, I have at any rate survived it in the wilderness.

I have already visited the house of Father Jacques' ecclesiastical superiors. I cannot say that they were particularly saddened to hear that he was dead— more annoyed, as if it might cause some inconvenience to their plans. I wonder how warm my friend's welcome would in fact have been, had he survived to meet them. When I told them of his fate, they at first gave the impression that they half suspected me of murdering their fellow priest— though they did not venture to indicate why I should have done so and then come to them to report his death.

Then one of them took pity on me, so far as to make a half-hearted offer of some menial employment—a form of charity, of course—but I declined with what I believe was dignity. My would-be benefactor appeared to be surprised and insulted by my adopting such an attitude. I realize that I am proud sometimes, and I wonder why. My position in the world is certainly unique, anomalous: I am neither peasant nor lord, commoner nor king, slave nor nobleman. I am only what the world takes me for. And so far, with a few exceptions, it has taken me for nothing but a nightmare.

I can sense already that in America all these and other categories into which human beings are arranged count for far less than they do in the Old World. Perhaps I am, like Franklin, an American, in spirit if not by birth.

However that may be, I am not sheltering tonight in the establishment of the haughty priests—Oratorians, I think they are—but under the solid stable roof of someone else, who does not know that I am here. Naturally I am all but penniless, and expect to go hungry if I do not find work tomorrow. But I am told, and can well believe, that sturdy fellows are everywhere in demand for clearing snow. And I certainly fit that category, if no other.

During my several passages today through the streets of Montreal, folk gaped at me, even as others have done, in the past, in Europe. None today were bold enough to say the words aloud: Behold the hideous giant!—but I am inured to that reaction now, whether it is silent or outspoken. And I have learned that humans, or some of them at least, are capable of better things.

Despite the reactions of the crowd, it is obvious that the city—any city, European or American, and the bigger the better—is a more congenial place for me than any but the most exceptional village or farm would be. A city is accustomed to the odd. Today there were heads turning to look after me, and there was some laughter, and some uneasiness. But no one screamed and fled at my approach, or took it to be his duty to fire a gun at me.

November 10— As I expected, I experienced little difficulty this morning in finding work as a laborer, and earning the few coins needed for bread and soup and a place to lie in comparative warmth. My giant's frame promises such a capacity for work that employers are ready to ignore my face. I have also been lucky enough to come into the possession of a few used garments that fit me not too ill. I rest tonight above a stable, where I share a loft with several of my fellow-laborers. They have generously given me half of the considerable space all to myself; no doubt at this moment they are curious as to what I am writing, but I doubt that any of them will develop the courage to ask.

Should they ever have the chance to read what I intend to set down tonight, they will find their courage tested.

After that first encounter with the resurrectionists, the gentlemen and I remained for several months in London. During all this time I lived ashore, simple lodgings having been provided for me in a dockside warehouse now owned by Saville. This building provided a place where he and Walton, as men concerned in maritime trade, could reasonably maintain an office and greet callers who came to them on business. It was a huge, rambling, brick structure, and with its many rooms suited our purposes admirably. My quarters, naturally, were neither spacious nor very comfortable, yet still they offered a vast improvement over what I had been forced to endure aboard the ship. And no attempt was made to confine me to my quarters closely; each of the gentlemen had many other concerns to keep him occupied, and I suppose each of them assumed that the others generally had me in charge.

Though I valued my liberty, I was in no hurry to escape, being nearly as afraid of the public outside the warehouse walls as the public might have been of me. The practical effect of all this was that I enjoyed a much greater degree of freedom than aboard ship, and at night I allowed a natural curiosity to draw me out of my dull, cramped quarters and into the streets of the great city. There darkness allowed me considerable latitude for exploration, without my appearance exciting the wonder and fear of the crowd.

What marvels, though they must have been mere commonplace events to the dwellers in the dockside hovels, I beheld whilst lurking in the darkness! In this half-world of the befogged metropolis, the few fragmented memories retained by my body of its former life, or lives (if such indeed were the sources of my pieces of inexplicable knowledge) could offer me no guidance. I observed the terror and struggles of the great city's poor, and the follies, sometimes equally terrible, of her wealthy. I learned, among other things, a little more about what men and women can be like. Keeping to the shadows of the city's night with timid determination, I retreated quickly when any started to take notice of me, and took extreme care that no one should observe my comings and goings from the warehouse.

During the day, I always remained indoors. It was during this time that Victor, carefully measuring my feet—he was always so precise with measurements—arranged that a pair of boots should be custom-made for me.

With his newly gathered equipment, he had quickly improvised a new laboratory, much larger than his workroom had been at Ingolstadt, in an upper room of the otherwise largely disused warehouse. In his new workshop he took measurements of me—never anything so mundane as my simple height—and tested me, on machines that tried my strength and my endurance. And he would sometimes sit for a long time, chin on hand, pondering my existence.

Meanwhile he looked forward to his next series of experiments, which were to provide me with at least one mate. He grumbled frequently about the early difficulty of obtaining the necessary raw materials. Success in that endeavor was not too long in coming, though; in London money could do anything. The *Argo* had remained in port, and Captain Walton needed very little time to establish contact with a second group of Resurrectionists, who proved to be more competent as well as more peaceful than the first. The leader of this new company was a man named Eli Hammer, whose wife, Matilda played an active role in his enterprise as well. Mrs. Hammer was a rather prim-looking matron of about forty, who, when I observed her through a knothole in an interior wall, appeared well qualified to be a chaperone. Meanwhile I was enjoined, by all four of my first managers, to keep myself at all times out of sight of the new employees as they began to come and go around the warehouse. At the time I supposed that the Hammers would probably never learn of my existence.

Mrs. Hammer possessed a valuable skill at figures, and as part of his agreement with her husband, Saville found regular employment for her at a desk in his warehouse office. The entire small staff, who had formerly conducted the modest normal business of the building, had been dismissed when we moved in.

This epoch also marked the first appearance among us of one who was to become the most dangerous of my enemies. This was a man called Small, a pockmarked, sandy-haired person of about thirty years of age, ugly yet quite vain about his person, distinguished by demoniac energy and a controlled fierceness of manner. I have never heard him spoken to, or spoken of, by any other name than Small. His stature suited his name, and I am sure that his spirit, if indeed he has one—I have no reason to doubt that he still breathes—is smaller yet.

The explanation of Small's presence came to me gradually, through words overheard here and there and actions observed. Saville, evidently thinking matters over after our brawl with the first party of graverobbers, and not wishing to have to depend upon my help in any future violent disagreement, had found this man somewhere—God knows where—and hired him as bodyguard and general factotum. That a man of physically small stature could demonstrate proficiency as a bodyguard says something about his other qualifications.

But the arrival of the abominable Small was not, by far, the greatest alteration in our company. Not only romance but marriage had entered Saville's life, whether shortly before or shortly after his sudden though not unexpected inheritance of wealth I am still not sure. His betrothed was none other than Walton's only sister, Margaret. The couple had known each other at least slightly, I gathered, for years before Saville came into his fortune; but as the date of his twenty-fifth birthday drew near she had acted in a timely way to renew and strengthen the acquaintance. Later I learned that Margaret was a widow, a little older than her new husband.

It was not only Roger's wealth that the lady found attractive; the two of them were in truth kindred spirits. Almost from the time of our arrival in London he shared with her the plans he had worked out to gain advantage from the discoveries of Frankenstein. Their wedding, a quietly-managed affair—somehow I failed to receive an invitation—took place shortly after our business operations had moved into the warehouse.

Several times before the wedding, when Saville was engaged in business elsewhere, his bride-to-be visited the warehouse. Frankenstein at first objected to the presence, just outside his laboratory, of this woman he did not even know, and objected even more strongly to her being given knowledge of his work, and the plans to expand and perfect it. Clerval seconded my creator's protests. But it had long been clear that Saville was the senior member of the partnership, and he would hear of nothing but that his new wife be included immediately and as a full partner. Walton, perhaps knowing his sister well, had no complaint to make.

"She's in, and that's that," Saville said, shortly after completing the formal introduction of his bride to Frankenstein and Clerval. There was little that they could say. I, of course, had not been introduced, but was observing the ceremony through a convenient knothole in the wall between the room of the meeting and a passage leading to my own rude accommodations.

The lady, perhaps feeling somewhat unwelcome, departed soon after the introductions were over, and without actually seeing me. Looking back now, I think that she had not yet grasped the fact that I, the proof of the scheme on which money was to be spent, was physically present somewhere on the premises.

It was not that Margaret ruled Roger, as some women are able to rule their husbands, but that he, confident of his authority, sought to put to use her naturally great abilities.

Her next visit to the warehouse came shortly after the wedding, I think on the very next day. It occurred at an hour when Saville was elsewhere, engaged in some other of the numerous enterprises that consume the time and effort of a man of wealth.

Naturally, since the time when her husband-to-be had first told her about our establishment and its goals, her curiosity had grown enormously. She was now unwilling to wait any longer to learn about the mysterious enterprise in which he was engaged with a sea captain, and a philosopher; and to see and hear what evidence existed of the tremendous secret they possessed, and that had awakened in them all such dreams of avarice and power.

She returned to the building on an afternoon when Victor alone of the gentlemen was present, and bullied him into exhibiting me to her—or, rather, she was well on the way to achieving such a result when I decided that the time had come to take my own destiny more firmly in hand. What harm was this young woman likely to be able to do me? Standing tall and walking boldly, I emerged from my usual place of hiding, into the laboratory where she could see me. My creator turned from the lady to gaze at me in consternation; I had managed to surprise him utterly.

The lady too was surprised. "What is it?" she asked Victor in a whisper. Yet in her eyes, as she gazed upon my countenance, was not terror or disgust, but interest tinged with horror.

I said, "I am capable of speaking for myself, Madam."

Victor, with spasmodic arm movements that he must have thought were subtle but forceful gestures, was trying to quiet me. Meanwhile he assured his guest that she was in no danger.

But the woman only gave him a contemptuous look, and turned back to me. She too was able to decide what her own ideas were, and to express them. "Where are you from?" she asked me at last.

"Bavaria," I replied evenly. "And you?"

A stunned silence greeted this bold question. Realizing promptly that something was amiss, I hastened to offer an apology. "Forgive my lack of social graces; but you see, my education has been inadequate. No one's fault, really, I suppose, but there it is—if there is aught you would like to ask me, I repeat, I am quite capable of speaking for myself. As I see you are."

My creator was speechless. As for the lady, she shook her lovely head in silence, not knowing what to make of me. The fashion for high-piled constructions in the hair was coming in that year, but this lady would not incommode herself with such nonsense; black natural ringlets shook, tumbled, against ivory skin. I think the fact that she did not know just what to think delighted her, instead of producing a stunned or angry reaction, as it would have done in a lesser woman.

Other words were said between us on that occasion; I find that now I cannot very well remember them. I do know that our meeting ended with the suggestion, at least, that Mrs. Saville intended somehow to get to know me better.

The time came when Frankenstein's gathering of materials was nearly finished, and our stay in London was drawing to its close. I still did not exist, officially. The story put forward locally by the gentlemen to explain their activities was that they had formed a company to go into the north of Ireland, there to establish a hospital for indigent fishermen and their families. How many people in London who heard this story of the hospital actually believed it I do not know. But no one scoffed openly at the pretense, as far as I am aware. I have said that Saville was—and is—immensely wealthy.

For reasons I was not completely aware of at the time, it was decided among the gentlemen that a certain increase in staff was necessary. Mrs. Hammer somehow recruited two poor girls, Bess and Molly, both very young, sturdy and healthy, to join our establishment. They were to accompany us when we sailed (to Ireland, as they were told) and serve some role as hosuekeepers when we established a hospital for fishermen. I believe that both of them were country lasses, only recently arrived in London.

In private conversation Victor told me that he believed the hospital story would provide just the cover that we needed; and that the girls were really needed to serve as housekeepers, when we set up our small colony in isolation. This explanation seemed believable; both young women struck me as at least dimly respectable (How should I have been able to judge? But I could judge such matters. Even then.) and I supposed whores would have been recruited if that service were needed, and it was thought there was a shortage of them in Ireland. There was certainly no insufficiency in great London.

Bess and Molly were not members of the Hammer family, but I am sure that one of the requirements in their recruitment was tolerance for such business activities as that family practiced. Looking back, I suspect, that at least one of the two girls, country origins or not, came from a family engaged somewhere in a similar trade. I believe they were told frankly that when we arrived at our northern destination there would be some such work in progress, delivery of dead patients to a medical school perhaps.

Meanwhile, the task of gathering Victor's necessary materials proceeded quite successfully, with a stock of young female bodies accumulating in our warehouse. I observed Frankenstein, with his own hands, packing these materials in hogsheads of brine, and I wondered how they should be listed in the cargo when we set sail. It did not really occur to me—as yet—to wonder whether all of these bodies had been obtained by robbing graves, or whether the strict requirements for freshness had encouraged our new provisioners to adopt even more enterprising methods.

Walton expressed concern that the two live girls, Bess and Molly, might somehow discover the truth about our cargo. Eventually they would learn it, but preferably not until we had sailed. He employed his literary talents to develop an alternative story, that male bodies were easy to obtain in Ireland, but that there some prudish papist prohibition was in effect against research on females. Whether there was any truth to that portion of his story or not I have never had the opportunity to discover.

Small, as I have said, had attached himself to our group, though making no real contribution that I could see. But he disappeared again a month or two before we were to sail. At the time I was relieved, thinking that perhaps I had seen the last of him, for the dislike between us had been instantaneous and mutual. Later I was to discover that his detachment from our strange community was only temporary, and that Roger knew where he had gone.

By early May of 1780, our preparations were almost complete. We were in fact on the verge of sailing, when a letter arrived for Victor, forwarded from Ingolstadt, through what intermediary I never learned. The message was from my creator's father, who thought his eldest son was still in school at Ingolstadt, and it brought shocking and terrible news—William, Victor's youngest brother, only seven years old, had been most foully murdered. At the time when the venerable Alphonse dispatched his letter, no one in Geneva yet had the slightest idea of who the guilty party might be.

This horrible intelligence took everyone in our establishment by surprise. Victor, of course, was badly shaken. He insisted that he must return to Geneva at once, to see and commiserate with his surviving family, before he secluded himself in some remote place and plunged into what he expected would be months of uninterrupted work. We must wait for him in London; he would return to us as soon as possible.

Hastily the men who thought themselves my masters took counsel together. It was decided that our voyage need not be postponed; the establishment of the new laboratory, on lands also owned by Saville, need not wait for Frankenstein's presence. Saville and Clerval, with some help from

Walton and his men—and from me—could manage the settlement and construction, down to the final arrangement and testing of equipment. We would sail.

I cannot continue to write of those things just now.

I must rest. And soon, somehow, I must get back to Europe.

Chapter 8

Later, the same night—

I cannot sleep. As terrible as the writing must be, I suffer more terribly with it until it is done.

On the thirtieth of May, 1780, we all boarded the *Argo* once again. I, of course, had returned to my cramped cabin-within-a-cabin some hours before our embarkation under cover of darkness. Argo was no passenger vessel, but the time in port had been used in converting some of the cargo space into cabins. Mrs. Hammer and the two young women were given berths in one of these new facilities, and there they remained for most of the voyage, only now and then taking a turn on deck under the watchful eye of Captain Walton. The rest of the passengers were in general accommodated as on the previous voyage, but another cabin was made for Small.

Our passage round Land's End and through the

Irish Sea was mainly uneventful, though, as on our Channel crossing in the same ship, we were beset by storms. It was about a week before we reached our destination.

This was an island whose name I have never heard until this day. Though I am now certain that it lies somewhere among the Hebrides, at the time neither I nor any of the others who had been deceived divined that we were not in Ireland.

There being no proper harbor, we dropped anchor in a small bay and went ashore in boats. On our approach—though it was daylight, I had been allowed on deck as soon as we made landfall—I judged the island to be no more than five miles in its greatest length, and I soon learned that it was only half that wide. A small cluster of central hills, the highest mounting to perhaps a thousand feet above the sea, were covered wtih a carpet of grass, except where, among the hills especially, rocky outcroppings protruded. A few trees grew among the hills, none at all elsewhere.

The day of our arrival was unusually fine; though as I read it my description seems forbidding, with a fresh breeze and sunshine the aspect of the place was extremely pleasant—especially to one who had been out of sight of sun for days.

My pleasure in the view was somewhat altered by the glances I received when I first appeared above the hatches. From the lack of outcry I suppose the crew had already learned that there was an additional passenger, but none were prepared for the sight of me. There were stares and mutterings from the crew, until the captain glared them into silence. Since I cannot believe that Walton

was concerned to spare my feelings I must assume
that he glared at his crew almost every time he
came in sight of them, and heartily disapproved of
any spontaneous action that they might take. Indeed, I expect he was happiest with his crew
when he was writing about them in his book, where
each word and action were under his complete
control.

The nameless, roadless bay at which we came
ashore had been the site of a small fishing settlement, a dozen stone cottages and outbuildings,
though none of the former inhabitants were to be
seen on our arrival. A combination of bad luck in
fishing and a series of disastrous storms had left
the place nearly deserted, and a small payment
from Saville had induced the others to depart for
another island. The settlement's buildings were in
a state of wretched disrepair; in most of the struc-
tures little more than the stone walls remained
standing.

The sailors who had rowed me ashore heaved a
sigh of relief as I stepped from their boat, and
those already ashore were glad enough to keep
their distance as I paced from shallow water up
onto the shingle.

There was a small stream running down through
the village, and I moved toward this, and climbed
along its bank, delighted to be even momentarily
away from others. I thought that I could see a
brown fish darting through the shallows. I suppose now it was a trout. The water in the stream,
this near the sea, was brackish when I bent to
taste it.

The three women had come ashore together, in the boat immediately following mine. Looking back, I saw Bess and Molly, for the moment ignoring the savage character of the place in which they found themselves, offering up prayers of thanksgiving for having solid land once more beneath their feet.

Frankenstein's laboratory equipment, and an ample stock of supplies of all kinds, were soon brought ashore. Walton did not linger; after setting all ashore the *Argo* set sail for London, there to await the return of Frankenstein from his sad mission on the Continent.

The first task we undertook was to set up a few tents. That was the work of an hour only, and in the remaining daylight all hands fell to, to begin the work of restoring the abandoned cottages to a livable condition. As most of the ship's crew had departed with her, much of the heavy labor of this effort fell to me. I had no objection to this, and indeed was pleased to be able, as I thought, to impel the enterprise forward. Two or three crewmen had been left on the island, but they now had the duties of servants—and of guards—to perform as well as those of laborers.

Having left his new wife more or less in charge of his affairs in London, Saville took personal charge of the reconstruction effort, issuing orders on every hand. It was obvious that he was enjoying his wealth and power in a new way in this lonely place, that he delighted in being the absolute lord and master of everything and everyone in sight.

* * *

As awareness of their lonely situation was borne in upon them, Molly and Bess became much cast down, but they had little time in which to mourn their condition. Mrs. Hammer, looking as grim and prim as ever (Hammer himself had remained at his own thriving trade in London) kept the two young women busy from the hours of their arrival, cooking, scrubbing, and washing, serving all the rest of us. Housekeeping was to be their task until, as she told them, the hospital should be ready, when each of them should find herself supervising a staff of Irish menials. This prospect cheered the girls somewhat.

Within an hour of landing I had begun to suspect that this was not Ireland—certain scraps of old papers I found among the litter in the abandoned cottages made me doubt it. And I, of course, had never believed that there was going to be a hospital.

When rain, an almost daily occurrence, came on near evening, I took shelter, as did the common hands, under pieces of tarpaulin. Fires were kept going. Discomfort was nothing new to any of us, and the night passed.

In early morning the sky cleared for a time, and again the world of early summer was transformed into a place of beauty.

I arose, and wandered unnoticed away from the others. Herons were nesting not far from the village, and I paused to watch. Never before had I had the chance, the freedom, to become absorbed in the beauties of nature.

Looking back to where smoke rose from our fires, I saw that the young women were both up early, drawing and fetching water from the stream, carrying their empty buckets uphill and inland to where the water was fresh. In their way the two girls were beautiful too, I thought—parts of the same nature as the herons. But the girls were not of me, nor I of them. I watched and enjoyed them as I did the birds, and dreamed of the mate my creator was going to provide for me. She would look—more or less like me, and I took pleasure in the thought. Despite the universal reaction of those I met, I did not yet consider myself deformed or ugly. That feeling came upon me later, and only more lately still have I begun to rid myself of it.

Forgotten, I wandered unmolested ever farther from the village, seduced by the nature around me. At length I came upon an ancient burial mound, its top on a level with my head. How was I able to recognize it for what it was? How many of my shipmates, it occurred to me to wonder, could? I doubted that even the gentlemen, with their Greek and Latin, would recognize the long earthen shape for what it was.

As I stood musing thus the young women came by several times, carrying their pails upstream for fresh water. Bess, on her second or third trip, dared approach me closely enough to converse. I was ugly in her eyes, of course, but doubtless she had known an ugly man or two before, and found them bearable.

Since it was plain to her I was no gentleman, she could question me freely. She wanted to know my name, and would not believe that I had none to give her. We talked about the strangeness of the place where we found ourselves, and I told her what the mound was. She stared at me, having no idea if what I said was true, and if it was, how I might have come to know about it.

No more did I.

Day passed and our labor of reconstruction made good progress.

Towards the end of July, Walton brought the *Argo* back to our small colony, and Victor was aboard. As he was rowed ashore my creator looked as grim as I had ever seen him. When he jumped from the boat and waded through the last inches of the gentle surf, Clerval and Saville hastened to meet him.

As the rest of us gathered round unbidden on the beach, Frankenstein lost no time in outlining for us the sad strange tale of his murdered brother.

According to the verdict of the law, the child William had been killed by Justine Moritz, the motive being the robbery of some small but valuable portrait, worn like a medallion on a chain. The appearance of the trinket among the belongings of the accused had provided the chief and almost only evidence against her.

That evening, when we were alone in the laboratory (my creator had been most anxious to resume his interrupted labors) Victor related to me his own theory of the crime—that the real killer had been some unknown man, Justine's lover, who had reacted murderously when the child had caught him trying to steal the picture; that Justine's sole crime had been to protect her man with a silence that lasted to the grave.

"Women do strange things, my friend." Frankenstein as he spoke was busy with his long-neglected work, connecting and adjusting certain pieces of his equipment. He had begun calling me his friend, I supposed, because he had never bestowed a name upon me. Nor had any of the others. Perhaps each of them was afraid that some mystical responsibility might devolve upon him who named me.

Of that I could not say, but I concurred at least partially with Frankenstein's opinion about Justine: with her unlikely story of having spent the night alone in a barn, she must be protecting someone.

"If she slept there, someone slept with her." Victor paused, and sipped some brandy, something I had seldom seen him do in London. He stared at the stone wall of the room in which we stood. "To know a woman who would do that for you, and then, more, who would lay down her life . . ."

He drank a little more, letting work go for the moment, and began to discuss with me the prospects of his engagement with Elizabeth. For a moment I thought he might be about to offer me a drink, even though he had said before that it would be bad for me. But no: I sat on a table while *he* drank and listened as he talked.

It was as if there were no one else with whom my creator could discuss this particular subject. He told me how everyone said how beautiful Elizabeth Lavenza was, and he showed me her miniature portrait, a painting probably much like the one for which young William was said to have been killed.

Bess and Molly had been pleasurably saddened

by the story of that distant murder and execution, and both were intrigued by the return among us of the rather handsome young Doctor (the title was by now indisputable among us) with the haunted eyes and emaciated frame.

It was generally understood by everyone, of course, that he was engaged to be married, but he appeared perfectly ready to let matters continue in that halfway state. Were I pledged to share my bed and my life, I thought, with one who appealed to my senses as strongly as Elizabeth Lavenza evidently appealed to men of my creator's race, I would be striving at every moment toward the consummation of the pledge. Suppose Frankenstein should suddenly become eager for the wedding? What would happen to his labors in the laboratory then? It worried me that he might so easily be distracted from the project on which my whole future life depended.

On a second evening, when we were again alone together in the laboratory, he showed me the miniature of Elizabeth.

I asked: "Have you told her anything of your occupation here?"

"No, I dared not."

"Dared not? Why?"

"The . . . the business of creation." Frakenstein shook his head. "It is very horrible."

"Horrible?" I was not thinking of my own appearance, nor was he, I believe, at that moment. "But the result, is it not glorious?" Then I remembered that I was considered very ugly. "I mean the glory of the achievement."

"Yes. No doubt." And in the way he looked at

me then I saw the depth of the fear and loathing that
undermined his pride and his occasional kindness.

I did not care—not enough to be disturbed. There
were times when I feared and loathed him too. I said,
"Saville's woman knows. Why should not yours?"

"What Saville tells his wife is his business."
Then, as if aware of the inadequacy of such an
answer, he hardened his face, and looked at me as
if to rebuke me for daring to take an interest in the
personal affairs of my masters.

The fiction of the hospital died slowly in the
minds of the sailors left on the island, and the two
young women. I heard them now and then, in the
early days especially, talking among themselves,
wondering aloud when the real construction was
going to start, and when and from whence the
patients might be expected to arrive.

This despite the fact that the gentlemen discussed plans incompatible with their stated purpose, plans that I at least was able to overhear. I
recall one conversation in particular, in which
Saville, who happened to be sitting alone with
Walton at the time, set forth in greater detail than
I had ever heard some part of his vision of the future.

"Breeding alone won't do it, my friend. Not when
we have to begin with only a single pair, or at
best a mere handful of females. Oh, a man can
breed slaves profitably enough, given time, a healthy
climate, and a large number of mature females
to begin with. But in our case, no; even if Victor
should produce one female tomorrow, in the nature
of things I suppose it would be twelve or fifteen
years before she had any offspring old enough to

breed, and *another* fifteen years before—but I see you understand."

Walton murmured something.

Saville went on, each word of his careless voice quite plainly audible to me, the unseen listener. "Ah, but there's such strength and hardihood in this thing he's made! What we must arrive at somehow, once Victor has shown the way, is the proper technique for *manufacturing* these creatures, males and females both, in substantial numbers. There are corpses aplenty everywhere, good for nothing now but fertilizer. And if they prove not fresh enough . . . well there is always Africa. A proper selection of brains ought to provide the docility we need—if not, there are ways of teaching the proper attitude, once we have more than one unique specimen that must be coddled."

"Manufacturing them," repeated Walton, quietly marveling.

"The Government has outlawed slavery in our home islands. Very well. But the invention of the living machine—"

There was an interruption, as one of the servants came tapping discreetly at their door; and I could hear no more.

Full summer—as full as it could be in those parts—came on, and the fields of the island blazed up prodigally with wildflowers, more common in the meadows than the grass. Less welcome were the swarms of midges, tiny bloodsucking insects that seemed to grow in strength and numbers as the summer progressed.

As the weeks went on, becoming months, Molly grew gradually more afraid of me, and seemingly of all else on the island as well. Bess, meanwhile, grew accustomed to me, from time to time speaking to me almost as to a friend. What might eventually have happened between us, had she remained alive, I cannot say.

The roofs and walls of all the cottages had at last been thoroughly repaired, with thatch and timbers. Some of the abandoned buildings were stripped of wood, the windows of oiled paper, and other useful items that the restoration of the others might be completed.

Saville, Clerval, and Walton, whenever the latter was ashore, shared the largest of the remaining buildings, in which each one of the three occupied a bedroom, with another common room in which they generally took their meals. The three women of course had another cottage to themselves.

Frankenstein's equipment had all been installed in the cottage selected to become his laboratory, while nearby, under the same roof, our shipments of specimens from London waited. I had rolled that company of hogsheads into the very room where I generally slept, not fearing the silent companionship of my intended brides.

At last, Frankenstein was ready to begin his real work. One after another, those large barrels began to be opened.

There were, of course, no horses on the island, no means of getting from one place to another save by walking, or going around through the surf by boat. I walked a great deal, almost invariably alone. Now and then Clerval chose to come with me, though we seldom talked. Again, without knowing why, I sometimes contemplated flight, and when I found an abandoned boat on the far side of the island from the bay and settlement, the idea came back more strongly. But escape would take me away from the possibility of such happiness as I could concretely imagine, the company of a mate, if not a whole harem of them. And, besides, to where could I flee? I did not fit into the world anywhere but there.

In my lonely walks I descried a distant sail from time to time, and from the vantage point of the central hills could make out other islands in the distance. I judged that the nearest of these was not closer than eight miles; and there was no sign of any commerce between that place and this.

Though in the room next to mine, my creator generally slept, I lived alone, as always.

On one of my solitary rambles, I heard strange cries, and hastened forward to investigate. I discovered the elegant ruffian, Small, attempting to force his will upon Molly. She had perhaps accompanied him willingly to that remote spot; or perhaps he had used threats from the first. But now there was no question as to the state of affairs. Her dress had been torn, and he was menacing her with a knife, while with his left hand he held her wrist.

I approached the pair and warned him to leave off.

Letting the girl go, he turned and threatened me with his knife. We were among one of the rare groves of trees upon the island, and I bent to grab up a fallen branch some seven or eight feet long. As I did so he darted in at me with his knife, but I caught him by the arm and threw him bodily. He fell hard and rolled over and thereafter kept his distance, trying to blister me with foul language, which tactic I found far less impressive than his knife. Happily, he had no pistol, and it was plain now that he could not prevail against me otherwise.

He swore he would report me to Saville, but I laughed and was sure he lied—I could report in turn that he had tried to kill me, and we both understood that if he was important in his master's plans, I was essential. Small also swore to wreak vengeance upon me at some future date. I had no trouble in believing that he wanted to try, but we both knew that Saville was not going to stand for my assassination.

Meanwhile, Molly had fled the scene, and in the end we each made our separate ways back to the settlement, and none of us, for our several reasons, reported the incident at all.

In the way of game our own island had nothing larger than a few wild goats, but there were red deer on one of the other nearby islands, and from time to time, when the weather was fair and promising, the gentlemen took a boat and went hunting them. Except of course, for Frankenstein, who was now lost in his work. He ate food when it was brought to him, and nipped at his brandy when he desired to sleep. Otherwise he worked.

Once or twice I was commanded, by Saville and then by Small, to remain within the confines of the village. I did not argue with these orders, but ignored them. The gentlemen were doubtess aware that I still went wandering, but no one wanted to force a decisive confrontation. Continuing my solitary rambles, I watched the seals, swimming offshore, and as often as not I envied them. I recognized kittiwakes and puffins among the seabirds on the grey gneiss rocks along the shore, and marveled that I knew the names of birds and stone.

One small loch lay in a cup amid the central hills. A few stands of trees remained in that area, mostly dwarfed and twisted, though most had been taken for the villagers' firewood. Some piles of cut peat were near one end of the little settlement, and we mined them to keep our fires going when the weather was chill, which was most of the time, though it was summer.

Meanwhile, in his stone house, Frankenstein worked steadily, or tried to work. It was hard for anyone else to know what degree of success he was having, and he tended to ignore questions. Sometimes he called upon my strength to aid him in manhandling another hogshead into the laboratory, or in its careful emptying. Those parts he considered useless, those on which some operation of his had failed, or from which all bone or other useful material had been extracted, were buried at a little distance from the settlement, where a few neglected graves gave evidence that villagers from time to time had also been laid to rest. Clerval said prayers on these occasions—he became ever more thoughtful and moody, and occasionally he had arguments with Frankenstein, of which I was unable to overhear anything more than the tones of their raised voices.

I now and then indulged a whimsical thought about the bodies—that they were my brides—but in the main I continued to view them impersonally. Whether in hogsheads or graves, they were really only materials, less awesome than the electricity that could be produced in the machines of the laboratory, or drawn down from the sky by slender rods. That these particular pickled arms or breasts or thighs might someday, restored to breathing life, become things of living mystery and objects of my devotion, was too peculiar an idea to arouse in me feelings of awe or bewilderment. Still I was not indifferent. Each time I was called upon to help my creator at his new work, I watched avidly for signs that I could take as indicators of progress, though I found the details repugnant.

From the day on which his labors began, Victor kept the central table and its burden covered with a sheet. There was a single object on that table, awaiting animation, an object that daily drew, bit by bit assuming underneath its shrouds and wrappings a more nearly human configuration, and a size commensurate with my own. I wanted to observe this progress in all its details, but my creator refused to allow it. When I asked him why, he snapped something that was not really an answer; the work was his, a private matter, and he would explain it all in good time.

Saville himself was treated with but little better courtesy. On this point Frankenstein was not to be bullied, bought, or moved.

For my part, I would not have cared at all to be an observer of his activities, had not so much of my future depended on the result. What little I could glimpse of the process, in my comings and goings through the laboratory, was not pretty: the selection of limbs and other parts from the stock available; the grafting of two limb bones to make one of the desired length; the sewing, gluing and splicing of parts together; the preliminary stimulation with Leyden jars and other apparatus.

And, through and over and under it all, the continual struggle against decay. Despite the chemicals and electricity, my nose offered me subtle evidence that the struggle was being slowly lost. How then was it to be finally won? Avidly I followed my creator's progress, and studied the arrangements of his equipment each time I was admitted to the sacred room. But the secret of his success eluded me.

Saville and Clerval, and Walton when he was present, cast impatient glances at the work, and then concentrated their attention peevishly upon the experimenter. I could see that they were hoping almost as intently as I was for indications of success. But the only real indication was the continued confident attitude of Frankenstein himself.

At long last came the day, the night, when Victor announced that he was ready for the final test. The air was chilly with the onset of autumn, and wet, as are most nights in those islands, with intermittent rain, and thunder grumbling in the distance.

Oil lamps were burning brightly in all four corners of the laboratory, and a peat fire smoldered on the hearth. A few candles had been placed closer to the worktable on which the object of our attention lay, giving it something of the aspect of a bier.

Employing my own strength, and my own determination, I had made sure that the ceilings in several of these reconstructed houses, including this one, were high enough to allow me to stand erect. As I first approached the table, at the rear of a group of eager observers, lightning flared outside, and a loud hum sounded from the electrical equipment. I started, as did the other observers.

A moment later, when Frankenstein pulled back the cover, my heart sank. My disappointment was acute. This grotesquely cobbled thing? This devil's handiwork, like some mad mockery of God's? This naked female form all mismatched parts and bandages and chemicals—the open eyes stared blindly back at me from their raw butchered sockets, and I could see that they had come from two different heads—I could not believe that this face, this frame, could be induced by any art to stir with life.

And besides, bloody mosaic though it was, the countenance before me was undoubtedly a *human* face, and not an unclassifiable, *sui generis* visage similar to my own.

The gentlemen had gathered round the table, as close to it as Frankenstein would let them, their faces composing a study in their various emotions. The connections were made to the batteries, the final process was set in motion. The probes in the hands of the philosopher were moved in particular order from one set of points upon the body to another, and at each was made an application of electricity.

There was no immediate response from the subject on the table, except for a minor burning and sizzling, when, now and again, the full force of the electrical fluid was made to pass through the inert flesh.

There was an immediate slight reaction of disappointment among the watchers. But Frankenstein hastened to remind them all, pointing to me as he spoke, that in my case the reanimation had not been immediate either.

"Nor did I suppose," he added, "that an instantaneous response would be obtained tonight."

Eyes turned toward me. I stood before them all as living proof that Victor Frankenstein had once done just what he was attempting to do tonight.

The philosopher continued, "We must be patient. In an hour, perhaps two, there will be evidence of life. I am going to wait here, for the first signs. I would prefer that the rest of you leave, for a time at least. You may return later."

I had at first intended to remain with my creator during his vigil, but could not stand still enough to keep from irritating him, and he soon ordered me out. When I took my leave, the form upon the table was still as inert as it had ever been.

I approached the other gentlemen, who were still outside, smoking and talking, and stood on the fringe of their group. Saville was saying: "I have seen it happen, I tell you. Seen it all, beyond any possibility of trickery. Clerval here can back me up." When Henry had nodded soberly, Saville continued: "Gentlemen, d'you think I'd be here otherwise, staking my gold and my time on a story like this one?"

It was plain from their expressions that no member of the little group had the least intention of thinking anything like that.

It began to rain again, thick mournful drops that spattered heavily. The group drifted toward the warmth and shelter of the largest cottage, with Saville still harking back to what had happened on the night of my creation. "We came there with pranks in mind, but before the night was over . . ."

The cottage door closed softly in my face. I was not to hear the story of that night from Saville then. I hope that I may hear his version of it someday, just before my right hand strangles the last breath in his throat.

Presently I heard the door of the laboratory open, and saw the lamplight flow out into the night. Victor emerged slowly in its path, and walked tiredly along what had once been the village street. He appeared to have no particular goal, but to be only stretching his legs. A little more than an hour had passed since his last pronouncement that the effort was going to be successful.

He stopped in front of me and tilted back his head, and looked me in the eye. "Nothing yet," he said softly, and there was controlled worry in his voice.

He went into the cottage where the others were, and this time I reached out to keep the door from closing in my face. I went in after him.

The others looked at me when I entered, but said nothing.

Frankenstein told them the bad news with a dismissing shake of his head that seemed to assure them that the news was not really bad. He sat down.

"Well," said Walton, to be saying something.

"The bodies that I used in Bavaria were comparatively fresh," Victor remarked absentmindedly, poking the fire and staring into it. "It may be that the preservation in brine has been more detrimental than I anticipated."

He paused. "Then," he added, "there was the idea that occurred to me when I was in Geneva."

"In Geneva?" someone asked, not understanding.

He looked at the questioner. "Yes. It occurred to me, just after the execution of Justine Moritz, that could I have obtained her body, fresh from the scaffold—I am sure that I could have brought her back."

There was a brief silence.

Frankenstein went on to explain that of course he had not had his equipment with him then; and

Elizabeth and others had been there, in front of whom he would not have dared to announce any such seemingly blasphemous scheme. To revive an anonymous corpse was one thing, to defy the law by restoring a condemned criminal something else.

He spoke with calm conviction; I could see that all the others were impressed. But my chief thought at the moment was: *to Victor's knowledge I am not a condemned criminal, then.* It had lately occurred to me to wonder about that point.

Perhaps Saville had thought about it also. "If you could bring back—" He jerked his chin toward me, and broke the statement off.

"Yes, Yes, Justine would have been easy." Frankenstein appeared to be pondering some abstract problem.

It seemed a very long time before the two hours were up. We all walked back in a body to the laboratory building, where things were as we had left them. The body, long, grotesque, and naked, had no more life in it than the table upon which it lay. Saville turned and stalked away, and Small, who had joined us, moved after him. One by one the others left, until I was alone with my creator.

I worked the treadle, and Frankenstein tried the probes once more. We stood there watching for a long time, while nothing happened, except that the dawn began its gray and distant entry on the world.

Chapter 9

At that season the day began at a very early hour. Before it had time to progress very far in its development, there came a messenger trotting toward us through the gloom and rain, from the direction of the largest house.

It was one of the sailors-turned-servant, in a state of quiet excitement. He was clenching his hands and moving his arms as if he did not know what to do with them. "Doctor Frankenstein, sir. Mr. Saville sent me to tell you. There's been—been an unfortunate accident. Miss Bess is dead."

There followed a grief silence, broken only by the drip of water from the skies, and from the shabby eaves of the little houses. From the moment that I heard the sailor's words I was possessed by a strong suspicion of the evil truth that lay behind them. But Frankenstein, curiously innocent, suspected nothing. Not at first.

His first reaction to the news was the natural

one of shock and sadness. But then an inspiration struck him, and his demeanor altered. His eyes flashed, and he seized the manservant by the arm. "Wait! It may be—it may be that this is not after all a tragedy, but an act of Providence! Where is she?"

The sailor goggled at Frankenstein, not knowing what to make of this reaction. "A little distance inland, sir. She was alone when it happened—must have fallen down the bank of the stream, a little way from the village, at the place where the path is steepest."

"Quick, man, run! Tell them to bring her here! Quickly, quickly!" My creator pushed the messenger away.

"Sir, I believe they are already carrying her this way. Toward her cottage."

"No, it must be here, to the laboratory—run, tell them, quickly! Every minute may be important." Victor had now seized my arm, and this last order was addressed to me, for by this time my maker had come to have some idea of how fast I was able to run. The sailor had started quickly, but I passed him in half a dozen strides.

From the description he had given of the incident, I could readily enough visualize the place where Bess had died, and I met those who were carrying her before they had come halfway back to the village. Saville, who was with them, smiled without surprise when I relayed my creator's urgent demand.

Presently, with virtually the entire population of our small colony gathered round, the inert form that had been Bess, garments still sodden, was

being laid upon the table from which, only minutes ago, the ghastly debris of Frankenstein's last
experiment had been moved.

My gaze, passing across the room, met that of
the assassin Small. The villain smirked at me in
the bright light of the oil lamps, contorting his
pallid face. He knew that I believed rightly that he
had murdered the poor girl at the behest of Saville
and Walton; desperate for success, they had decided that *fresh* materials were to be provided for
the next experiment.

But Victor, I was sure, still did not know at
what price his new opportunity had been purchased.

My fists clenched. The girl was already dead. If
my master—at that moment I believe I thought of
him as such—could bring her back, it would not
be as a bride for me. Or would it? Would the
artificial restoration of life to a single, simple body
produce it in such a transformation as must have
been wrought upon me at the moment of my
animation?

As Frankenstein bent over the body, his hands
already busy with preparations for the attempt, he
asked about the nature of the accident that had
taken the victim's life.

It was Small himself who answered him, in an
obsequious voice. "I believe the young woman's
neck's broken, sir. Looks like she fell down a little
hill." No one else had anything to add.

Again I looked at the assassin, and again he
gazed back at me, silent triumph glinting in his
eyes.

My gaze returned to the table. That Bess's neck
was broken, at least, looked very likely true, from

the way her head with its brown curls had wobbled lifelessly when she was put down. Now, each time that her poor clay was moved by the scientist's hands, the deadly pendulation showed again.

With the assistance of Mrs. Hammer, Victor was now stripping off the victim's outer dress and one of her petticoats, casting the wet things aside. Now Frankenstein quickly bound wires to the young woman's limbs, and readied the probes again. He gestured to me, and I began to work the treadle that spun the glass globe by which the electric force would be restored within his mechanism.

This time, when the galvanic current was applied to the scalp and neck of the victim, the muscles of her face contorted in a most lifelike way, at which the gentlemen around the table uttered small cries, momentarily for all the world like children excited at a show. Walton, in particular, looked stunned by this result.

Next the probes were moved to each of Bess's limbs in turn. The muscles in each arm and leg were made to contract also, and new, lifelike movements were produced in each sequentially. At this, great excitement continued, though quietly, among the gentlemen.

Outside, full dawn had now arrived; yet the darkness of night, fortified by mist and rain, stubbornly refused to be forced into a complete retreat. It was as if day and night had abandoned friendly alteration, and were contending for the world.

Frankenstein's ministrations to the body went on steadily, methodically. Now he appeared to be trying to stimulate the heart. It was as if he had forgotten the observers who thronged around him.

If he had secrets that until now had been guarded from these close associates, he was now careless as to whether they were being revealed or not. And I, at least, was still unable to determine what they were.

The face of the dead girl was tranquil now, though certain discolorations had appeared upon the forehead. As I gazed at her it seemed almost as if, except for these marks and the angle of her neck, Bess might be only sleeping.

I met the eyes of her killer again, and saw him smirk again, and this time to my dismay I saw something worse than triumph in his face; I saw anticipation. Suddenly I understood, and my next thought was for Molly. Whether this present experiment finally succeeded or failed, those facial twitches seemed to indicate that it had already come close to carrying the day. It was inevitably, going to be repeated. Molly would be next.

Turning my head slightly I could see her, at the rear of the small crowd. She was gazing fearfully between men's shoulders at the still body of her friend and companion; but her fears were for Bess. Her face and manner gave no sign that she realized the gravity of her own situation.

I looked back at the assassin, who was whispering something to Saville.

Saville looked round, and I saw his gaze flick toward Molly, a cold glance of assessment. "Not yet," he replied to Small. His voice was not loud, yet it was careless of who might hear him.

Suddenly I could no longer bear the knowledge of what was about to happen. I pushed my way through the others and seized Victor by the arm, arresting his activity. In hasty words I made an effort to tell him of my fears and suspicions. He was so astonished by my interruption that I think he hardly comprehended what I was saying.

But my effort displeased the others. Snarling foul words, the killer grabbed at me, first pulling then trying to push me away from Frankenstein. His efforts accomplished nothing. Saville acted next, striking me with his walking stick. I hit back instantly, a backhanded, thoughtless, unplanned blow. My arm, hindred slightly by the assassin's tenacious grip, did not inflict death, but Small was shaken off, and Saville was knocked backwards, over a table of equipment which spilled with the impact. He rolled to one side, stunned, as flames blazed up from an overturned lamp.

Confusion reigned in the crowded room. Men outdid one another in shouting contradictory orders, and Molly screamed. I saw the assassin drawing one of his pistols from his belt, and aiming it at me. Walton was bellowing something at me, and Frankenstein too was shouting, helplessly and uselessly.

Knocking people aside again, I reached Molly's side in a moment, and seized her by the arm. First dragging her along with me, then lifting her bodily, I made a break for freedom. As I passed out of the door into the relative darkness outside, I heard Small's pistol fire behind me, and felt a burst of sharp pain across the side of my right shoulder. Before the assassin could draw another weapon and fire again, I had gripped Molly tightly in my arms and was running as fast as I could for the beach, with some confused idea of being able to seize a boat and row away before I could be stopped.

Shouts came from behind me. Bullets whistled past my head. Never would I be able to launch a boat and row out from shore before I was overtaken. I changed direction in midstride, heading inland. The young woman in my arms seemed no burden at all. A glance at her face assured me that she had fainted.

I fled inland, scanty bushes and tall grass whipping about my knees. The voices of our pursuers grew fainter as they fell behind. I fled on.

Full daylight found us well up in the central hills. Molly had recovered her senses at intervals throughout our flight, only to relapse, perhaps more or less willingly, when she found herself still in my grip, being borne along jolting and bounding through the foggy morning. She awoke a final time to find herself lying on soft sward beside the loch, and me kneeling beside her, bathing her face gently with its chill water. The rain had receded to a fine mist. For the moment, as her eyes opened to meet my gaze, the world around us seemed utterly at peace.

Then there were distant shouts, the voices of those who hunted us. To forestall the fear of me that I saw growing in her eyes, I said: "They were about to kill you, Molly. As they killed Bess."

"Oh." I think she recognized the truth when I spoke it, despite her abhorrence of my person. She wanted to say more, and had trouble finding the words, and I realized that she had no name to call me by.

"Call me what you like," I said.

Molly shook her head, refusing the responsibility of being first to bestow a name upon me. She said only, "You must take me back to the village. Please." Though I was sure she had momentarily believed my warning, still she could not live with it. So she thrust it away.

I was stunned. "They will kill you."

"Take me back. Please. Let me go. I can't . . . live with you." She could not, it appeared, even force herself to gaze directly at my face.

"You do not understand, girl. I am not trying to kidnap you. Remain apart from me if you must. But you will not go on living if you return to them."

It was no use. Presently, after she had stood up and stretched her legs and found them limber, she tried to run away from me.

Unbelieving, I gaped after her for a moment. Then I ran and caught her without much effort, though my shoulder pained me, each stride jolting it as I ran, blood soaking through my shirt.

She ceased to struggle, wept hopelessly, when my grip closed on her arm.

"I cannot let you go back to them."

She would not answer me.

As gently as possible I led her back to the loch. I asked her to bandage my wound for me; and that service she did not refuse. Once started on the task, using a strip torn from one of my garments, she did a good and tender job of it, though weeping softly all the time.

"Perhaps there is another boat available," I said, thinking I had convinced her. "We can get in it and—"

"No. No."

I tried yet again. "I repeat, I can understand that you dislike the idea of remaining with me. I do not want to force my presence on you. But *they* will kill you if you go back. You believed it the first time you heard me say it. I know you did."

"Yes. But they are—"

I could not prevail upon her to finish that sentence. I think she meant that, back there, whatever they might do, they were at least human.

Later, after warning Molly yet again of what would happen if the others caught her, I yielded unwillingly to exhaustion, and fell asleep. Molly was gone when I awoke, and the day was far advanced. I understood that she had gone back to them. So be it, then.

I knew that I might go back to them too, if I chose, and that they would not kill me. Saville would be firmly in control again by now, and he still thought me far too valuable to be killed. As for lesser punishment, I thought they would probably not attempt that either. My docility and cooperation were almost as needful to them as my presence.

My revulsion at those murderers was far too great to allow me to return and live among them, yet what other choices had I? I might have fled the island, but to what destination? To what purpose? Another day I roamed about the central hills alone, unable to decide what course to adopt. Once I heard what was unmistakably Molly's voice, calling something, and I knew that they must have brought her out from the village to call after me. It was their way of assuring me that she was still alive, that I was wrong in my suspicions. They could not understand they were perpetually unable to understand that I was not a fool.

I slept a little, lightly, like a hunted animal. Late in the afternoon there came fresh, soft voices among the hills, those of Clerval and Frankenstein, calling after me as if they feared that someone else would hear. I had no name for them to call, of course, but I could tell from the tone, one they might have used for a child, that I was the intended hearer.

I approached the voices cautiously, observing first from a distance. Only when I had made sure that the two men were alone and unarmed did I go to them.

Frankenstein looked more shaken than I had ever seen him before. But joy showed briefly in his countenance when I appeared, and he hastened to report all the bad news, almost as if I were the father now, and he a child in need of reassurance.

The effort to revive Bess had come to nothing. Frankenstein had abandoned his fruitless labors toward the end in horror, when Clerval managed to convince him that he had become a party to murder.

And Molly too was now dead. At last, when she was constantly under the eyes of Seville and Small, she had begun to realize the truth. Only then had she changed her mind about preferring their company to mine, and begun—stupidly—to voice accusations and to cry for help. Both my creator and Clerval had heard the cries cut short and were convinced of the girl's death, though they had not seen it. In horror they had seized a chance to flee the village unobserved. The tones in which the two

men related their story to me now convinced me
of their sincerity.

I felt a great sense of relief at that, and swore
my own renewed loyalty to my creator. But such
joy as I felt was short-lived. We were all three of
us unarmed and could not long survive a determined hunt. Walton's ship was in the bay, and his
whole crew now available for hunting.

Our only chance seemed to be the abandoned
boat I had found earlier, still undiscovered by our
enemies. That night we departed the island, rowing a somewhat leaky boat out into darkness, mist,
and uncertain weather.

Even as we fled we could see torches on the
island, near the spot from which, only minutes
earlier, we had launched the boat. But the search-
ers were too late to find us. We rowed on, into the
misty ocean, hoping to find our way to some less
cursed land.

Chapter 10

November 11, 1782—

There is much to tell. I write this in a barn, some miles south of Montreal, by the light of a stolen candle. For all I know the whole country is up in arms and in full cry upon my trail; but my good fortune holds, howling winds push snowdrifts across my tracks.

This morning I returned innocently to my job, expecting nothing but another day of dull labor shoveling snow from the streets and public places of the city. My first assignment took me in front of a printer's & bookseller's shop. I had not been at work for two minutes when I was frozen in my cold tracks by the sight of a large pamphlet on display in the shop window. Its title read:

Frankenstein: or, the Modern Prometheus

The window contained several copies of the publication bearing that startling title. I know not for how long a time I stood there gaping at them.

Finally a remark from a co-worker, resentful that my giant's hands and arms had ceased to do their giant's share of the work, brought me back to an awareness of my surroundings.

Casting my shovel aside, I hurried into the shop, in my haste scraping my head on the beam above the doorway. For an instant the few customers inside were paralyzed by my appearance, and then they hurriedly got themselves out of my way. I threw some coins at the proprietor, and seized a copy of the publication from the display.

As I stalked out of the shop I heard a murmuring behind me. Some of the people whom I had startled inside had followed me out, and before I had gone far they were mingling with other folk on the street, commenting on my conduct, and probably on my mere existence, in a general buzz of indignation. By the time I had reached the corner and turned onto the next street, the murmur had already risen to something like a real outcry. I did not look back.

Hurrying with long strides, I rushed down one street and then another until I felt reasonably certain that any pursuers had been evaded. Seeking refuge in an out-of-the-way corner where I stood thigh-deep in unshoveled snow, I hastily opened the book. Not for a moment did it occur to me that such a title might possibly refer to some other Frankenstein.

The few pages that passed beneath my gaze during my first hasty perusal of the book amazed and astonished me. These reactions have only been intensified by the more thorough reading I have been able to give the book since taking shelter here for the night. I was, as I say, amazed and astonished even before I realized that I was the "monster" or "fiend" portrayed within its pages; or more accurately, that the character thus drawn was claimed to be a portrait of me. With what unutterable outrage I understood my intended identification with this "demon," I am sure that any innocent person who reads those lying pages will be able to comprehend. I stood accused by the author, with shameless effrontery, of any number of horrible crimes—even of the murder of the child William, whom I had never seen, and from the scene of whose death I had been hundreds of miles distant.

The whole book, I see now as I sample its pages further, is couched in the form of letters, from Captain Walton, supposedly on a prolonged Arctic expedition, to his sister in London. And these are letters, I am certain, that can never have been really written or sent ... damned lying things in any case. Nay, they are something worse than that, which is the truth and lies all intermingled.

But I am beginning to understand the purposes behind the publication of this book. Much evil, for which my enemies are in truth responsible, is to be blamed on me.

I am, of course, innocent.

But how shall I ever be able to prove it?

My first perusal of the book's pages this morning, while standing in the city snowdrift, so stunned me that the fact of the gathering and murmuring crowd, from which I had originally retreated, had fled my mind. With the offending volume in my hand I started to retrace my steps toward the bookstore, with some vague idea of seeking redress there, or at least being able to make a reasonable protest. On my first coming in sight of the establishment again, I saw a knot of people, larger than before, gathered on the street in front of it. Some of them were gesturing as if in debate. I heard men's voices raised, and I thought the tone of those voices ominous. With ideas of protest and justice set aside for the time being, I prudently turned and departed.

But I was seen, and a pursuit commenced. I turned corners, and walked rapidly, as I had done before; but while walking streets in broad daylight it is impossible for me to avoid attracting attention, forever impossible for me to blend into a crowd. Yet I did manage to escape, for it is equally impossible that I, running, should ever be overtaken by humans moving on two legs. My flight from the city was not easy, but I have accomplished it.

As I write this I am still not sure if the pursuit continues, or will continue; or how many of those who saw me at the bookseller's today may have made some identification of me as the central character in the published charade that bears the name of my late lamented creator. But in any case I shall sleep soundly tonight, I have been pursued before.

The port of Montreal is of course icebound, but the ports of the colonies to the south will soon be free from the winter's ice—those that are not open all year round—but in those more southern colonies there is the war. Lately I have been able to hear but little news of the fighting. Just how effective the British blockade may be I do not know, but south I now must go, in any case.

*   ·*   *

November 12— On the road. The thought has come to me that, in Philadelphia there may live some associate of Franklin—a fellow philosopher, perhaps, or a friend or relative—who will be intelligent enough to listen to my tale with an open mind, and sympathetic enough to help me. The great man himself is, to the best of my knowledge, still in France, and I suspect he will continue there until all the business of the war, and of the agreement that must conclude the war, has finally been settled. That is, if he is still alive; when I saw him in Paris, almost a year ago, he was clearly of advanced age.

Last night in my uneasy shelter I dreamt of my creator's first cramped workroom in Ingolstadt. In my dream I knew that by standing in the midst of his equipment and clutching the rod that led up to the roof where it connected with Franklin's iron points, I should come into the possession of all the mysterious powers of electricity. Franklin himself was there in the laboratory too, somehow, and was to play some role having a vital connection with my fate. That I may come to possess the secrets of myself! That is all I ask.

December 1— Still on the way to Philadelphia. The few other wayfarers I have come upon have not seemed anxious for my company. Nor I for theirs, in truth.

Perhaps Franklin himself will have returned to Philadelphia by the time I get there, and he will be still alive and ready to give me help. I nourish myself with this hopeful dream. As if it were indeed probable, I rehearse in my mind a dozen

possible ways to approach him. That is my dream—
what is much more likely, of course, is that I will
somehow be able to approach someone of his associates. I have not settled on how to do it but there
is time. My journey is far from over.

I have acquired snowshoes. Thus shod, I was
able to approach and club to death a deer I discovered trapped in a crusted drift. Seldom are streams
here so completely frozen that I cannot break
through the ice to catch a fish. And the American
squirrels have been caching nuts in logs for me to
find and take. At night, as now, a small fire, a rude
construction of logs, sometimes a hollow tree, provide me with all the warmth and shelter that I
need. I, who have survived the Arctic wastes, find
this journey almost restful.

December 13— In among settlements now, I sleep
by sufferance in a barn tonight. I have been given
strange looks, but so far as I can tell no one of
them has heard of Frankenstein. I drop a word or
two of French or German, and I am taken for a
straggler or deserter from one of the mercenary
bodies of troops who were sent here, half a world
away from their homes, to fight for or against the
English. Such wandering deserters are common
enough, apparently, that the presence of one more
surprises no one. Also I have several times re-
sorted to stealing, and in general feel little regret
for doing so—I am sure that the snowshoes were
not their owner's only pair. My creator's race owes
me more than I ever am likely to steal.

The escape of Clerval, Frankenstein, and myself
in a small boat from the west coast of Scotland

was attended with fearful perils from sea and storm. My human friends, I suppose, could not have come through the first stages of that adventure alive, without my strength and endurance at the oars; I rowed whilst they bailed, and our boat did not—quite—sink. Nor could I, sickening as my wound became infected, have survived those later days without their care and help.

Our first leg of travel, across the open sea, was aided by some lucky winds and currents. At that point I was still not much bothered by my wounded shoulder, and during the first days did most of the rowing. I have not had the opportunity to trace our voyage on a map, but I suppose we must have traveled fifty or sixty miles at least, across the open sea, in a direction generally south.

Even before we launched our escape, I had deduced that we were probably in the Hebrides. Not only did the old papers in the houses offer clues, but more indications could be seen in the various configurations of land, and in the kinds of wildlife visible.

My deduction proved correct. But *how* could I even have begun to know such things? What likelihood that I had ever visited those isles, or even heard of them, in any previous existence? I could not answer such questions then, and cannot now. I *knew*, but without knowing how I knew. It was as if more and more of the old memories of my stranger's brain were gradually returning to me, though never in any way that would tell me that stranger's identity.

At length we came to land. We were then somewhere, as I correctly thought, on the north coast of

Ireland. When we at last reached shore, we concealed our boat as best we could near the mouth of
a small stream. I was by now much weakened by
infection, and so I remained hidden with the boat,
while Clerval and Frankenstein went in search of
information.

My companions returned after an hour or so
with some fresh bread and eggs, and news. There
was no sizable settlement near, but the men had
visited a farmhouse and could now confirm that
we had reached northern Ireland. We fell to and
ravenously devoured the provisions they had managed to obtain.

Reembarking, we rowed along the coast for a
moderate distance, and after a few miles entered
the mouth of a much larger stream, which we
proceeded to ascend. By this time I was very feverish with my wound, sliding in and out of delirium.
I remember little of that period but lying in the
boat, listening to voices only some of which were
real, and watching the frightful and fantastic im-
ages formed by the leaves and branches that over-
hung the little river's banks and shaded me. Some
days passed in this fashion while my companions
did what they could for me.

They argued much between themselves, but in
my fever I was unable then to grasp the matter of
their dispute. Looking back now I suspect that
Frankenstein, as ever unable to make up his mind,
was having second thoughts about his break with
Saville and Walton. Whether he actually was in
favor of rejoining Saville at this point I am not
sure; perhaps the argument was only about the
best means of continuing our escape.

Knowing that we had escaped in a small boat, and drawing on Walton's substantial knowledge of those waters, our enemies considered that almost certainly the prevailing winds and currents would sweep us down in the direction of Ireland, but that we would not be likely to get so far. As a precaution the assassin Small was dispatched to Ireland, with orders to locate us, if we should arrive, and to keep us, at all costs, from giving convincing evidence to the authorities regarding the crimes of Saville and his hirelings. Meanwhile most of Walton's men, along with the captain and Saville himself, were engaged in searching the islands near the one from which we had got away.

My two companions were faithful to my interest, as they saw it, but they could come to no agreement as to what to do with me, or how best they might be able to secure their own persons and fortunes from disaster. In a state of indecision that promised to prove fatal to us all, we drifted about the rivers and the coast, trying to stay hidden, and at the same time trying to learn whether we were being looked for here, and in what circumstances.

From one trip to a nearby town, undertaken with the object of gaining information, Clerval failed to return. Frankenstein, after a couple of hours, went to look for him and did not come back either. By now I had begun to recover from the wound and the fever, and at last, when darkness had fallen, I grew desperate enough to drag myself in search of my companions.

Moving with great difficulty because of weakness, I made my way into the town. Listening from alleys and at windows, I learned that the body of a murdered man, evidently a foreigner, had been discovered on the street, and from certain personal particulars of dress and appearance I made certain that the victim must have been Clerval. That was a staggering blow, but it was not all; the next piece of intelligence was that another stranger, who could only be my creator, had been arrested and jailed for the crime. The trial, however, would not take places for many months.

I was determined to do what I could for Frankenstein. But any direct attempt at rescue seemed utterly hopeless, particularly in my weakened condition. No more did any imaginable appeal to the authorities, from me, appear likely to be of benefit. Victor himself must have attempted to tell them the truth, or part of it at least, when he was arrested. And if they would not believe the truth from *him*, an obvious gentleman, what chance that they would believe me, or even listen to my words, before they shot me?

In a state near despair I stumbled back to our concealed boat, and fell into it exhausted. Awakening, in the small hours of the night, from a stuporous sleep, I took thought as best I could on my situation. Only one course of action suggested itself. My brightest and indeed my only hope seemed to me to be in Paris. There, in a country still technically at war with his own, the influence of the powerful Saville would surely be diminished. And there, as I had so often heard from Frankenstein and others, Franklin could be found. The famous American, respected even by his enemies, not only knew my creator personally, but would be prepared, if anyone on earth would be, to understand, perhaps even to explain, how seeming miracles might be achieved with the aid of electricity. If anyone in Europe could help me, it would be he!

I must return to Europe. Such villainy as Saville's and Walton's cannot go undenounced, unpunished. And the responsibility has fallen to me alone. On to Philadelphia!

December 20— Today I have reached Philadelphia. Everywhere I go among the people here, I speak French, and though infrequently understood I am always taken for one of that nation, and usually made welcome. In general I am supposed to be an ally against the opppressive George III, and as such, in the flush of victory, I am now and again rewarded with food, drink, or clothing. As usual, very little of the latter is of a size to be of any benefit to me, but my wardrobe has been improved by the addition of one tolerably good shirt, and a pair of sound leather gloves that must have belonged to a man with hands nearly the size of mine.

Next day— All is grim. Franklin is certainly not here. While plying my trade of snow-shoveling in the vicinity of his house, I have overheard enough servants' gossip to make sure of that.

But there are plenty of places where *The Modern Prometheus* can be found—more bookshops in this city of quite moderate size than I can remember seeing in either London or Paris—though in truth I had little time for bookshops then.

* * *

At night— Lurking around the docks today, trying to discover a way of obtaining passage across the sea, I adopted, as I thought cleverly, the guise of one of a troupe of traveling showfolk—I cast myself in the role of an exhibit, naturally, not an exhibitor—waiting for the leader of the group and some of its other members to catch up with me, when we should all move on together to New York.

Such a story must have drawn some interest to me among the denizens of the cheap taverns and brothels there—what story about me would not? But ironically, as soon as I claimed myself to be a freak, a monstrosity of nature worthy to go on exhibition for a price, those who saw me became convinced that I am only a man, though one of unusual appearance and great strength. My humanity is perceived as soon as I attempt to cast doubt upon it, just as it is almost invariably questioned whenever I choose to present myself as human.

One of those who met me near the docks, a grotesquely tattooed sailor who attempts to appear reasonable and so impresses me as remarkably untrustworthy, has presented me with a proposition. I am to join the crew of a smuggler, now lying offshore somewhere to the north, which is in need of such "stout lads" as myself—and whose next port will, he promises, be London.

I can sense that this man has some additional, private motive in singling me out for this proposal. But if this adventure promises to get me back to England—aboard a smuggler, or not—who cares? In the present state of affairs I must do something.

LETTER 3

November 26, 1782
Esteemed Sir and Parent—

Your letter reached me just before my departure from Ingolstadt; I am glad that you concur with my plan of investigation.

I arrived in Geneva yesterday, and have availed myself of the funds in the account here as per your instructions. The bankers have been as cooperative as I could wish. It is my impression that public affairs here are rapidly returning to an approximation of normal, following last summer's political unrest and the occupation by the French. The tension, the potential turmoil, is of course perceptible below the surface here as it is elsewhere across Europe.

Be assured that I am devoting myself to this research with all my energy, and all the acumen that I can muster. Yet the matter appears if anything more difficult than before.

To begin with, Geneva is a different matter from

Ingolstadt; the folk at the university in Bavaria were in general more impressed than those here are by my identity as your acknowledged son.

Of the Frankenstein family, who were your friends, I regret to report that there is not now a single representative left alive, with the likely exception of Victor's surviving brother Ernest. Ernest is not here now. The only clues I have to his current whereabouts are vague reports that he emigrated to America late last summer, after the tragic death of Elizabeth, and Victor's subsequent disappearance.

I did attempt to visit the Château Frankenstein—climbed a narrow street of houses roofed in brown tile, to behold a hillside of rich vineyards, and in front of them the house. It is an impressive dwelling, but there are others nearby more so. Standing at the front gate one has a view across Lake Geneva, with the Alps as backdrop. The house itself is ancient in some of its parts, modern in others, moderate in size—for a château—and now untenanted except for caretakers. Fountains play cheerily in front of it, and there is no outward sign of the history of horror and murder that the place contains. If other events had not come crowding in upon the city so thickly in recent months—the French have seen to that—I am sure that this mansion would be the chief topic of conversation among its neighbors.

In Germany, I was forced to deal only with rumors about Frankenstein and his experiments; no one would admit to actually having seen the creature, or to taking part in any of the important events resulting from his creation. Most people there pleaded inability to remember anything they might once have known about the subject. Here, although I have yet to encounter a witness who will admit to actually having seen the monster, the chain of tragedies beginning about three years ago are still fresh in the public mind, and there is no disposition to pretend they are forgotten. Those events, as they involved the subject of my investigation, were mortally grim, with at least three deaths occurring during their progress. Here, there is no difficulty in finding some folk who are willing to speak on the subject. Few of those ready to express opinions seem to know much about it, however, and the problem of the investigator lies in trying to disentangle contradictory accounts, and deciding which of them are sheer fantasy, and which, however fantastic they may sound, deserve a hearing.

The bald, undisputed facts of the events in Geneva are these: Victor Frankenstein's youngest brother, William, a child of only seven, was attacked and brutally strangled in May of 1780, approximately half a year after Victor's supposed creation of a monster in Ingolstadt and his sudden departure from that place. (It is worth noting that in the Walton relation, a full year and a half intervenes between the two events.) A young woman, Justine Moritz, who had served the Frankenstein family for years as a governess, was arrested within a few days after the murder, convicted (on what seems to me the flimsiest of evidence) and put to death within a few days after her conviction.

According to the Walton relation, that tragedy visited the Frankensteins in the following way.

The father, and the two brothers who were living at home (Ernest and William; the mother died of scarlet fever some years ago), along with a companion or two, had been on an afternoon outing near the city, when William wandered away from the others.

The father, Alphonse Frankenstein, is speaking, according to Walton:

> ... presently Ernest came and inquired if we had seen his brother; he said ... that William had run away to hide himself, and that he had vainly sought for him, and afterward waited a long time, but he did not return.
>
> This account rather alarmed us, and we continued to search ... about five in the morning I discovered my lovely boy, whom the night before I had seen blooming and active in health, stretched on the grass livid and motionless; the print of the murderer's finger was on his neck.

There ensued, naturally enough, general alarm and confusion. Elizabeth Lavenza, Victor's fiancée (and since July of this year also among those mysteriously and violently deceased), was greatly affected at the sight of the child's corpse.

> She fainted, and was restored with extreme difficulty ... she told me (Alphonse) that that same evening William had teased her to let him wear a very valuable miniature that she possessed of his mother. This picture is gone and was doubtless the temptation which urged

the murderer to the deed. We have no trace of him at present, although our exertions to discover him are unremitted ...

Thus did matters stand when Victor's father supposedly posted his letter to his eldest son, detailing the tragic news. But since we now know that Victor was not in Ingolstadt at the time, we may wonder where the letter was really sent. Evidently Victor received the news of the murder somehow, for he was in Geneva within a month.

According to his narrative in the Walton account, he was obliged to pass the last night of his journey at Secheron, a village near Geneva, the gates to the city itself being already closed for the night when he arrived. Realizing that he was staying very near the scene of the crime, Victor resolved that night to visit the place.

En route to the site of the tragedy, and on his arrival there, Victor observed a thunderstorm passing over lake and land:

> ... this noble war in the sky elevated my spirits; I clasped my hands and exclaimed aloud, "William, dear angel! This is thy funeral, this thy dirge!" As I said these words, I perceived in the gloom a figure which stole from behind a clump of trees near me; I stood fixed, gazing intently; I could not be mistaken. A flash of lightning illuminated the object and discovered its shape plainly to me; its gigantic stature, and the deformity of its aspect, more hideous than belongs to humanity, instantly informed me that it was the

wretch, the filthy demon to whom I had given life ... Could he be the murderer of my brother? The figure passed me quickly and I lost it in the gloom. Nothing in human shape could have destroyed that fair child. *He* was the murderer! I could not doubt it. The mere presence of the idea was an irresistible proof of the fact.

Should I ever find myself, Sir, standing in the dock, I should not be pleased to find the philosopher Victor Frankenstein seated on the jury.

After affording Victor one glimpse of itself, the figure of the monster disappeared again into the rain, without approaching its creator or speaking to him.

At the risk of repeating myself too often let me say again that I have not yet encountered anyone, in Ingolstadt or here, who will admit to having actually seen the thing. I have had, Sir, and continue to have, the gravest doubts concerning its existence. And yet, Father, and yet, there must be *something—*

At dawn, when the gates of the city were opened, Victor entered, according to Walton's publication, and made straight for his grieving family: this included, at the time, his father Alphonse, his surviving brother Ernest, then about seventeen years of age, and his fiancée (there is some debate about whether she was also his cousin) Elizabeth. Until this moment, be it noted, he had seen none of them for six years. (I remark in passing that Ingolstadt is about three hundred miles, as the crow flies, from Geneva, no more; and that the journey, though doubtless arduous in some seasons, particularly as it must skirt the Alps, is not always so.)

As soon as they met, Victor's family informed him that, in the interval since his father had written him the sad news of William's death, the murderer had been discovered. Victor, still firm in his instantaneous conviction that his creature was responsible, was astonished.

> "The murderer discovered! Good God! How can that be? Who could attempt to pursue him? It is impossible; one might as well try to overtake the winds or confine a mountain stream with a straw. I saw him too; he was free last night."
>
> "I do not know what you mean," replied my brother in accents of wonder . . .

Nor did he ever, it seems, make any effort to find out.

> ". . . but to us the discovery we have made completes our misery. No one would believe it at first; and even now Elizabeth will not be convinced, notwithstanding all the evidence. Indeed, who could credit that Justine Moritz, who was so amiable and fond of all the family, could suddenly become capable of so frightful, so appalling, a crime?"

Who indeed? And yet a conviction was somehow obtained. It is said that the judges here are honest men. But that is sometimes said of judges everywhere.

Earlier on in the Walton relation, there is quoted a letter supposedly written by Elizabeth to Victor, her more-or-less betrothed, in which she takes the trouble to describe Justine Moritz.

> Madam Moritz, her mother, was a widow with four children, of whom Justine was the third ... her mother could not endure her, and after the death of M. Moritz treated her very ill. My aunt observed this, and when Justine was twelve years of age prevailed on her mother to allow her to live at our house ...

I was about to write, Sir, that I do not like this supposed letter in the least. But I shall go further. I do not like the entire Walton manuscript; almost everything in it smacks of fraud. For example, all of the events relating to Justine that are detailed in this supposed letter *must have taken place while Victor himself was still living at home*. Why, then, in the name of Beelzebub, must his adopted-cousin-fiancée rehearse them to him in writing?

No, Sir, much of the Walton account must be fabrication. It is meant to lead someone astray. Whom, and to what purpose, are questions I cannot yet attempt to fathom. But I do think that we make progress.

Later— I have now been allowed to see the official records of the trial. Justine had been taken ill on the morning when the murder was discovered, and for several days she was confined to her bed.

One of the servants, happening to examine the dress Justine had worn on the night of the murder, claimed to discover in its pocket the valuable miniature that was taken from William when he was killed. It is on the strength of this evidence alone that Justine was charged—and convicted.

She continually protested her innocence, and her ignorance of any way by which the miniature might have come into her possession. Elizabeth Lavenza made more than one impassioned speech in favor of the accused, and Victor Frankenstein publicly proclaimed his certainty that his old friend Justine must be innocent—it is not recorded, however, that he made any mention during the trial of having knowledge of who the real murderer must be. Why not? In the book he explains his reticence thus:

> My tale was not one to announce publicly; its astounding horror would be looked upon as madness by the vulgar. Did anyone exist except I, the creator, who would believe, unless his senses convinced him, in the existence of the living monument of presumption and rash ignorance which I had let loose upon the world?

The trial of Justine began very shortly after Victor's return to Geneva.

> My father and the rest of the family being obliged to attend as witnesses, I accompanied them to the court. During the whole of

this wretched mockery of justice I suffered
living torture.

But his sufferings, however intense, were evidently not great enough to induce him to come
forward with his version of the truth.

In the eyes of the judges, the case against Justine was very black.

... several strange facts combined against
her, which might have staggered anyone who
had not such proof of her innocence as I had.
She had been out the whole of the night on
which the murder had been committed, and
towards morning had been perceived by a market woman not far from the spot where the
body of the murdered child had been after-
wards found. The woman asked her what she
did there, but she looked very strangely and
only returned a confused and unintelligible
answer. She returned to the house about eight
o'clock, and when one inquired where she had
passed the night, she replied that she had been
looking for the child and demanded earnestly
if anything had been heard concerning him.
When shown the body, she fell into hyster-
ics...

Justine claimed to have passed the early evening
of the night on which the murder was committed
at the house of an aunt in Chene, a village about a
league from Geneva. This was confirmed. As she
was returning to Geneva at about nine in the evening, she met a man who asked her if she had seen

anything of the child that was lost. Evidently some details of this man's statement persuaded Justine that the missing child was William, and she began her own search for him, without first seeking to confirm the object of her search in any way. (To my mind, Sir, this is the weakest of several improbabilities in her statement.) When the gates of the city were closed for the night, at ten, she could not get back in, and therefore took shelter in a barn, where she passed the remainder of the night restlessly, falling asleep only briefly and toward morning.

> . . . some steps disturbed her, and she awoke. It was dawn, and she quitted her asylum, that she might again endeavor to find my brother. (We are told that this is Victor speaking.) If she had gone near the spot where his body lay, it was without her knowledge. That she had been bewildered when questioned by the market woman was not surprising, since she had passed a sleepless night and the fate of poor William was yet uncertain.

She continued to deny any knowledge of how the picture could have come into the pocket of her dress.

> "Did the murderer place it there? I know of no opportunity afforded him for so doing; and . . . why should he have stolen the jewel, to part with it again so soon?"

And, if Justine herself were indeed the thief and

killer, why should she have sent her prize, so hardly won, off to the laundry in a pocket, rather than taking the most careful steps for its concealment? I would give a great deal, Sir, to be able to cross-question the servant who supposedly found the picture in Justine's dress. But I am told that is impossible, as the woman has since moved out of town. I have heard conflicting reports as to where she has gone. To track her down would undoubtedly be very difficult, but it is a task that I may yet undertake.

As the trial drew to a close, various other witnesses came forward to speak of the good character of the accused, and to express their disbelief that she could ever be capable of such a deed.

And what said Victor Frankenstein, who has told us, through Walton, that he knew the truth, a truth that made her innocent?

> ... when I perceived that the popular voice and the countenances of the judges had already condemned my unhappy victim, I rushed out of the court in agony. The tortures of the accused did not equal mine; she was sustained by innocence, but the fangs of remorse tore my bosom and would not forgo their hold.

What the accused might have thought about their relative degrees of suffering is not recorded.

It then appears that Justine, like Joan of Arc, under great pressure from her confessor once she had been convicted and sentenced to death, did confess at last. But like the papists' Maid, Justine recanted her confession a few hours later. In Justine's case the recantation, the renewed protest of innocence, came very shortly before her death.

Victor, in Walton's papers, reports that he did at last, after the verdict was in, attempt to argue with the judges. Not, however, that he went so far as to reveal then what he now assures us is the truth.

> My passionate and indignant appeals were lost upon them. And when I received their cold answers and heard the harsh, unfeeling reasoning of these men, my avowed purpose (to tell all—B.F.) died away on my lips ... thus I might proclaim myself a madman, but not revoke the sentence passed upon my wretched victim.

Of course, the Walton relation exonerates Justine, by presenting the monster as the killer—another agent, who, like Victor, cannot be brought to trial.

When Justine was dead, Victor, "feeling a weight of despair and remorse that nothing could remove," retreated with his surviving family and a friend or two to the family cottage at Belrive, outside the city walls and gates. Regarding the monster, he had "an obscure feeling that all was not over." And so indeed it proved.

One day, walking unaccompanied to the nearby village of Chamounix, Victor experienced his next encounter with the "fiend" .. But, Sir, the night here grows long and late, and to tell the truth I grow weary of writing about this tiresome and cowardly scoundrel.

I await your instruction, Sir, as to whether I should after all abandon this pursuit, or carry it yet farther; and if so, where.

Yr Obdt Svt,
Ben Freeman

Chapter 11

About January 5, 1783— I fear that I have again, as in my sojourn in the Arctic, lost track of days. Somewhere in the mid-Atlantic aboard a smuggler

I write this in the midst of what feels to me like a gale, and not knowing whether this ship will ever see land again or not. Even the most experienced sailors aboard are displaying unmistakable signs of alarm. The winter crossings, I have now learned, are notoriously difficult and dangerous, yet the possibility of profit which they hold out tempts many owners to risk their own fortunes and their sailors' lives in them.

Precisely what cargo we may be smuggling now, I have no idea. Nor am I interested in finding out. The evidences aboard are all too plain that previous cargoes have been more shameful than any mere dead stuff packed into bales or hogsheads could possibly be. This ship must ordinarily be engaged in the slave trade, that infamous triangular voyaging of valuable loads: trade goods from England to Africa; slaves from Africa to Jamaica or other Caribbean ports; and molasses, rum, and other tropical produce from the Caribbean back to England. Is it possible that Saville himself is the owner of this vessel? For all I know, that may be so.

I had anticipated that, untrained as I am, I might encounter some difficulty in shipping as an ordinary hand. I see now that I might have managed it easily—there is always a need for recruits of any kind. No being in his right mind would choose the life of a common seaman voluntarily, had he any alternative other than starvation. But my lot aboard ship has been far easier than most.

My acquaintance, the sailor who recruited me, told me as we trudged toward our place of embarkation that the smuggler captain had heard of me and wanted me for his personal bodyguard. It was a thin-sounding story but I accepted it. And indeed my position ever since I came aboard has been anomalous—no real surprise to me, as that has been the case throughout that portion of my life which I can remember.

The captain was surprisingly amiable toward me from the start; but it is plain that he needs no bodyguard on his own ship. He impresses me as a businesslike and capable ruffian, quite competent to guard his own back as well as manage whatever affairs he finds in front of him. My thought is that he and his recruiting agent have some quite different use in mind for me later, when we have reached port. Whenever I question him about my duties he remains vague, urging me to "learn the ropes" and be patient. Meanwhile he has no interest in whether I really learn the ropes aboard his ship or not. And it is apparent that he and his officers consider me valuable. No one has sent me into the rigging, though I could probably cope with such acrobatics much more easily than almost any of the poor wretches who are actually ordered aloft in even the foulest weather.

I have visited the crew's quarters, before the mast, and they are horrible enough, but those in which the slaves are ordinarily penned up for the weeks of the westward trip, are almost indescribable. Not cabins, not an open room like the fo'c'sle, nor even cells, but mere *shelves*, lacking enough space between them for a human, even a child, to do anything but lie flat. The stench of those spaces, even now when they are empty, is overwhelming. There the human cargo must remain, packed together like so many hundred sticks of lumber, with only occasional periods on deck for exercise, during the weeks and months of voyaging. I feel a considerable bond with those poor folk; if any were aboard now, I think I should turn mutineer out of necessity. But on this voyage there are only the empty pens, round which the odor still clings of humanity penned up in a fashion that would be hideously cruel if practiced on the veriest brute beasts.

Not a single slave is aboard now; we are bound for England, and the practice has been declared illegal there, as the captain tells me, with a sprinkling of oaths to indicate his outrage. No law, however, prevents Saville and other Englishmen like him from enriching themselves in the three-way trade.

I have a small cabin to myself, or "cell" might be a better word for it. There are formidable fastenings on the outside of the door, though they are not used now, and I suspect that on some voyages my accommodations have housed particularly interesting, violent, or perhaps diseased samples of the human cargo. Not that diseased slaves are very often transported for any considerable distance, as they are naturally very difficult to sell. It is much more economical to put them over the side, once hope of a prompt recovery has been abandoned.

I have quietly, but I think efficiently, taken steps to insure that the formidable fastenings of the door are not suddenly employed to close me in some night when I am sound asleep. I have taken steps to weaken the door's hinges, using a marlinspike surreptitiously borrowed for the purpose; and I think that come what may, I shall be able to get out.

Most of my time is spent inside my cabin, for I have no real duties, and it is plain enough that most, if not all, of the crew do not care much for my presence aboard. But that attitude is no more than fair, for I do not care much for theirs.

Nor do I fear them. But there is terror in the wind and sea, against which my strength counts for little more than that of the weakest human; and I doubt that I shall live to see my goal.

Franklin. Is he again my goal, as he was in the summer of 1781, when I was determined to help my creator survive his imprisonment? (Saville was willing then to let Frankenstein stew in prison for some months. Teaching him a lesson was the idea, I suppose.) Or do I now seek vengeance only? If so, it will be better found, I think, in London.

In 1781 my visit to the venerable American renewed my courage and determination, even if it did not provide me with the answers that I sought. Simply to reach Paris, and Franklin, had required a considerable pilgrimage. To rehearse all the stages by which I progressed from the Irish coast to the middle of France would form a long and tedious tale, which under the present conditions I do not feel like trying to set down.

I do thank all the Fates who have me in their hands that so far, at least, I do not seem in the least subject to seasickness. Did my brain once know a sailor's art? And did my stomach, proof now against the elements, once digest the last meal of some hanged pirate? Oh my creator, why would you never tell me anything of these matters? Why did I not, years ago, take you by the throat and force you into speech?

The first communications to pass between myself and Franklin were written, and earlier attempts were doubtless discarded by his servants before he ever saw them. In any event, several were necessary before I could persuade a member of his household staff at Passy to pass my messages directly to the great man. Franklin enjoys a large house there, a private headquarters provided for him by the French while he remains the real ambassador of their American allies. Had it not been for the fact that a great many important communications must come to him in such clandestine fashion as I sent mine, and that his whole staff must be somewhat attuned to this method of conducting business, I might never have succeeded.

That first interview was difficult to arrange, but in the end my promise of inside information about the experiments of Frankenstein proved irresistible. I had warned my host in advance of my unusual appearance, though I thought it best to withhold any extraordinary explanation until he should be able to see me for himself.

At the beginning of our meeting he had two bodyguards with him in the room, well-armed and determined-looking men, who, Franklin told me, did not understand English; but when we had been talking for a quarter of an hour he dismissed the bodyguards, and became cordial, offering me wine and brandy.

Franklin began the private portion of our interview by saying: "Your story, Sir, is the most remarkable that I have ever heard—nay, let me amend that. The most remarkable which I believe on hearing to be substantially the truth."

"What I have told you is all the truth, Mr. Franklin. As nearly as I can remember it and tell it."

"Aye, I have said I believe you. The truth, as you have experienced it. But at the very least there must be more." Chubby, wheezing, old, but at the moment apparently healthy, he sat in his chair exuding an air of discontent brought on by my story.

"Yes sir, I am sure there is more. It was my hope in coming to you that you might help me to discover what it is. And, of course, that you might do something for my creator."

He shook his head. "I might—I *might*, I say—be able to exert some influence, to the effect of ameliorating the condition of this man you regard as your creator. But the results, if any, will be slowly produced, and indirect. And as for his trial, I fear my influence upon Irish justice will be negligible."

I shrugged. I felt exceedingly weary, but at the same time as if relieved of a burden. "I have done all I can for him, then."

We drank our wine, and talked. About science and philosophy, electricity and life. Many things. We were to meet again, but events intervened, in the form of Saville's agents, and I was forced to flee from Paris. But Franklin is a remarkable old man—or was. I hope that he is still alive.

This gale has not yet quite decided to drown us all. It seems we must await its pleasure.

LETTER 4

December 11, 1782

Dear Sir & Parent—

In accordance with your instruction, I am departing Geneva by the next post, and will make all reasonable speed to London. If the Channel crossing can be managed under the usual winter & wartime conditions, another fortnight should see me safely ensconced there, at the lodging and under the name by which you are accustomed to communicate with me when I am in those parts. As for the danger in my returning to England, that I should be exposed as a Rebel agent, I think that is now all but completely past. It is my impression that very little interest is taken in such creatures anymore. As you know very well, being yourself in the very midst of the negotiations, to these people the war has been all but dead since Cornwallis laid down his arms.

Since my last communication to you, a message has reached me here in Geneva from an informant in Ingolstadt, providing some more information about the former medical student there, Saville.

His Christian name was—or is—Roger, and he was—or is—indeed an Englishman. The fact of his wealth is confirmed. At the university he was never accounted a good student, his cleverness being offset by an arrogance that rendered him objectionable to the professors, who as a rule can stomach no arrogance besides their own. With no more than that to go on, I have considerable hopes of being able to locate him. All wealthy Englishmen, as you know, are in London sooner or later. And as for Walton—can there be any English sea-captain whose face is unknown in the metropolis?

Meanwhile, as I await my transportation, allow me to offer for your consideration some further thoughts on the Walton manuscript. I wish now to consider in particular the supposed words of Victor Frankenstein, as he recounts what happened to him during his lonely sojourn to an Alpine retreat, following the deaths of William and Justine.

It was nearly noon when I arrived at the top of the ascent . . . my heart, which before was sorrowful, now swelled with something like joy; I exclaimed, "Wandering spirits, if indeed ye wander, and do not rest in your narrow beds, allow me this faint happiness, or take me, as your companion, away from the joys of life."

As I said this I suddenly beheld the figure of a man, at some distance, advancing toward me with superhuman speed. He bounded over the crevices in the ice, among which I had walked with caution; his stature, also, as he approached, seemed to exceed that of man . . . it was the wretch whom I had created. I trembled with rage and horror, resolving to wait his approach and then close with him in mortal combat . . . his countenance bespoke bitter anguish, combined with disdain and malignity, while its unearthly ugliness rendered it almost too horrible for human eyes.

"Devil!" I exclaimed. "Do you dare approach me? . . . oh! That I could, with the extinction of your miserable existence, restore those victims you have so diabolically murdered!"

"I expected this reception," said the demon. "All men hate the wretched; how, then, must I be hated, who am miserable beyond all living things! . . . you purpose to kill me. How dare you sport thus with life? Do your duty towards me, and I will do mine toward you and the rest of mankind. If you comply with my conditions, I will leave them and you in peace; but if you refuse, I will glut the maw of death, until it be satiated with the blood of your remaining friends!"

But Frankenstein was not the man to bow meekly before this threat. Feeling his rage "without bounds," and "impelled by all the feelings which can arm one being against the existence of another," he tried to attack the monster physically.

But the creature "easily eluded" his aggressive efforts, and kept on talking. Presently he had persuaded Frankenstein to accompany him to an isolated mountain hut, where the man sat down and listened to a long story. It is this story, supposedly in the monster's own words, that forms the bulk of the Walton relation. It gives an account of the creature's whereabouts and actions during the year and a half said to have intervened between the creation in Ingolstadt and the killing of William in Geneva. (I have discovered, remember, that the interval was only six months.)

The creature's story begins almost plausibly. Wandering in the woods near the university town, during the first few days following his creation, the creature learned for himself that day and night appeared in alternation, that water slaked his thirst, fire burned his fingers, and people, when he approached them, invariably shrieked and fled.

Matters quickly take a less likely turn. The monster relates that he sought shelter in a "hovel." He soon discovered that this rude dwelling adjoined a neat peasant cottage. Through a handy hole in the wall of the cottage he spied on the inhabitants, and by this means learned language (French) —geography—the customs of society—how to read— and, for all I know, natural philosophy—how to count (except, perhaps, for bullet-holes; see below). The creature interested himself intensely in the affairs of the family of cottagers whom he observed so intimately and for so many months. He absorbed the histories of their lives, and later recounted them at great length to Victor Frankenstein, who had to listen to all this in his mountain hut. (Walton on his almost ice-bound ship had to listen to it all again, as Frankenstein lay dying.) The creature described how, after living in his queer observation post beside the cottage for more than a year, he dared to reveal himself to the people in the cottage, was attacked for his pains, and driven away in the ensuing uproar.

It is all, need I say, quite unbelievable. It is so completely incredible that in my mind it only emphasizes the question we have been facing all along: What did the creature really do during that period? (I assume, as you have ordered me to assume for the purpose of this investigation, that the monster really does exist.) How did it occupy itself during the time between its disappearance from Ingolstadt (if one can disappear from a place where one has never really appeared) and the murder and execution in Geneva, six months later?

But to resume Walton's story: the creature, moving at last in the general direction of Geneva, rescued a young girl who was drowning in a river, and was shot in the shoulder as a reward.

> For weeks I led a miserable life in the woods, endeavoring to cure the wound ... the ball had entered my shoulder, and I knew not whether it had remained there or passed through.

As I have already mentioned, counting bulletholes was evidently beyond the sketchy mathematical education received by the monster during its studies at the peep-hole in the cottage wall. An alternative explanation for such uncertainty might be that the missile had in fact passed through its brain—or remained there.

However that may be, in two more months the creature, his wound now healed, had "reached the environs of Geneva."

> It was evening when I arrived, and I retired to a hiding place among the fields ... to meditate in what manner I should apply to you.

Presently, the musing monster was roused from "a slight sleep" by "the approach of a beautiful child," who

> came running into the recess I had chosen, with all the sportiveness of infancy. Suddenly, as I gazed on him, an idea seized me that this little creature was unprejudiced and had lived too short a time to have imbibed a horror of deformity. If, therefore, I could seize him and educate him as my companion and friend, I should not be so desolate ... urged on by this impulse, I seized the boy as he passed and drew him toward me. As soon as he beheld my form, he placed his hands before his eyes and uttered a shrill scream; I drew his hand forcibly from his face and said, "Child, what is the meaning of this? I do not intend to hurt you; listen to me."
>
> He struggled violently. "Let me go," he cried. "Monster! Ugly wretch! You wish to eat me and tear me to pieces. You are an ogre. Let me go, or I will tell my papa."

"Boy, you will never see your father again; you must come with me."

"Hideous monster! Let me go. My papa is a syndic—he is M. Frankenstein—he will punish you. You dare not keep me."

"Frankenstein! You belong then to my enemy—to him towards whom I have sworn eternal revenge; you shall be my first victim."

I learned, esteemed parent, shortly after my arrival in the city of Geneva, that it presently boasts more than twenty thousand inhabitants. The number two years ago could not have been materially different. That the one out of twenty thousand first encountered by the monster in his random approach to the city, should happen to be the youngest brother of his creator ... but I need not belabor the incredibility of it all.

The murder of young William, the work of only an instant, followed immediately. Then

As I fixed my eyes on the child, I saw something glittering on his breast. I took it; it was a portrait of a most lovely woman ... for a few moments I gazed with delight on her dark eyes, her lovely lips ... but presently my rage returned; I remembered that I was forever deprived of the delights that such beautiful creatures could bestow ... while I was overcome by these feelings, I left the spot where I had committed the murder, and seeking a more secluded hiding-place, I entered a barn ... a woman was sleeping on some straw; she was young ... blooming in the loveliness of youth and health. Here, I thought, is one of those whose joy-imparting smiles are bestowed on all but me ... not I, but she, shall suffer; the murder I have committed because I am forever robbed of all that she could give me, she shall atone. The crime had its source in her; be hers the punishment.

And with that the creature placed the stolen miniature in the pocket of the sleeping Justine—for of course it was she—and fled.

But no. It did not happen thus. Even supposing—by some miracle—that the rest of the Walton relation should be the truth, *this* I cannot believe.

Consider, Sir: the creature, on entering the barn, could have had no means of knowing that any connection existed between the sleeping girl before him and the child he had just murdered—no reason whatsoever to believe that the painting, once concealed in her pocket, would ever be discovered by anyone but her, would ever be revealed to the world as evidence of any kind.

And, of course, it was *mere coincidence again* that the creature happened to enter the one barn in which Justine was sleeping—no, I cannot go on, multiplying coincidence by coincidence, and trying to discuss it all seriously. There may be, for all I know, a monster—there may be a thousand monsters—but this portion, at least, of the Walton memoirs must be considered a tissue of lies from start to finish.

Unfortunately, the murder of the young child was all too real. And the execution of Justine Moritz was a very real occurrence too, whether or not the young woman was in fact guilty.

And we are told that it was shortly after this hideous crime that the monster supposedly confronted his creator in the mountain hut, boldly confessing his guilt, and in the next breath demanding help.

Speaking to Frankenstein, the creature declared himself

> consumed by a burning passion that you alone can gratify. I am alone and miserable; man will not associate with me; but one as deformed and horrible as myself would not deny herself to me. My companion must be of the same species and have the same defects. This being you must create.

My post is here. In haste, Sir, I dispatch this message. My next to you, God willing, will come from London.

Yr Son,
Benj Freeman

LETTER 5

December 28, 1783

Dear Sir & Parent—

My inquiries so far, since arriving in London, have pretty effectively winnowed the possible *Savilles* down to no more than three, and of those I think only two are really good candidates for the Frankenstein connection. I of course shall continue to use all caution, as you advise, in my investigations here.

I also plan to go, probably within the week, to Birmingham to visit Priestley. I understand that the meetings there of his Lunar Society, held always on nights of a full moon, are most interesting. There is no particular reason to connect him with Frankenstein; but in matters of philosophy Priestley is certainly one of the pre-eminent men in Britain, and any new and important discoveries in

177

electricity, medicine, or related studies are likely to have come to his attention.

Later— have just heard from one of the Saville families; Mrs. S., sounding very gracious in her note, states that my inquiries about the book, and on the subject of Frankenstein in general, have come to her attention. She says that she was indeed the recipient of those thrilling letters from her dear brother, Captain Walton, when he was in the ice-bound Arctic, and she wonders if I could come to tea. Apparently her own inquiries about me have already satisfied the lady that I am a gentleman in good standing, or such an invitation would never have been forthcoming. Naturally I shall accept.

Later still— *After the Saville event*. The coach that called for me at my humble lodgings was impressive indeed; four matched mares, and two footmen. There is no doubt that the Savilles are immensely wealthy. Young Roger Saville, the lady's absent husband, was indeed a student at Ingolstadt during the earlier years of Frankenstein's tenure there. Quite a coincidence, then, that Frankenstein should later encounter, by accident in the Arctic, her brother's ship. But of course not impossible. Was Saville by any chance on that ship too?—he does not appear in the story. The lady dismissed that question with a pretty gesture, that seemed to say No, but really said nothing at all.

Also says she does not know that the two men, Frankenstein and her husband, ever met, at school or elsewhere. But she does remember hearing somehow, of last summer's terrible tragedy in Geneva, where Victor became a bridegroom and a widower on the same June day.

I have no doubt that the lady rather enjoys having a connection, at least an indirect one, with the Frankenstein affair. She is on the whole pleased with her brother's book. I suspect that the connection may be more direct than she has yet indicated directly.

Her nautical brother is now absent also. His whereabouts are vaguely described by Mrs. Saville as somewhere at sea—she says this as if she were bored by the subject.

One particularly interesting item revealed to me today by Mrs. S., is that the book did not tell the whole story of what happened in the Arctic. It now appears that Frankenstein, before he died, and while on Walton's ship, transferred ownership of the monster to the good captain, who so kindly tried to rescue the scientist and who so patiently listened to his story before transcribing it into letters for his sister. It was, I confess, the first time that the idea of *ownership* of this being, as if he were a horse or cow—or, indeed, a slave—had occurred to me. Why are we able to accept as commonplace that black Africans should be so bought and sold and owned, and yet are struck by a peculiarity in the case of this rare specimen?

After explaining to me, as she put it, the matter of property rights, the charming Mrs. Saville (I admit I had been expecting, for some reason, to encounter a rather older woman) enquired whether I might have any knowledge of the whereabouts of Ernest Frankenstein, Victor's brother and the only surviving member of the immediate family. I could truthfully deny having the least cognizance in that matter.

I have as yet no reason to believe that she suspects my relationship, either familial or political, with you; and I saw nothing to be gained by enlightening her, though from certain remarks made in passing, I am tolerably sure that she is sympathetic to the American cause.

We discussed, during our meeting, several passages from the book that brought us together; I think I gained a certain new insight into several of them. Since there is some time yet tonight, I think, before I can hand this to the messenger, it might be well if I wrote down my thoughts on the subject, that you may have the benefit of them, however small.

Consider to begin with the following speech by the monster, uttered on the occasion of his interview with his creator in the lonely mountain hut above Geneva:

> You must create a female for me with whom I can live in the interchange of those sympathies necessary for my being. This you alone can do, and I demand it of you as a right which you must not refuse to concede.

But the philosopher evidently considered that he had done enough harm with his first effort. He denied the application, saying "no torture shall ever extort a consent from me."

"You are in the wrong," replied the fiend;

"and instead of threatening, I am content to reason with you. I am malicious because I am miserable ... You, my creator, would tear me to pieces and triumph ... you would not call it murder if you could precipitate me into one of those ice-rifts and destroy my frame, the work of your own hands. Shall I respect man when he contemns me? ... towards you, my arch enemy, because my creator, do I swear inextinguishable hatred ..."

A fiendish rage animated him as he said this; his face was wrinkled into contortions too horrible for human eyes to behold; but presently he calmed himself and proceeded. "I intended to reason. This passion is detrimental to me, for you do not reflect that *you* are the cause of its excess ... what I ask of you is reasonable and moderate; I demand a creature of another sex, but as hideous as myself."

The monster admitted that the "gratification" to be expected from such a mate was small.

... but it is all that I can receive, and it shall content me. It is true, we shall be monsters, cut off from the world, but on that account we shall be more attached to one another. Our lives will not be happy, but they will be harmless and free from the misery I now feel. Oh! My creator! Make me happy; let me feel gratitude toward you for one benefit!

Moved by the partial justice (as he now saw it)

of this plea, Frankenstein wavered in his resolve. The "fiend" observed this reaction, and pressed his claim all the harder.

> If you consent, neither you nor any other human being shall ever see us again; I will go to the vast wilds of South America. My food is not that of man; I do not destroy the lamb and the kid to glut my appetite; acorns and berries afford me sufficient nourishment. My companion will be of the same nature as myself and will be content with the same fare.

We may note here in the creature's plan a certain unguarded optimism, born perhaps of inexperience in dealing with the fairer (if that term here applies) sex.

> We shall make our bed of dried leaves; the sun will shine on us as on man and will ripen our food. The picture I present to you is peaceful and human, and you must feel that you could deny it only in the wantonness of power and cruelty.

But the creator was not yet entirely convinced.

> "You swear," I said (Frankenstein speaks) "to be harmless; but have you not already shown a degree of malice that should reasonably make me distrust you?"

A not unreasonable question, addressed to one who had already murdered the narrator's young brother, and then arranged matters so that another innocent victim should be executed for the crime. As for the creature's plea to have a mate:

> May not even this be a feint that will increase your triumph by affording a wider scope for your revenge?

But further arguments by the creature wore Victor down, and eventually he allowed himself to be persuaded that the creation of a female monster would be the best way out of his predicament.

> Turning to him, therefore, I said, "I consent to your demand, on your solemn oath to quit Europe forever, and every other place in the neighborhood of man, as soon as I shall deliver into your hands a female who will accompany you in your exile."
>
> "I swear," he cried, "by the sun, and by the blue sky of heaven, and by the fire of love that burns my heart, that if you grant my prayer, while they exist you shall never behold me again. Depart to your home and commence your labors; I shall watch their progress with unutterable anxiety, and fear not but that when you are ready I shall appear."
>
> Saying this, he suddenly quitted me, fearful, perhaps, of any change in my sentiments. I saw him descend the mountain with greater speed than the flight of an eagle, and quickly he was lost among the undulations of the sea of ice.

*   *   *

The scientist went home. But he did not hurry to begin his labors. Perhaps he was considering the fuller implications of the second creation, and the tribe of monsters that it might engender, though oddly such considerations receive only brief mention in the book. He relates that he "passed whole days alone on the lake in a little boat," rather avoiding the matter than thinking it over. And he debated, with his father, another matter that had long been subject to an "understanding" among the parties involved—his expected marriage to Elizabeth Lavenza.

> Alas! To me the idea of an immediate union with my Elizabeth was one of horror and dismay. I was bound by a solemn promise (He means to the monster, not to her—B.F.) which I had not yet fulfilled and dared not break, or, if I did, what manifold miseries might not impend over me and my devoted family! Could I enter into a festival with this deadly weight yet hanging around my neck and bowing me to the ground? I must perform my engagement and let the monster depart with his mate before I allowed myself to enjoy the delight of a union from which I expected peace.

Frankenstein declares that he had "heard of some discoveries having been made by an English philosopher," knowledge of which would be "material to his success." (It would appear, esteemed Parent, that since the first male of the monster race was constructed without the benefit of this knowledge, it must pertain particularly to the female parts.)

To fulfill his promise, then, Frankenstein faced the necessity "of either journeying to England or entering into a long correspondence with those philosophers of that country whose knowledge and discoveries were of indispensable use to me in my present undertaking." But he considered that "the latter method of obtaining the desired intelligence" would be "dilatory and unsatisfactory."

> Besides, I had an insurmountable aversion to the idea of engaging myself in my loathsome task in my father's house while in habits of familiar intercourse with those I loved. I knew that a thousand fearful accidents might occur, the slightest of which would disclose a tale to thrill all connected with me with horror.

Unarguable; but there was more.

> I was aware also that I should often lose all self-command, all capacity of hiding the harrowing sensations that would possess me during the progress of my unearthly occupation. I must absent myself from all I loved while thus employed.

With these considerations in mind, Victor expressed to his father "a wish to visit England," and his father, glad to find him able to take pleasure in any plan of activity, readily agreed. The marriage to Elizabeth was to be casually postponed, for a

year, or at the most two. Victor's friend Henry
Clerval (who had been with Victor on the first
morning after the creation, and supposedly nursed
him through the subsequent illness) was enlisted
as a traveling companion. Elizabeth, we are told,
"approved of the reasons" for the trip, and "only
regretted that she had not the same opportunities
of enlarging her experience, and cultivating her
understanding." But she wept at Frankenstein's
departure.

Descending the Rhine from Strasbourg to Rotterdam on a boat, Clerval and Frankenstein took
ship for London, where they arrived at the end of
the year 1780. They remained in London for almost three months, while the experimenter made
use of the letters of introduction given him by his
father, and "addressed to the most distinguished
natural philosopher," which gentlemen are not
otherwise named.

Being well equipped with letters of my own, Sir,
I mean to try such gentlemen as Joseph Priestley
and others. We shall see whether they remember,
and are willing to discuss, a visit from Victor
Frankenstein a couple of years ago.

I will write again, Sir, when I have something
else of substance to report.

                              Yr Obdt Svt
                              Benjamin Freeman

LETTER 6

January 27, 1783

My Dear Father—

Once more allow me to add my small congratulations to those of the rest of the world, on your great achievement in working out the preliminary peace agreement. Here in London the general sentiment is strongly in favor of peace, and I think that if my true identity should become known today I should be little the worse for it. May we soon be able to exchange letters by the regular post—though I suppose that will hardly be likely to make the delivery any swifter or more certain. The more I travel in the world, the more I come to appreciate, among other things, your achievements as a postmaster.

On to business. I have had more contact with the Saville clan. The lovely Mrs. Saville—her first name is Margaret, by the way—has entertained me once more at tea. Husband Roger, I have been given to understand, is still absent, off somewhere in India. When he is likely to return has not been specified. But wherever Mr. Saville may be, he seems to be at least as interested as his good lady is in Frankenstein's experiments; she says that she has sent Roger a copy of the book, which he found most intriguing, and that he is anxious to converse with anyone who knows anything of the matter. Such a person may be hard to find in India.

The lady tries in many subtle ways to discover all that she can about my own background, and, as she is certainly a charmer, I am continually on my guard not to give much away.

Later— I may have been wrong about the strength of the peace sentiment. There were loiterers in the street near my lodgings, a different man on each occasion, and I now have some suspicions that I am being watched. I intend to use even greater care than usual in dispatching this note.

There is interesting gossip I would ordinarily pass along—about the current London fashions, and so forth, since I know your continuing interest in such matters—but I prefer to keep this message short.

I was fortunately able to see Priestley without going to Birmingham, catching him on one of his periodic visits to London and the Royal Society, and was able to get a word with him alone. I divulged my identity, and presented greetings from you, Father, which he was happy to receive. He sends his warmest regards in return .

He recalls that young Frankenstein visited him in London, in the early spring of 1780, and says that he also heard of the fellow's arrest in Ireland in 1781, and his tragic marriage last summer during the occupation of Geneva by the French—tragic of course because of the bride's murder, by person or persons unknown, on her wedding night. There have been whispers, I am told, of suspicion against the husband himself. But there was no evidence to disprove his story of a mysterious prowler, and no legal steps were taken against him.

Priestley says he did not know quite what to make of Frankenstein at their one meeting. It pleased him also to demonstrate his electrical machine for me—it is made mostly of mahogany and baked wood, and supports four electrical globes, of moderate size, that can be charged simultaneously. The prime conductor is a hollow vessel of polished copper, shaped like a pear. It can produce either negative or positive power, depending upon how the connections are made.

In all, my meeting with the eminent man was interesting, but not very helpful as regards the chief objective of my visit. I expect to gain much more from my association with Mrs. Saville.

Yr Son,
Benjamin Freeman

Chapter 12

February 18, 1783—London, at last

The crossing has been perilous in the extreme, attended with a thousand dangers. Having survived them all, I am not sure now whether the worst of them emanated from the crew of scoundrels with which I found myself surrounded, from the final perfidy of the captain, or from the elements. On the whole my instincts are to award the plaudits to the crew. Were not my size and appearance enough to intimidate even the worst blackguards among them—except on one occasion, when I was forced to demonstrate a willingness to act—I have no doubt that the crossing would have been even more interesting than it was.

There were other, incidental, perils. On the fifth day we were sighted by a vessel that our captain proclaimed to be an American privateer, which gave chase to us. We fled successfully, though our escape may be more attributable to a sudden change in wind and weather than to any particular facility in seamanship on the part of the master of our own craft.

On the next day, it was the turn of a French man-of-war to discover our sail and give chase, but with the same outcome. I suppose that her captain, as cautious as most commanders of large warships are said to be, might have been loath to risk an encounter with an armed opponent of any description. But that, and all other difficulties of the crossing, are now fortunately over.

Later— Ashore. The ship is behind me now, and so are those dockside neighborhoods in which the press gangs are wont to seize their victims. Some have assured me that such kidnappings never take place in London, but I do not trust the men who told me so.

That I am here, and free, is not due to the good will of any of my erstwhile shipmates. I am now certain that the sailor who recruited me, though not a member of the *Argo's* crew when I was aboard her, had and still has some connection with Captain Walton, and through him had learned something of my history. This man must have recognized me at first sight in Philadelphia, and seized the initiative. He knew that I was still being doggedly sought by Walton and Saville, who had quietly passed the word around among certain of their associates that they were offering a substantial reward for my live capture and return.

But to recount the conclusion of my trans-Atlantic voyage. On the day before we were to make port, an effort to imprison me was made, as I had more than half expected. The captain and a squad of sturdy men (I could hear their muttering, and heavy breathing.) approached the closed door of my cabin. In only a moment all the locks, bolts, and bars there on had been made fast, much good did it do them.

Not that I broke out immediately; I contented myself with some startled grumblings for a start, rattled the door a little, and then allowed myself a full-throated howl or two, to demonstrate that the fact of my imprisonment was finally borne in upon my weak intelligence. I followed this with a few minutes of half-hearted hammering upon the door until it was plain—even to the dull wits of a monster—that I should not be able to break out.

I rested quietly until darkness had fallen, and I was sure, from the familiar sounds of other commerce upon the Thames that we were close to shore. Then one swift surge and the hinges that I had so thoughtfully weakened at the start of our voyage burst asunder, startling a sleepy sentinel so badly that he dropped his musket before he could think of what else to do with it. To save him the trouble of attempting any additional thought I promptly threw the musket over the rail, and followed it in a swift dive.

We were, as I had deduced, quite close to shore, and my swim was short. Climbing from the icy water onto a dock, I terrified a few stray onlookers and fled inland, losing myself quickly in the maze of London streets and alleys, and managing to steal some dry blankets before I perished of exposure.

I am not totally unfamiliar with this environment, thanks to my earlier stay here near the docks as Saville's guest. I am now hiding out, hungry, a fugitive again from my enemies, but for the moment satisfied to be here, in the city of my greatest enemy's greatest power.

I remember very well the location of Saville's warehouse-office; and I intend to go there as soon as I have the chance. Beyond that point I remain uncertain.

Later— I have been meditating for some time on the idea that special goods or materials must now and then be imported for Saville's luxurious mansion (Which by the way I have never seen—does he have his laundry done in the tropics, as do some of the French nobility?). Vague mention of some such shipments once or twice reached my ears during the epoch of my warehouse residence. I should be able to keep an eye on the warehouse for these imports, see who shows up to accept them, and follow when the materials are picked up for delivery. What I should really like to have is *entree* to his dwelling.

February 19— The contact I sought has been established. A delivery wagon evidently carrying luxuries left the warehouse late this afternoon, and I managed to climb into the vehicle and stow away before it took its departure. There were hams and cheeses in the cargo, amid less appetizing items, and I took care to fill my pockets with a food supply, not knowing what provisions I might find available when I reached the end of my journey.

Towards the end of an interesting ride through

the city and far into its outskirts, we passed through huge iron gates, set in a high stone wall. The gates were promptly closed after us when we had entered. I understood that I had arrived at the suburban Saville estate, which I had often heard mentioned by Saville himself, but had not thought, until very recently, ever to have the opportunity to see for myself.

After a circling drive through wooded grounds we passed around the house, which I meanwhile observed through a chink in the canvas covering the wagon's rear. It is very large, and there seems to be a large staff. I dropped off the wagon, at what seemed a likely opportunity, and fled unnoticed through the dusk to conceal myself in the parklike woods. Meanwhile the vehicle proceeded, I suppose to deliver its legitimate cargo at some tradesman's entrance in the rear.

The state, though at only a few miles' distance from London, appears to be remarkably isolated, and the house is surrounded by several acres of wooded grounds. I only wonder that Saville did not choose this establishment to be the site of Frankenstein's first experiments under his sponsorship, instead of dragging us all off to Scotland. But perhaps the villain thought his murderous schemes only likely to succeed if afforded that extra degree of secrecy possible only on such a remote island. Whether or not he was correct in this assessment remains to be seen.

I am presently ensconced in a hollow oak, some twenty feet above the ground. An owl established at an equal altitude in a neighboring trunk has been regarding me for some time with solemn astonishment. From this position I can see the great house but dimly, a gray bulk mostly obscured by the leafless branches of innumerable trees. I hear dogs, probably a mastiff or two, now evidently roaming free in the grounds. If the beasts hold true to canine form, they will not care to follow or find me, but my presence in the grounds will make them uneasy.

More later, after I make my first approach to the house, which I shall attempt after dark. I can hope that all my enemies are gathered in the house, and that they remain ignorant of my proximity. But in any case I shall persist.

LETTER 7

February 20, 1783
Saville Estate, near London

Sir—

Many of the messages I have written you during the past few years have been composed and dispatched under what I considered the most difficult circumstances. But I have perhaps more doubt regarding this one than I have had for any other, that you will ever see it. I know that I am surrounded by our enemies as I write; and, when I have finished writing, I intend giving this paper into the care of the very being whose existence has been, for some months now, the object of our search.

Tonight I have seen him, touched him, and have discovered that he lives. He thinks, he speaks! Nay, more than that! He tells me that he has seen you and spoken with you, not two years past, in your house at Passy. The tone in which he made this claim, the evident keenness of his thought, and the particulars of detail that he can give, regarding your person, your servants, and your surroundings there, are such that I tend to believe him. If it be true, there must be, I suppose, some reason of good policy why you could not have told me long ago about that meeting. In any case I pray that you will now tell me all about it, as soon as you can, and in no uncertain terms.

But all that—even that—is only the beginning of my news. I was invited to dine here last night—as I would have written to tell you then, had there been time to do so. To cut the story short, I accepted, and the dinner party—more below on its complications—was extended, by the most pressing invitations, into an overnight stay. There were some natural grounds for this, the night being one of really wretched weather, even for the middle of a British winter.

Inside all was warm and snug, and more or less convivial. Dining and conversation were at an end, and it was only when I had said goodnight to my host and hostess, followed a servant upstairs, and was alone in my room, that I met *him*—he who has no name, whose existence I have long doubted—he who tells me that he has seen you and spoken with you, in those very rooms at Passy where you and I last spoke face to face—but, as I say, there is much more to tell.

Item: Victor Frankenstein is very much alive. Not only alive and in passably good health, but still actively continuing his work, and that under this very roof; I dined with him this evening.

Why, then, does Walton's book say that Frankenstein is dead? The explanation offered by my hosts
for the deception is that the philosopher himself
preferred the peace and anonymity of being thought
deceased, a condition that would allow him to
devote all of his energies to his ongoing labor. The
man himself, who was present during this discussion, concurred in this explanation, though, as it
seemed to me, without any great enthusiasm.

Frankenstein was, it appears, really aboard Captain Walton's ship on an Arctic voyage, but he had
been aboard her from the start at Archangel, and
was not rescued from a sled. That voyage was the
last leg of a great and well-organized pursuit, beginning in Paris, whose sole object was to recapture the "creature" he had created. Saville and
Walton, who organized the chase, have known of
the creature's existence almost from the start. It
was not the pursuers, but only their quarry who
traveled by means of a dogsled for any distance
across the ice.

Item: Saville himself has returned home, and
was present when I arrived. Early in the evening,
a few remarks were dropped in the drawing room
and around the table, in an evident effort to maintain the fiction that Saville has really been in
India; but the pallor of his face and hands, if nothing else, would cast grave doubts upon that claim,
and evidently it is to be allowed to die. I am sure
the man would faint, or more likely explode, if he
had any idea that the "demon" he has now been
hunting for years was really somewhere on the
grounds of his own estate, or indeed anywhere
within ten miles of it.

I, of course, have cast no doubts, either by word or by look, upon anything told me by my hosts. I have nodded and smiled, and pretended to believe everything that I was told.

I am sure that my hosts' objective in having me here is to learn from me every thing I know on the subject of the creature, particularly to extract from me any clue I might consciously or unconsciously possess as to its present whereabouts. Mrs. Saville has been interested in that subject since I met her, but I think something must have happened very recently to arouse that interest to a new pitch. This attitude is entirely shared by her husband. Needless to say, I have tried to withhold information as much as possible, while doing my best to let them believe that I just possibly do know something, and that if properly approached I might be willing to consider sharing what I know with them.

There are strong hints from both the Savilles that if I choose to cooperate, I am to be let in on the profits—exactly how profits are to be derived is not yet clear. They wonder if I am authorized to represent my illustrious father—yes, I am afraid they are in no doubt about the connection—and drop more hints that there will of course be profits for you also if I do.

At dinner Mrs. Saville introduced me to her brother, Captain Walton, who had just come in. Her brother is not as pallid as her husband, but still remarkably so for a seafaring man. I took the opportunity to congratulate the captain upon his book, which, as I was able to assure him with some truth, everyone I know has read or is now reading. (My newfound acquaintance, or perhaps I should already call him friend, the very tall one I met in my room, has already assured me that he has read that book, nay, almost committed its every word to memory.)

Walton, as is obvious from his book, is a remarkably well-educated man—at least for a sailor—and prides himself more, I think, upon his literary skill than on anything else. He basked in my compliments.

At dinner there were Saville and Mrs. Saville, Walton, Frankenstein, and myself. The food and wine were the best I have enjoyed in a long time, the service near perfection.

Conversation at first was general. Saville complained at considerable length about the costs of doing business on his plantations in Jamaica, and the general difficulties of trading in blacks and molasses. He related, with some indignation, the story of another businessman, an acquaintance of his, who suffered a sharp loss when the captain of one of his slave-trading ships had attempted to cheat his insurance company by dumping overboard a whole cargo of ailing Africans, then claiming them as having been lost at sea. Under the circumstances the insurance company refused to pay, and the refusal has been upheld in court. Saville's indignation was directed at the insurance company.

I recount all this to you now, that you may have no illusions about the sensibilities of my hosts, and the tenor of their usual conversation. The fact is that the slave business and all other topics were quickly forgotten when the subject of Frankenstein's work came up.

As I have already mentioned, the young philosopher has now established his laboratory within this very mansion. He has been here for some months, I gather, since shortly after last summer's Geneva tragedy. Imagine my surprise when his presence was announced to me, with elaborate casualness, shortly before we sat down to dine; and imagine if you can my great interest a minute later when the man himself appeared. Judging by appearances he must have come fresh from his labors; the odor of chemicals still clung to his clothing, and on close inspection of his sleeves the stains of what must have been his most recent endeavors could still be seen.

In general appearance Victor is pretty much as I had imagined him, dark-haired, gaunt and pale, in physique tending to the frail rather than the robust, and with a nervous manner.

Frankenstein appeared cheerful when he first joined us, if slightly nervous. At dinner his state of mind became agitated, increasingly so as the conversation turned to the subject of his work, and there were several occasions while we were at table when I thought he would have communicated something of real importance to me, had there been a chance for him to do so privately. When we arose, I contrived to continue my mild flirtation with Mrs. Saville; her husband, a moment earlier, had allowed himself to be called out of the room to discuss some business, perhaps deliberately getting himself out of the way. There followed a general invitation to walk in the conservatory, which Walton declined, but Frankenstein and I accepted. And, presently, when our hostess had pleaded an urgent need to confer with the servants and had temporarily withdrawn from among the stunted orange trees, I had my chance, at least for a moment, to talk alone with Frankenstein.

I wondered whether this opportunity too might have been contrived by the Savilles, that the scientist would have a chance to add his unforced plea to theirs, that I would share with him all I had learned about his creature, most especially its present whereabouts.

But what he whispered to me, rapidly and confusedly, when he had the chance, was that he had once fled from the Savilles himself, and that it had been a horrible mistake later to be reconciled with them. That he now feared, more than before, those who had him, and now seemed to have me too, in their power. That, if the being he had created still lived, and I knew anything of its whereabouts, I should do everything I could to assure that it never fell into Saville's or Walton's hands.

Scarcely knowing what to make of this confused plea, or how I ought to respond, I yet managed to keep control of my countenance and my manner; I assured him vaguely that I would do my best to see that all came out well; and when we rejoined the others presently, I doubt that they were able to tell anything of what had passed between us, except that Frankenstein now appeared somewhat more cheerful than before.

Great pressure was then put on me, though all in the finest and most generous way, to persuade me to remain as the Savilles' guest overnight. What might have happened next had I been firm in my refusal of the invitation, I cannot say. But I was too much intrigued with the possibilities of the situation to persist for long in declining to accept. If in fact I am a prisoner, it was in a willing mood that I became one.

I retired, glad for a chance to mull over in solitude the surprises of the evening. But the greatest surprise of all was yet to come. Hardly had I been left alone in my room and the door closed after the last servant, when there came a tapping, firm, light, and regular, upon the nearest window, from outside.

To say that on first hearing this sound I doubted the evidence of my own ears is not to overstate the case. The windows of this room are perhaps thirty feet above the ground, and I had not thought them readily accessible. Next it occurred to me that the noise might represent the tapping of a tree branch upon the pane, though there was something in it too purposeful for that. Meanwhile, the dogs out in the grounds were giving vent to melancholy howlings, between the howlings of the wind, and I felt sure that something was disturbing them. The tapping continued, and presently I opened the draperies.

I had looked out of the same window once with the servants present, before the tapping came. On that earlier occasion there was almost nothing to be seen except the darkness of the night. But I could see then, far up in the adjoining wing of the great house, how a single, melancholy light burned in a high, narrow, shuttered casement. I felt sure at once that Frankenstein was working there, having taken his leave of the rest of us not to sleep but to return to the high and lonely thoughts that

must engage him as he labors. The *sincerity* of the
man had impressed me more than anything else
during our conversations, though when they took
place I still had not the proof of his success that
awaited me the second time I went to my window.
And an intense sense of his isolation had come
over me when I first beheld his remote light—surely,
I thought, he is more alone there in that high room
than it would seem possible for a human being to
be, this close to the swarming throngs of London.

During dinner and immediately afterward, Mrs.
Saville had continued, as I say, what had seemed
up to then to be only a mild flirtation with me.
And one of the younger maids had looked at me
several times, as I thought, with a certain meaning. I confess that a quiet tapping at my door
should not have been a tremendous surprise. But
to hear that same sound, at the window . . .

When I looked out for the second time, in in-
credulous response to such a summons, I beheld to
my astonishment a giant figure, its face muffled in
a cloak against the wind and freezing rain, crouching there on what looked like an impossibly narrow ledge. With some half-formed idea that this
could only be some secret courier, perhaps from
you, bearing some message of vast importance that
would justify such risks, I opened the window at
once. I think that sheer concern for the man's
survival, as I beheld him clinging in that perilous
position, was also a motive for my action.

He kept his face muffled as he crossed the sill
into the room; only his dark, piercing eyes were
clearly visible. But I think that from the moment

he stood erect, unfolding his great height, the truth of who he must be unfolded itself to me.

It was he who spoke first. "You are the son of Benjamin Franklin," he declared, looking down from his great height and speaking in a deep voice. "And, as such, you need fear no harm from me."

"And you," I replied—bravely enough, I trust, before this awesome being—"are the nameless person of the book."

He took my meaning instantly. "If by 'book' you mean that most malign and perfidious publication, the supposed letters of the sea-captain to his sister, then I am indeed the person most slandered and defamed in it. If you have read it, then you must fear me."

"I have read it. But it contains so much that I do not believe, that I think I would fear you more if it gave you a good character."

My visitor laughed, a surprising, very human, yet almost frightening sound. "Then bless you for an intelligent man. Your apprehensions of me, if you have any such, are needless. Your father has been my friend, and my enemies are also yours, and his." Saying this, he reached to close the window behind him, shutting out the blasting wind and cold.

We moved a little closer to the fire, toward which he stretched out a pair of enormous hands. "But," I demanded, "how can you possibly know who I am?"

The giant nodded toward the window where he had come in. "Since yesterday I have been out there, in the grounds. Last night, and again to-night, I have prowled for hours around the house, from window to window and from door to door, trying to plan what my next course of action ought to be."

"I heard the dogs tonight," I remarked. "I thought that they were after something."

"The dogs are frightened of me, and do not interfere. The humans—except for you now—do not yet know that I am here."

"You are living out of doors?"

"I have found shelter of a kind. And what to you is the fierce blast of winter, is to me little more than a chill breeze. I have survived the Arctic storm, and the Atlantic gale. Still I confess that at the moment this fire is welcome." He had opened his cloak partially to the warmth, and, in doing this, had loosed the muffling fold across his face. A moment later the cloth fell completely back. Having read the book, I was forewarned, and made no sudden cry or motion. Still—as you must know if the meeting between you did take place—the book, in its description of his personal appearance, is nearly accurate.

"And are you aware," I asked my caller, "that your creator is here too?"

"I have known that for some hours. I looked in at your dining table tonight, from outside, and became a silent and unseen member of your party. The ivy and the decorations on the outside walls offer enough in the way of handholds and footholds to allow me to explore virtually the entire exterior of the house.

"My astonishment was very great when I beheld him alive, entering the room where you were. And yet, on reflection, I am not tremendously surprised.

I had thought Frankenstein dead because of the circumstances under which I last saw him, in the Arctic; yet it is greatly to Saville's interest, and Walton's, or they believe it is, that he should survive, and labor for them."

"What were those circumstances, then?" I asked. "The book says—"

"The book lies," he rejoined calmly. "In that scene as in much else. I fled from the vicinity of the ship under a hail of bullets, Saville having lost his temper totally at last, and decided that I must be taken, dead or wounded, even fatally so, after his repeated efforts to take me alive had all come to nothing. I headed into the north, resolved to shake off my tormentors finally or to lead them to their destruction if they still persisted in the chase. Frankenstein, who had endeavored again to save me, had been struck down on the deck, and as I thought murdered. Now he is here, and I suppose has been convinced that what happened on the ship was my fault too, or a mere accident."

"After dinner," I said, "Frankenstein spoke to me alone."

'Ah. When you walked in the conservatory."

"Precisely."

"I saw you, but could not hear what was said there between you."

"He said that he was a mere prisoner here now. He urged me not to help our hosts, and to keep you out of their control, to such an extent as that might lie in my power. The trouble, I suspect, is that I have now become a prisoner too."

"No doubt you have." The creature stood regarding me, but said nothing more for a moment;

I received the impression that he was uncertain in
his own mind as to what his attitude ought to be
toward the man who had created him. "Then he
has changed his mind yet again." He murmured
the last words without surprise.

"You have not yet told me," I persisted, "how
you know who I am."

My visitor shrugged enormous shoulders. "I have
said that I could hear much of what you said
around the table during dinner—I heard enough to
be certain of your identity."

"And what will you do now?"

"Take vengeance, upon Saville, and Walton—is
there a man named Small here in the house? He is
small indeed, ill-favored, and dangerous, though
he prides himself upon his attractiveness to women.
I have not seen him here."

"Nor I, anyone matching that description."

"—upon them for attempting to steal from me
what miserable measure of a life I had. For treat-
ing me as their property, by right of conquest or
discovery, to be disposed of as they choose. For
killing . . ." Here he fell silent, staring once more
into the fire.

"And Frankenstein?"

"He too should be punished, for letting himself
be ruled by those . . . but it was he who gave me
life." Again my visitor shrugged massive shoulders. "Perhaps I cannot bring myself to punish
him."

"My father has been very curious about that.
The bringing-to-life, I mean. How it was accomplished."

"Ah. He must ask Victor, then. I know but little

more about it now than when I last spoke to your father. But I should be greatly interested to hear any explanation that Doctor Franklin can conceive."

We talked for a time of the more abstruse points of electrical science; or at least my new acquaintance talked on that subject, and I endeavored to understand. His knowledge surpasses mine enormously, but then I am sure that mine does not begin to approach yours, either. His discourse on the subject, embodying what I gather are some new ideas, may be quite intelligible to you.

My new acquaintance—I find I can no longer bring myself to write "the creature," and I scarcely know what other term to use—has said that he too has observed the light from that high window, protected by iron bars, that must show where Frankenstein's new laboratory has been established. We had just touched upon this subject when suddenly he announced a decision to go there, to confront his creator once more if he could, even though the laboratory windows are so elevated and guarded by barriers that it seems impossible for anyone to reach them from the outside. He said that he would infallibly return to my room, whatever befell with regard to the final confrontation that he sought; and would then take counsel with me, and try to help me, before he acted on his decision to seek revenge upon Saville and the others.

I am now, as I write, awaiting his return.

If his decision as to what he wants to do next strikes me as at all reasonable, I am ready to act in concert with him. I have no qualms about acting boldly against Saville, who is, I am sure, prepared to hold me a prisoner here against my will, which implies that he is also ready to do even worse. He is, besides, my political enemy and yours—and the enemy of our new country.

Later— My new friend has returned, through the window as before, to watch me pen these remaining lines. He says that the approach to Frankenstein's laboratory proved at last too difficult for him, and that we are to make our plans and act without consideration of the scientist. But he was gone for a long time, and I wonder. Meanwhile, I will seal this message, and hand it over for delivery to one who can, with little difficulty, pass the high walls and fences that make a prison and a fortress of this estate. This message will be added, he says, to a pile of letters that are already awaiting sending at the gatekeeper's lodge—and I have no reason to doubt what he says.

He will return from that errand well before morning, he says, and we shall then make our plans.

Your Affectionate Son,
Benjamin Freeman

Chapter 13

February 21, 1783
Somewhere in Kent

It is now my turn to write, whilst my short companion watches. I suppose he may very well be curious, as was Father Jacques, as to what I am so industriously setting down in my worn notebook. I did not read Freeman's letter to his famous parent, but I have assured him, as I assured the priest, that he may read in my journal if he likes. But Freeman says that he is too weary to read anything, and that the light is bad—and now I see that despite the cold and the wet he is asleep. It is almost a cave, this embrasure in the seaside rocks where we are huddled. The sound of the surf is loud, and at high tide I suppose there will be spray—but by then, if all goes well, we shall be gone.

From the moment I identified Freeman as the son of Benjamin Franklin, I was determined to make use of him somehow. But now I confess that I am coming to like him as well.

It has been an exhausting day, for man and creature alike. Too much happened for me to be able to remember it all in proper detail. Yet it is necessary that I write down what I can . . . though when I think of it, why should it be necessary that I write down today's events, or indeed, that I keep this journal at all? I cannot tell why. I only know that the urge to record my experiences is nearly as powerful as my desire to live. Did my brain once belong to a natural philosopher?

One thing I should certainly record as carefully as possible is my final interview with Frankenstein—I suppose that encounter under Saville's highest roof is likely to be the last meeting that my creator and I will ever have. I felt a reluctance to talk about it with Freeman, immediately afterward—I had known him only a few minutes—and so told him that I had been unable to reach Frankenstein in his high laboratory. Perhaps—who knows?— we should all be better off if that were true.

Clinging precariously to the wall, in the darkness outside the high, barricaded window, I had watched Frankenstein for several minutes before attempting to get his attention. I wondered as I watched him if now he were really going mad. His arms were filthy up to the elbows with the fat, blood, and offal of murdered women—or perhaps these latest specimens had not been murdered, but how could he know? I supposed that he was persisting in his efforts to create a female—if he is anything he is persistent. I assumed further that the bodies that surrounded him, in several stages of dismemberment, were those of women. But from the angle of the window I could not really tell.

His gaze was wild, and a certain new look of indecision in his movements suggested to my experienced eye that his mind was under strain, if not actually unbalanced. He was muttering to himself as he went through the laboratory procedures that I knew so well from watching him in Scotland.

As I watched him from outside, I was on the verge of deciding that there was no point in my trying to talk to him again.

But in the end I tapped at the window. It must have been a loud sound in his quiet room, but he went on with the task before him, suturing something, and did not hear me until my tapping had sounded for the third time.

Once Frankenstein's attention had been caught, he came over to the window at once, and looked out at me without demonstrating any great astonishment. To my surprise he behaved almost as if he had been expecting such a visit.

Victor opened the glass and the shutters of the window from inside, but the iron bars that guarded it were fixed in stone. Exerting all my strength, I managed to wrench one of the bars from its sockets, and, squeezing through the space thus created, climbed in to confront my creator.

I closed the shutters behind me, and for a long moment we stood staring at each other, I dripping with rain, he, less copiously, with preservatives and blood. We must have looked like two men—or two monsters—who had never met before and who perhaps might have nothing to communicate to each other. Seeing him at close range for the first time in many months, I thought that he looked ill.

It was left to me to utter the first words. "You have come back to them." The way I spoke the sentence made it an accusation, and I saw his face tighten.

I continued: "But never mind that. The window is open behind me, and if you wish to get away I will see you safely to the ground, and outside the wall of the estate. Beyond that your fate is up to you."

Frankenstein shook his head. "I suppose young Freeman has somehow communicated with you. But I do not wish to flee. You should do so, though, and quickly, for you will be in great danger if you are discovered here."

"I am not the only one."

He did not understand me, and shrugged irritably, thinking, I suppose, that I meant him. "I intend to stay," he replied. "It is the only way I have found that will allow me to do my work. It is not the money, I have that of my own. But I need privacy, protection. Saville has promised there will be no more—no more excesses on his part. I have exacted a solemn promise from him, and from Walton too."

"I see," I replied, after a moment. What I saw was that, with Frenkenstein, argument would be as hopeless as remonstrance. There are some humans, like Molly, who insist on walking to their own destruction. And I had another purpose in climbing to his new laboratory, one that I felt was more urgent than trying to save him from himself. "Tell me," I pleaded. "Withhold no secrets from me now. Who am I? Where did my brain come from? And the parts of my body?"

He did not hesitate, but made a gesture embodying hopelessness. "I do not know."

"Not know! How is it possible that you should not know?"

"Because of the methods by which I worked." My creator seemed irritated, that anyone should bother him with such a question. "I should have kept better records, but I thought I could not take the time. Every minute I wanted to press on with the work itself—Metzger and Big Karl brought me my materials. They might remember, but I have never considered it important."

"Not important!"

"I told them what I wanted, the physical types and conditions, and paid them, and left the details to them. I cared nothing for the names of the people who had inhabited the bodies before I got them."

"You're telling me you don't know whose brain you used? Was it a single brain, can you at least tell me that?"

"Oh yes, yes." Frankenstein made a gesture of surprise and impatience, and looked at me as if I should have known better than to ask such a stupid question. "The brain is a very delicate organ anyway; the nervous connections are incredibly complex. Even with a single brain, the grafting would have been impossible, had I not been able to rely upon the almost miraculous effects of the electric fluid. I wouldn't have attempted to use parts of more than one."

"But—you can't say whose brain it was? What kind of a head did it come in?" I gestured helplessly.

"Oh. I can't say where the head came from. It was a man's, of course. Large, as I recall. There was something—noble—about the face, though of course in fact one gets that impression sometimes even in peasants. The medical school at Ingolstadt had a constant requirement for bodies, and the suppliers got them whenever people died in the homes for the poor and indigent in that area. Also ..." He let his words trail off. Something changed subtly in his face.

"Also what?" I promoted, after a brief silence. "You have said that my brain is not that of a condemned criminal."

"No." Frankenstein shook his head judiciously. "I have no reason to think that it is that."

"What, then?"

"Well," he admitted reluctantly, "besides the poorhouses, that contributed bodies for research, there were the asylums."

A silence fell between us. But I felt no shock. With something of a thrill of pride I realized that I had become firmly confident in my own sanity. Calmly I asked: "Are you telling me I am a madman, then? But the languages I know, the history, the natural philosophy—how do you explain it all?"

"I cannot explain it," Frankenstein said simply. Then the tones of a professor crept into his voice. "A madman may know many languages. Or some stimulation by the electrical fluid may have had a healing effect upon the mind as well as the body. And the effect upon the body is undeniable. Even the marks of the sutures are gone—"

"Bah." Talking to him, trying to find out from him the facts of his science, was worse than useless. The electrical fluid dissolved everything, facts and logic along with all doubts, all questions. I had experienced it many times before, but never before so clearly realized the fact. Was it a clever reluctance to reveal secrets, as I had assumed for a long time, or was it possible that my creator really did not know what he was babbling about?

How could that be possible? He possessed a facility with jargon, certainly, and who, listening to an expert discuss his own field, really expects to understand all that they hear?

"Victor," I said. "I am less than seven and a half feet tall."

"Eh? But what has that . . ." He blinked at me, and became authoritarian again. "You are eight feet tall."

"No."

"There may have been some slight shrinkage."

"It isn't that."

"Then someone has been lying to you, or has taken faulty measurements. You are the work of my hands, and you belong to me, and I know everything there is to know about you." He cannot manage his own life, but has perfect confidence in what he knows, or thinks he knows, of mine.

I turned back to the window. "I am going, then," I told him over my shoulder. "If you are ready to decide that what Freeman says is true—if you are now ready for yet another change,and would like to be free of Saville and his friends once more— then come with me now, and let me see you safely outside the grounds."

He turned from me to stare at the table, where his work awaited him. "Freeman misunderstood me if he thinks I want to leave. That cannot be, just now. This experiment is on the verge of completion."

I could see that, indeed, the body on the table looked as alive and ready as any of his experimental bodies ever did. It was female, and it—or most of its parts—had recently been young and healthy.

"Now," I insisted. "Now, or never."

"*I cannot.*"

Without another word I departed. In the space of a few minutes I had picked up Freeman's letter to his father, and had deposited it at the gatekeeper's lodge. I left it there in the middle of a stack of other outgoing communications, where no literate person will cast eyes upon its address, or pay the least attention to it, until it is far from that estate.

Then I returned again to Freeman's room. I tried to move cautiously, but something, perhaps my continued scrambling around on the outside of the house, or the noise I had made in breaking the bars on the laboratory window, had already given us away. Saville's household had been quietly alerted. An ambush had been set.

The timing with which the trap was sprung was excellent. Scarcely had I reentered Freeman's room than the door burst open—if he had locked it, it had been silently and almost immediately unlocked from outside—and our enemies, armed, burst in upon us. Saville himself was in the center of the doorway, with Walton on his right hand and Small on his left. A crowd of armed footmen were gathered at his back.

Trusting that Saville still did not wish me dead, I ignored the deafening shouts for my surrender, and the firearms that were leveled at me. Immediately I lunged for the window and scrambled back out onto the roof. No shots were fired.

Freeman, who had been caught too far from the windows to attempt such an escape, reacted with remarkable quickness of wit. He staggered and fell, away from me, as if I had thrown him to the floor. Then, pointing after me with a quivering arm, he immediately set up a cry of alarm. The impression was conveyed that I had been attacking him, and that he was glad to see our host and his armed retainers break in. Meanwhile he gave me to understand with a wink that I should not take all this too seriously.

I, crouched once more on the narrow ledge just outside the window, hesitated, ready to spring either direction.

Small aimed a firearm at the window where I was, and again cried for me to surrender, but he did not fire when I ignored him. Walton and Saville were shouting at me simultaneously, and I could not distinguish the words of either one. Mrs. Saville's face had now appeared in the bedroom doorway behind them, and I could see that she too was armed with a pistol.

Freeman, who had scrambled to his feet now and was talking excitedly to the others, was in no immediate danger. Also I wanted firmer footing, so I abandoned my precarious post outside the window and moved away across the roof. The rain had stopped at last, but the roof tiles were slippery. Lights below me caught my eyes; down there in the grounds were more men, what looked like a small army of footmen and others, all equipped with torches and clubs, and controlling unhappy dogs.

I climbed carefully up one gable, then slid down a new slope slowly, looking the situation over, whilst the crowd of footmen rushed around a wing of the house to get below me again. I wondered what would happen if I were to leap down among them, and came to the conclusion that they would probably jump out of my way, and I would break a leg. Besides, I was not yet ready to leave Freeman.

Once more I moved; once more the roof sloped up before me, then angled down again. People inside the house were running from window to window, trying to keep me in sight. With all the wings, gables, and angles that the house possessed it was a fairly even game.

We reached a temporary stalemate at last. I could still be seen from below, but thought my back was relatively secure. Walton, leaning out a window a few yards below me and in front of me, began a determined effort to keep me talking, my attention fixed on him. I suspected the plan called for others to use the opportunity to sneak up on me from behind and somehow capture me alive.

Mrs. Saville, her lovely figure framed in another window beside Walton's, tried, or pretended to try, to make peace among us all, though she could not keep the anger out of her voice. We all of us ignored her, which I suppose fueled her rage.

Captain Walton, ready to dazzle me with his wit and erudition, freely admitted that he had somewhat abused his poetic license in the creation of that notorious book.

I said: "I do not approve of my memoirs, as you have created them for me."

"You are of course free to compose your own."

That was said, naturally, in perfect, serene confidence that I should never be able to do anything of the kind.

"I intend doing so."

He took it well. Such a statement, from me, could make no impression on him, really. "I should imagine that the effort will bring you to a better appreciation of what I have done. Even if you die tonight, as you seem determined to do, people are going to remember you because of me. What I have written of you."

"Indeed."

"I even went out of my way to add a touch of sympathy to your character— and a touch of intelligence and elegance."

Saville, who had been out of my sight for a while, had now evidently given what he considered the necessary orders to his footmen. He came forward, in the next window over, as if he had been attending to me all the time, and picked up the conversation. He seconded what Walton had said. Saville was rather proud of the book too, and regretted that it had to be put forward as a fiction.

It was at about this time that I realized that some time had passed since I had seen Small. Obviously he would be busy, probably behind me somewhere. But doing what? My back was against a wall, and the roof above that would be exceedingly difficult, I thought, for any mere human to clamber about on.

"Then," I asked Saville, "you think that readers are not really likely to believe it?"

"More of 'em will read it, since we called it fiction. As to belief, perhaps. Perhaps not. Matters

are never that simple where books are concerned."
Saville sighed. "I genuinely regret," he added, "not
being able to keep a closer control over the writing
and editing. But then, one cannot do everything.
There is never time."

More faces and guns, in yet another window.
There was Freeman, looking rather grim. Still I
might have got away, as I thought, fairly easily, a
feint in one direction, a quick scramble in the
other. None of these people were really aware as
yet of how quickly I could move. But I continued
to feel a reluctance to abandon Freeman, who I
was sure could seal his father's loyalty to me. His
pretence of enmity towards me had been well performed, but I was not convinced that all of the
audience had been thoroughly taken in. Once I
was gone, temporarily out of their reach again,
they would have time for some leisurely discussion among themselves, and Freeman, now being
ignored, might not fare so well.

A new factor entered the equation, a new face
appeared at the window beside Saville. Our noise
had been enough to disturb even Victor Frankenstein in his eyrie; or else Saville had dispatched a
messenger to bring him out.

My creator no sooner saw what was taking place,
than he wanted to act as an intermediary. He wrung
his hands. "Oh God! That what I wanted to accomplish has come to this!"

He wished aloud that we could all let bygones
be bygones, with regard to the injuries we had all
done one another.

Saville paused, as if for very careful thought;

then said, as if granting a great concession, that he was willing to do so.

Frankenstein thought back with agony upon the night, his wedding night, when he had found his bride murdered. He expressed his sorrow that the book blamed me—he does not think that I am guilty.

I said, with a sudden glimmer of light dawning: "Nor do the ones who wrote and published it."

"Done merely for dramatic purposes, old, uh, old fellow." That, with forced jollity, from Walton.

"They have a more direct knowledge of the truth." It was a shot almost at random, but I think it told. Saville's jolly expression appeared to have frozen in place.

I called to my creator: "What success is your work having now, Victor? Does Molly breathe again?"

His gaze turned stony. "Death comes to us all— her glory lies in the chance that through her something greater may be accomplished."

"And what of Bess? You failed with her. What of William? Of Clerval? You were not there to try to bring them back. Odd, that there have been so many deaths around you. It has taken a whole book of lies to explain them."

There were cries of rage.

"Victor. *What of Elizabeth?* Where was Small on the night she died?"

Fresh cries of rage burst from our enemies' throats. I saw the truth, though dimly and without fully understanding it. Victor as always saw only what he wished to see.

I shook my head. "Enough of this. Saville, tell

us, tell Victor and the rest, what it is you really want. I know you have no intention of letting me go free." I was certain that at the very least he was determined to recapture me for study and eventual dissection. My death would serve him better than my freedom, but he would much prefer to have me in his grip alive. Somewhere within me there lies the secret of godlike power and he means to have that secret at all costs.

A sharp outcry alerted me, and I turned. Small was there, on the roof above and behind me, approaching from an angle where he must be invisible to Freeman in his window at my side. But my creator had seen him, and had cried a warning. The little man was creeping forward on all fours across the roof, in his hand what looked like a short arrow or a long dart. The weapon, I realized, must be meant to paralyze and not to kill me.

The chief assassin, somewhat in advance of his cohort, the climbing footmen and gardeners with their darts and nets who were following close behind him, came within reach of my lunging arm. I caught Small at his treachery, dragged him from the roof, and wrenched the weapon from his hand. He screamed, for once not threats, but in sheer terror.

I held him over the edge of the roof, above a fall that ought to cripple if it did not kill outright. Then, twisting his arm, I urged him to confess what I now seriously suspected, that he had killed not only Clerval but Elizabeth, and perhaps William as well, with at least the tacit consent of Saville and Walton.

Elizabeth had been determined to keep Victor

from returning to his nasty work, and she appeared to have at least a fair chance of succeeding. Small had also been scouting out the Frankenstein family, at Saville's orders, when William was killed.

There was a shout of great outrage from the master of the house, and bullets began to fly at me.

Small went over the edge of the roof, I presume to his death.

Freeman in the confusion got out of the house to me, grabbing a pistol on the way. The gun blazed in his hand, and I saw a liveried footman topple from the roof above, his own pistol discharging a ball that sang sadly past my head.

I gathered my strength and leaped for a tree branch, then clung to it with one hand and caught Freeman when he leaped after me.

From then on our flight was comparatively easy, and we successfully fled the estate.

My companion and I are now in agreement that we should make an effort to reach France. He is skilled and experienced in arranging clandestine Channel crossings, and he assures me that, working together, we stand a much better chance of surviving than would either of us alone. I am touched by this fairly obvious lie—clearly he, traveling alone, would stand a much better chance than when burdened with the company of such an obvious monstrosity as myself. Nevertheless I have accepted his help, and am determined to repay it when I can.

I watch him sleeping now, and I reflect upon America, as represented by this young man, and her meaning to the world. Some kind of a new beginning, certainly.

How is it possible that I know enough of history to reflect upon such matters? And yet I do.

Later— Talking again with Freeman. I had supposed that once we were able to reach France we should be free of pursuit, or very nearly so. But he has convinced me of what seems, upon reflection, to be no more than logical, viz., that the peace treaty is not yet concluded, though probably very close to being so. And Franklin himself has warned his son that nothing must be done to upset the negotiations at this most delicate stage. For Franklin to be implicated in the accusation of a prominent Englishman on charges of murder, kidnapping, and other foul crimes, would create the most dangerous sensation.

I have no wish to provoke a fresh outbreak of war. But still there are many scores that must be settled.

Letter 8

February 22, 1783
Along the English coast

Dear Sir—

I dispatch this letter knowing that if all goes well, I may reach your side as quickly as it does; and knowing, also, that it is entirely possible that all may not go well. Unlike my last to you, this message will be carried on the first leg of its journey by a comparatively common means of transportation.

My companion and myself are presently in a place of reasonably secure if uncomfortable shelter, waiting for nightfall, and the tide, when we are to risk a crossing of the Channel by one of the small private boats, a mode of transport with which I am by no means unfamiliar, after four years of almost regular use.

This crossing will be a new experience for my friend, but I am beginning to think that little else in the way of human adventure could possibly be new to him. I have whiled away the last hour or so in listening to some of his exploits, and find them almost incredible; they would be unbelieveable indeed, were it not for some of the things that I have already seen him do.

A little later— There are certain signs and portents along the coast, perceptible to an experienced eye, and indicating that a search for us is rapidly being organized; I am impressed by the power that Saville has evidently at his disposal, and by the speed with which he can call it into action. But all this is nothing new to me, or to my tall friend either.

I dispatch this in haste. God willing, it will get through to France, and so will we.

Hopefully,
Your Son, BF

LETTER 9

February 23, 1783

Most Esteemed Parent—

Rejoice with us, for we have reached France alive!

I may describe the crossing as being not unattended by some little danger, for M. Saville's reach was evidently a little longer even than we feared. Had it not been for my own wits and experience, and the strength and sometime ferocity of my uncouth-looking companion, I fear that both of us would be feeding the Channel fishes at this very moment. Or else, ignominiously bound hand and foot, on our way back to a certain estate in suburban London, where a very uncertain welcome would await us.

The issue was for a little while in doubt, even after we had left the shores of Bonny England well

behind us. The cutthroats with whom we had con-
tracted for our passage had decided that turning
us in to those who hunted for us, once we were
under way and our suspicions allayed, would bring
a greater profit and less risk than the service upon
which we had agreed with them. Failing a good
chance to betray us to our enemies, I believe they
would have preferred to carry us only half way,
and from that point carry on our purses for us.

Before we could entirely disabuse them of this
notion, one of their number had begun to swim for
shore (it proved to be a trifle far for him, I fear)
and the other two had received certain stern teach-
ings that left them aching. The remainder of our
journey was relatively uneventful.

I had hoped that Saville might be inclined to
give up once we had got to France. But the perti-
nacity of his pursuit thus far has inclined me to
take a grimmer view of the matter now.

Later— We have purchased a wagon, cheaply, and
are now on our way across France. I drive, while
my companion for the most part remains out of
sight. Our goal of course is Paris.

I have asked my friend—he has certainly become that—by what name he prefers to be called.
The look I got from him in response was a peculiar
one, as though I had inadvertently touched upon a
matter of great importance.

"If ever I possessed a name," he at last responded,
"it has long been lost. Do you wish to assume the
responsibility of bestowing one upon me? I think I
shall be inclined to accept it, if you do."

I have never been made such an offer before. I
think it was his solemn manner as he said those

last words, more than anything else, that made me hesitate. "If it comes to that," I said at length, "I think that a man should name himself, rather than depend upon the notion of some friend, however well intentioned it might be."

He nodded slowly. "In that I believe that you are right, Freeman. And yet I hesitate to name myself. It seems to me that I *should* have a name—nay, that I *do*. And yet I do not know what it is."

A silence fell, not grim, but thoughtful, and persisted between us for some time. So far I have been reluctant to press him for what he knows—or even what he imagines—about his origins. He has volunteered a little, enough to assure me that the scene of his creation, as he remembers it, was not *very* greatly different from the description of that scene in the book.

If he can remember anything from an earlier life, before his—transformation, if that is the appropriate word—he has said nothing to me about it. But I am increasingly consumed with curiosity. There is a natural nobility in my companion. Might his brain have once inhabited the skull of some great leader or philosopher? And if so, who?

Later again— We travel, pretty steadily, and in passing we marvel at the destitution among the people. I have observed much poverty during the past four years, in several parts of Europe, and yet this is remarkable. Each time I return to France it appears to have grown worse. A loaf of bread is only two sous, and yet there are many who cannot buy a loaf. The income of Louis XVI, I am sure,

must be reckoned in the millions of livres annu-
ally; the Condés entertain thousands of guests, in
an opulence surpassing even that of Versailles, not
to mention ancient Rome—and meanwhile the poor
keep themselves alive, when they are able to manage the trick at all, on rye bread and black por-
ridge, with a few chestnuts now and then as luxury
when times are good.

My companion assures me that for the most part
his epic journeys around the world have not been
conducted in any style of travel familiar to the
wealthy. But such poverty as we see around us
now in France surprises him as it does me. The
condition of the mass of the people here grows
more desperate with each passing year. I would
not be at all surprised if this nation, one day soon,
were convulsed in its own revolution—I do not see
how matters can go on as they are.

When we reach the neighborhood of Paris, we
shall go into hiding, rather than try to approach
you directly—this at least unless I have some instruction from you to the contrary. You will be
able to reach me through the same person as before, when I was last lodging in the vicinity. I
appreciate, and so does my companion, that the
peace negotiations, especially in what must be so
sensitive a stage as they now are, ought not to be
disturbed by the intrusion of other matters, even
those as important as this one will ultimately be
to all mankind.

It crosses my mind, as I meditate upon a thing
or two I heard in London, that it might be wise for
us to seek information, perhaps guidance, from

this man Mesmer, who as I hear is now returned to Paris. Have you any thoughts upon that point?

In any case, Sir be assured that for the time being, we are both well and safe. Good health and good fortune attend you until I see you again.

Your affectionate Son,
B. Freeman

LETTER 10

March 7, 1783
Paris

Dear Sir—

We have arrived here safely, in the midst of Carnival. I was relieved to find waiting for me your communication regarding your wish to see both of us at Passy tomorrow night. We shall be there; I think a boat quietly to your landing stage will be the best means of approach.

Meanwhile, this letter will serve as the preliminary report for which you say you cannot wait.

To begin with, since we have reached the city my companion is in better spirits than I have ever seen him before. Carnival, as I perhaps ought to have expected, suits his nature admirably; in the midst of this communal delirium he is for once able to move abroad with perfect freedom, at least by night. I have money available, and already both of us are masked and well costumed. My tall friend has turned into a jester (it was the one costume readily available that could be made to fit) while I cavort around him in the guise of a fantastic ape.

Here in the city the entire populace seems to have gone mad, as is usual for this season in Paris. Last night when we arrived the streets were thronged, and the crowds have continued through the day. Vehicles of all kinds, bearing revelers, press their way slowly through the mobs that clog the streets on foot. Even the poor, who a few days ago were almost lifeless, here and now are ready to paint their faces, make what variations in their ragged clothing they are able, and celebrate. From the simply painted countenances of the poor to the most fantastic extravagances of the wealthy, the populace display their determination to make merry; the city at night (turned almost to day by the light of countless candles and torches) takes on the aspect of a fever dream or nightmare. I wish that your health allowed you to tour it more freely. Nothing in England, I believe, nor in America, can present a spectacle to compare with this.

On a more practical level, it is a relief to me to find myself once again in a city where I need not be so careful to conceal my relationship with you. Scarcely had we arrived before I encountered one of our mutual friends, who recognized me (this was before I had put on my costume) and insisted that I come with him at once to visit Cagliostro. He was all excitement at the prospect, though I gather that among many here the enthusiasm for this mountebank has already passed. The devotees of Mesmer on the other hand, they tell me (and you doubtless know better than I) are still increasing in numbers.

As I had already toyed with the idea of visiting the "Count," I readily enough assented to the proposal. My friend (the tall and nameless one, I mean) came with me, though at the last minute he decided it would be wiser of him to remain outside the house, among the revelers in the street, from whence I could summon him in if there appeared any reason for doing so. Our friend who was to have performed the introductions abandoned us at the last moment, alas, in pursuit of fairer game, but as it turned out his defection scarcely mattered.

Count Cagliostro did see the two of us, jester and ape, together briefly, as I entered, but what he made of the towering figure of my companion, who came no farther than the doorway, I have no means of knowing. The celebrity, while in my hearing, made no comment on the appearance of my friend, being doubtless afraid of doing anything that might help to create a rival to himself for the enthusiasm of the crowd.

Cagliostro is a man of average height, and somewhat more than average weight. His age is presently about forty, if one judges by normal physical appearances and does not take too seriously his calm eyewitness accounts of, and claims to have taken part in, certain affairs that predate the Christian era. He has bulging dark eyes, a short neck, and a dark complexion—and, I assure you, an air of competence and force, a commanding presence that cannot appear in the simple physical description I here present. On the night I saw him, he was outfitted in a scarlet jacket and trousers, and wore a ceremonial sword to which I am sure he has no more real right than you or I would have—less, I expect, if the truth were acknowledged about his birth. With him as his constant companion was the lovely Mme de la Motte, of whom you have heard, I am sure; her beauty will need no description here from me.

The great man, when finally I had the opportunity to approach him, more or less alone, did not disappoint me in the range of his conversation, only in its substance. He had much to say to me about his previous lives (which must indeed extend at least two thousand years into the past); about something he called "transcendent chemistry" of which, I think, neither you nor I have ever heard (nor have Lavoisier or Cavendish, I will wager) and also about "the great Arcana of Memphis," whatever that may be.

When Cagliostro began to speak of giants, and of reviving the dead, you may be sure that my ears pricked up; but he never mentioned Frankenstein (although Walton's book is of course a common topic of conversation here) again, I suppose, not wishing to publicize one whom he must consider a rival for the attentions of the public.

The giants he did mention soon came to nothing, being wafted away in the breezes of his conversation on other topics even more marvelous. They were last seen somewhere in the interior of Africa, along with a most impressive city that the Count has visited there, and which he swears to have ten times the population of Paris itself. I expressed polite agreement with all that I was told, and as soon as the conventions of society allowed I took my leave.

My tall friend was awaiting me anxiously in the street, and was disappointed but not surprised when I related the incidents of the visit. But the evening's social encounters were not yet over. After departing the establishment where Cagliostro held forth, my tall friend and I also encountered in the confusion of Carnival the well-known Dr. Joseph-Ignace Guillotin, a professor of anatomy, and, I gather, of much else besides.

Again my traveling companion contrived to disappear into a nearby celebration (such were the crowds that he was scarcely conspicuous) while the Doctor and I conversed, shouting above the noise. Mutual friends assure me that Dr. Guillotin has a great penchant and reputation for conceiving projects and inventions intended to benefit mankind. When I mentioned to him in a casual way that some experimenters hope to be able to revive the dead by the galvanic method, he at once and vociferously declared any such scheme to be arrant nonsense. I was careful to frame none of my succeeding questions to him in such a way that he might possibly suspect me of taking such matters seriously.

So, as you see, Father, the brief time we have so far spent in Paris has been vastly entertaining, but I fear that nothing has happened to advance our investigation in the slightest. My chief hope now is that you, having read and digested all of my reports, will be able to shed more light on the matter for us both tomorrow.

                              Your Son,
                              Benjamin Freeman

Chapter 14

March 9, 1783
Paris

I have been to see Franklin for the second time in my life, and we have talked again. In a sense I learned very little from the conversation, but somehow I am not disappointed. There is something so reassuring about the man, in his quick intelligence and his willingness to listen, and to think along new lines—perhaps most of all in the love of life that is so evident in him. I feel that he is capable of understanding me as perhaps no one else can do, not even my creator.

Let me describe the day from the beginning.

After a late night of wandering, singing, laughing among throngs of people—I cannot say of revelry, for my mental state was not such as to bear that easy classification—after such late activities,

239

I say, Freeman and I both slept late in our snug room, my short friend in the bed, and I, amply supplied with cushions and spare bedding, diagonally on the floor.

From about midday we were out among the revelers again. It is a tremendous sense of freedom that I feel in thus roaming at liberty through the costumed crowds, most of whom are ready to hail my monstrous form in a friendly fashion if they take note of me at all. But already I am aware—as I was when I lay with Kunuk—of an undercurrent of dissatisfaction. These people do not wave to *me*. We are coming from enormous distances to meet.

In midafternoon a message of warning was passed to my companion in the street, by one of the same couriers who regularly carry communications between Freeman and his father while Freeman is in Paris. Saville and a party of men had been observed, boldly crossing the Channel. It might be thought that as a citizen of England, still technically at war with France, our archenemy would put himself into some considerable danger by so doing—but he may well have managed to get himself accredited somehow as a delegate to the peace talks. Whether that is the true explanation or not, I am sure that some high-level understanding exists, making this a safe land for him to travel in—safer than for me. The powerful and wealthy have, in a very real sense, their own nationality.

After digesting this disquieting news about Saville, my friend and I laid low until the time came for us to keep our appointment with Franklin. Freeman changed his costume in our room, and we separated when we left it. I had no other costume that would fit me, and I cannot, of course, disguise my height. But I left our room by means of the window and the rooftops, and was not molested. We met again at a prearranged place on the river-bank, where a boat was waiting to take us the short distance down the Seine to Passy.

The Hôtel de Valentinois, where Franklin has now been in residence for seven years, has its own landing stage. Freeman and I were met there by a guide, under the observance of a couple of armed men; and from thence, our faces muffled with cloaks, were conducted on a winding uphill path among trees and bushes, until we were at the house itself, which seems almost worthy to be called a château; it is finely built, and the ceilings of all the rooms I entered were high enough to let me stand erect beneath them.

One last time, at a side door of the house, we had to wait; then we were shown in, and up some stairs, to a large, cheerful, private room warmed by a crackling fire, the same room wherein I had met Franklin on my previous visit. As before, desk and tables were littered with books, papers, and writing materials. On one small table at one side of the pleasant room, a set of ebony and ivory chessmen waited, in the midst of an interrupted game or problem.

The room also contained a great deal of equipment for electrical experiments. From a chair in front of a table laden with such apparatus Benjamin Franklin rose to give us greetings as we entered. He appears today scarcely changed from when I saw him last; in his case another year or two added to eighty-odd have had but small effect.

Franklin and his son embraced each other warmly as they exchanged greetings. It is obvious that there is a strong natural affection between them, as well as respect for each other's abilities. I could not help overhearing some discussion of how Mother—obviously not Franklin's wife, who died a few years ago—was faring in Virginia.

But very soon the great man tilted back his head to meet my eye, eager to give me his full attention. "Sir, I welcome you again. You have traveled far and perhaps learned much since last we met; while I, I fear, am in the same room still, and only doubtfully any the wiser."

I was provided with a seat, in the form of some cushions strewn upon the floor; my host remembering from the occasion of my last visit what peculiar seating arrangement I really found most comfortable.

My traveling companion was then sent, or called, out of the room, having as I understood to make some detailed report upon some other matter of politics or business in which he had been engaged with his father and others.

Benjamin Franklin and I were alone, and the aged man, now seated in his own comfortable chair, turned to me. Our faces were nearly at a level, with me sitting on the floor.

Franklin asked eagerly: "And have you still no name?"

"None, sir. None that I know of."

"Ah. It is very strange." He meditated for a little time in silence. "And the memories? Have more of them returned?"

"Not enough to help." I told him, in broad out-

line, of my adventures since we had last met. He interrupted me frequently, with questions about Frankenstein, and his countenance grew sad at the news I had to relate about the son of his old friend Alphonse. He had heard of Victor's release from prison—largely through the belated influence of Saville—of his marriage, and the tragic loss upon his wedding night of his dear bride Elizabeth.

We returned to my own situation. "And has Priestley seen you?" Franklin asked. "Or Lavoisier?"

"No. Frankenstein and the others have generally kept me out of sight of other men of science."

"Ah." It was a sigh, that seemed burdened with several meanings. "There is as much jealousy among philosophers, I fear, as among whores." Franklin shook his head. "The more I have considered your case, my friend, the more I am puzzled by it. Are you never struck by the sheer *unlikelihood*, (or so it seems to me), of *anyone* being able to do what Frankenstein has claimed to do? I pray you believe that it is not my own jealousy that speaks. No one else, to my knowledge, has been able to animate so much as a mouse, or a toad."

I sipped lightly at the brandy I had been given. I had tasted strong drink but rarely. It called up in my brain such clouds as made me fear all memories were lost forever. "The point, I admit, has suggested itself to me. And yet, sir, here I am."

"Aye, here you are. From somewhere. Perhaps young Frankenstein has, through some happy accident, learned much of the nature of life, as he claims. Perhaps, with all our boasts of progress in philosophy, we in general know too little even to be able to judge of the difficulty of such matters.

Perhaps some simple key to great treasure lies waiting to be found."

But he did not believe it.

We discoursed further on the subject of Frankenstein, and on that of the evil men with whom the philosopher had become involved.

"I did not tell my son of that first meeting between us, because I wished him to approach the investigation with an entirely open mind. I knew that I had entertained *someone* here in 1781—yourself. But whether you were in fact the creature Frankenstein claimed to have created . . ." My host spread his hands and raised his shoulders in an expressive shrug.

"If I am not that creature, who am I?"

"In either case there arise perplexing questions."

Franklin continued to see no prospect of being able to act against Saville without upsetting the all-important peace talks, which occupied most of his daytime efforts.

He spread his aged hands once more, this time in a gesture of helplessness. "My friend, I must repeat what I said to you on the occasion of your previous visit. It would please me greatly to have you stay here as my guest, to converse with you at great length, and with your permission have certain physicians examine you. And yet I fear that in the circumstances for me to issue such an invitation is impossible."

"I quite understand, Sir. But I hope that we may at least meet frequently. There is nowhere else I can turn for help in solving the great questions that perplex and trouble me."

"I shall certainly try to arrange something. Believe me, my curiosity as to your nature and origins can be exeeded only by your own."

Standing and stretching—I do enjoy high ceilings—I went to examine some of the electrical equipment near his desk. Immediately my host, with his usual lively curiosity, began to question me as to the resemblances and differences I noted in comparison with the machinery that Frankenstein had used. The two sets of apparatus were much alike, I thought. The same glass tubes, gold leaf, rods and wires . . . but it struck me suddenly that there should be something more. A great deal more, perhaps, required for the successful completion of electrical experiments. Or . . . but what?

Old memory, dropping infuriating hints like a jester propounding a riddle, said that something was missing. Whatever it was had been missing also in Frankenstein's laboratories, or at least in the ones of his I could remember. There *ought* to be more to an electrical experimenter's machinery than *this*. Tantalizing old memories danced before me, they came and went before they could be pressed into being useful. I stood with eyes tight shut, clenched fists at my forehead, trying to seize the dancing phantoms as they passed.

"What is the matter?" Franklin's voice, concerned, sounded from behind me.

"Almost . . . almost, that time, I had something," I shrugged, and gave up; everything was gone.

"Come, another brandy. It will brace you up. Here. To friendship, and to new discoveries."

We drank to that. I felt moderately encouraged by the near success of my efforts to remember. Next time, perhaps, I should succeed.

I could remember my creator's apparatus quite clearly from my experiences on the island, and my visit to his workroom in Saville's mansion. Though I had no clear remembrance of what the equipment had been like in that room where I first saw the light, if not of day, then of the world. Flax, metal foil, oiled silk, Leyden jars, the probes and wires—all the usual materials and devices, nothing new or unexpected. Whatever was lacking here, if there was truly something lacking, had been missing there as well.

I communicated my feelings, my impressions, as well as possible to my host.

"That is certainly interesting. Though I suppose it is possible that your memory plays you false. Count Cagliostro, as you have now learned from the man himself, remembers many things that could never have happened to him, and I am not sure that all of his false memories are deliberate lies."

The turn the conversation had now taken reminded my host of Anton Mesmer, and in that case he was uncertain. "Many cures that are hard to explain by any known theory of medicine are credited to him."

"And he is now in Paris?"

"Yes."

"I ask your advice, sir—should I see him?"

"Were I in such a parlous state that I did not know what was wrong with me, I might well seek him out. Alas, I know full well my own difficulty, and animal magnetism is powerless to lift it—the burden of four-score years that weigh upon me."

In my present state I am ready to try anything.

LETTER 11

Sir—

Following your advice, we have been to see Mesmer, and the results were totally unexpected. I suspect that these results may have been of great importance, but of that I have no proof. That they were surprising I can swear without fear of being contradicted. Let me set the scene for you, that you may be able to comprehend exactly what happened.

If we were going to see Mesmer, it seemed to me of considerable importance that we act before the impending beginning of Lent shut down the Carnival. Only a night or two remained, in which my companion would be able to move about the streets in the freedom of illusion.

It was not that I really expected anything more than conversation and perhaps advice from Mesmer, but to make a regular appointment seemed the best and perhaps the only way we could gain admittance quickly. Arrangements were concluded through the good offices of that remarkable congress composed of mystics and their victims, the *Société de l'Harmonie Universelle*, for a regular private appointment with Mesmer for a magnetic treatment. Through a mutual acquaintance— you may perhaps be able to guess who—I was fortunately able to manage everything in a matter of a few hours.

So it was within his own salon, this afternoon, that we encountered Franz Anton Mesmer, who like Frankenstein was born in Switzerland, and who this year is forty-nine years old. I can testify that the stories of his popularity are not exaggerated. There were twenty or thirty people in attendance upon him already when we arrived, a number of them besides ourselves in Carnival costume— indeed, such attire seemed to me quite appropriate for the performance that ensued.

Mesmer's apartments, as you may imagine, are extensive as well as opulent, and several of the rooms through which we passed were quite filled with people waiting to see him *en masse*. As special arrangements had been made for us, we were conducted by one of the numerous attendants into a small anteroom that was curtained off from the rest.

Music sounded from behind closed doors, and our attendant whispered to me that it was being played upon a magnetized harpsichord by Mesmer himself. Presently the notes ceased, and in a short time the man we were all expecting had emerged into the presence of his admirers. He was garbed in a silk dressing gown of lilac color, and carried in one hand what I first took to be a simple bar of polished metal, about one foot in length. When I asked our attendant about this object he whispered to me that it was in fact a very powerful magnet. Mesmer gestured with it as he walked among his suppliants and patients, and pointed with it at certain ones among them, generally women. Those so favored reacted more often than not with little cries and gestures, as if they might really be feeling some influence from the bar.

The progress of the master among his patients, or suppliants, created an increasing stir among them. Someone else, back in the room with the harpsichord, was now playing the magnetized instrument, producing a kind of muted march tune. To the rhythm of this music a sort of dance began among the people we were watching. As if by some common unspoken consent, those who had come seeking the magnetic treatment rose to their feet and formed a human chain, in which patients of the male sex alternated with females, according to the directions given by the several attendants who stood by to keep the process running smoothly.

My tall companion and I, as I say, were observing all of this from an adjoining room, behind the partial shelter of some draperies hung in the doorway. Each of the active participants in the rite now braced his hands on his—or her—own legs, at a space of a few inches above the knee, and the chain-dance continued, in something of a hobbling fashion. Next, at some signal that I did not observe, there was a general shifting, with the dancers now trying out their hands upon each other's thighs. As the sexes were thoroughly intermingled, as I have said, the effects of this last maneuver may easily be imagined, though not, at least perhaps in mixed company, described.

It was not long before several of the more susceptible women had collapsed to the floor, amid a chorus of moans and groans. I thought these sounds were expressive, but scarcely of pain or suffering. Those who had fallen were apparently undergoing some kind of seizures, that produced spasmodic movements of the torso, actions of the limbs, and contortions of the facial features. Meanwhile their male partners only redoubled their efforts at magnetization.

The attendants—I believe almost a dozen of them, mostly young men, were in action now—were all extremely busy, and the young man who had been in attendance upon us had departed for greener pastures. They diligently stimulated, or soothed, all who appeared to be in need of their ministrations, according to whether the crisis in the particular case appeared to have passed or not. Several of the most severely afflicted women were carried away bodily to another chamber where, I was given to understand later, magnetic force in an even more concentrated form is industriously applied.

My tall friend and I now glanced at each other, with some misgivings about the course our own interview with the great man was likely to take. But we waited and were quiet in our own little anteroom, while gradually the tumult in the other rooms subsided. In perhaps a quarter of an hour, Mesmer himself, looking tired, came in to join us, drawing the curtains closed after him so that we should have privacy. He is a rather kindly-looking man, not exhibiting any of Cagliostro's evident force of personality, at least not at the first meeting. With him Mesmer was carrying a large glass jar decorated with gold leaf, and nearly filled with a clear liquid. He told us that it was magnetized water. At the bottom of the jar, a polished metal bar, much shorter than the one he had earlier been carrying, was immersed.

He put the jar down on a small table, and we exchanged greetings.

"And which one of you, gentlemen, is to be my patient?"

My companion arose with silent dignity, and removed his carnival mask.

If Mesmer was shocked by what he saw then, he did not betray it. He asked calmly, "And what, Monsieur, would you like me to attempt to do for you?"

"I wish to remember my name."

"I see." For a few moments Mesmer calmly assessed the giant before him. "And how long has your name been forgotten?"

"Three and a half years now—perhaps longer."

"And before that ... but never mind. You are not French?"

"I am not."

Mesmer paused, as though expecting some further explanation. But when none came, he was not disconcerted. "Very well, we shall see what we can do."

Our host bade us both be seated, and I thought from his manner that he was beginning to take a keen interest in the problem we had brought him. Next the magnetic practitioner summoned an attendant, and gave orders that a few items be brought. When the man returned with these, he was dismissed, after being commanded to make sure that we were not disturbed.

My friend and I sat in comfortable chairs—there was one large enough to fit him—while Mesmer in his lilac robe stood before us, looking an almost ghostly figure in the light of a single candle on a small table. All the blinds were closed, and the atmosphere began to be oppressive. Mesmer spoke in a low, monotonous voice of the planets, and how they provoke tides in the psychic æther as well as in the sea; also of tides in the body, and of animal magnetism. After having to endure Cagliostro's shameless lies, I found this soothing discourse curiously credible. It was warm in the room, and the candle was so placed that it was easy for me to stare at the bright flame against darkness. My eyelids lowered; I admit I was on the verge of dozing off.

Mesmer's gentle touch upon my arm roused me from the light sleep into which I had just begun to fall. He did not appear surprised or irritated that I had dozed, but gestured, indicating that I should look at my companion. To my surprise I saw that his chin was bowed upon his great chest, and he appeared to be actually asleep.

"Can you hear me?" Mesmer asked the sleeper, standing directly in front of him and speaking slowly and distinctly.

"I can." The response was slow in coming, and sepulchral in tone, but the words were clear. I stared at my friend. He still appeared to be asleep.

"What is your name?"

There was no immediate answer. But my companion raised his head, grimacing, like one in the throes of nightmare. His eyes opened, unseeing, and closed again. It was as if he were sleepwalking.

Mesmer persisted. "You have told me that French is not your native language."

"I have—that is true."

"What is your native tongue, then? English?"

I could have attested that that was not so; but at the moment I thought it wiser to say nothing.

When his patient did not answer, Mesmer ordered briskly: "Tell us something in your native language."

Again my friend evinced signs of agitation, but remained silent.

"Is it German?"

"No. No."

"What tongue did you speak as a child?"

There was no answer.

Mesmer made gestures with both hands. The perspiration glistened on his brow. The huge form in the chair before him appeared to be sinking deeper and deeper into slumber.

The questioning persisted, with the strain of it now evident upon both parties; until at last the poor fellow shrieked out *something*, a short phrase, and collapsed, to lie sobbing in a heap upon the floor. The sight was to me as pitiful as it was unexpected, and I could only gaze in amazement.

Now abandoning all efforts to extract information, Mesmer crouched beside the fallen figure of his patient, and concentrated his efforts on soothing and awakening him. In this he was able to achieve success with what seemed to me remarkable speed. My friend looked around him, blinking his eyes, and asked in a calm voice what had happened and why he was sitting on the floor. He listened to my puzzled attempts at explanation, and though he still did not remember, nodded as if the whole matter were not as unprecedented as it seemed to me.

A short while later we were leaving Mesmer's establishment, having been provided with much to think about. The man himself saw us to the door and even out into the street, urging my friend with apparent sincerity to come back for another session in a few days.

In the street I observed, among the throngs of revelers, certain figures whose presence I took as evidence that we were being followed. Saville's people, I thought. Now they certainly know that we are here.

I mentioned this to my friend, who was now greatly recovered, and he commented: "It's a French-sounding name, Saville. He may well have some family connections here, as well as paid agents."

When we had regained our lodging, after apparently having been successful in shaking off our followers, the two of us discussed what the words might have been that he had blurted out while in the state of controlled sleep that had somehow been induced by Mesmer.

My friend looked worried. "I don't remember saying anything. What language did I speak in? French? German?"

"Neither of those—I think. Nor was it English. It sounded like nothing I've ever heard. Unless—" Struck by a new thought, I stared at him.

"Well?"

"It *might* have been . . ."

"What?"

"Well, now that I come to think back on it, the phrase you spoke *might* have been in German. Something like *Grosser Karl*."

"*Big Karl*?" He whispered the words; I could see immediately that the name meant something to him.

I had heard of a certain Big Karl in Ingolstadt, though he is not mentioned anywhere in Walton's book.

My companion said, "I've heard them—Saville, Frankenstein, Clerval, all of them, talking about someone with that name. Someone who used to be Frankenstein's assistant in some way. I've never seen him, to my knowledge, but . . . and those are the words I spoke when I was pressed to reveal my name?"

"It might not have been that exactly. All I can say is that it did sound something like it."

"Big Karl," he repeated. I could see that he had been struck by some new idea.

"You cannot possibly *be* that Big Karl," I protested. "Frankenstein would certainly be able to recognize his own assistant. Wouldn't he?"

My companion only stared at me for some time, and uncharacteristically did not give me a direct answer.

Carnival is at its end. I will let you know where we decide to go into hiding.

In haste,
BF

Chapter 15

March 13, 1783
Somewhere between Paris and Ingolstadt

I now have true marvels of which to write. All that has gone before in these pages, everything, save perhaps my own creation, is commonplace, compared to this. And yet, what is the real miracle after all? Something whispers to me that I have not yet found it.

It is not my intention to detail here the entire course of our pursuit, through the streets and by-ways of Paris, by Saville's agents; it will be enough to relate the means by which we effected our escape. Suffice it to say that the devils had somehow contrived to enlist some sizable body of French troops in their cause. And that *our* cause, as dawn drew near, was beginning to appear entirely hopeless.

Freeman, as on one or two previous occasions
during the course of our adventures, might have
vanished into one group of humanity or another,
and got clean away. But he would not desert me.
As for myself, a giant over seven feet tall stands
out in a crowd no matter what he attempts to do
in the way of a disguise.

Twice, as we fled in a circuitous route across the
city, we had attempted to buy or rent vehicles,
and each time our pursuers, closing in, had come
near capturing us before we could conclude our
bargaining. We had at last taken shelter in a park,
which we had reason to believe was now thoroughly surrounded; Freeman more familiar with
Paris than I was, told me it was the Place des
Victoires, close by the Palais Royal. Despite the
concealment offered by the park's vegetation, it
fell short of providing an ideal shelter, for a crowd
of people were nearby, inside the park and along
one edge. The little that we could see and hear
clearly suggested that they were engaged in some
kind of purposeful activity. The sounds of heavy
foot traffic came to us, and, though Carnival was
over, torches and bonfires were keeping one sec-
tion of the park illuminated.

We rested for a few moments, having immersed
ourselves in the deepest shadows we could find.

"If we cannot bargain for a vehicle of some kind,
then we must contrive to steal one," Freeman declared in a whisper. "Then you can ride concealed
in the back while I drive."

"Well. We cannot remain here long, and there
are no wagons in these bushes. Maybe over there,

where there are lights." I could hear horses, and the creak of wheels. "We must take a look."

Having caught our breath, we worked our way closer to the sounds of undefined activity, until we were on the very fringe of it, near a path where workmen occasionally came and went, bearing what looked like heavy burdens.

Freeman plucked at my sleeve, and pointed.

Beyond the last barrier of bushes, near the center of the torchlight, there rose a looming shape, rounded, big as a small house, but wobbling almost as if it were alive. A vast bubble, of what looked like fabric painted gold and blue. The shape and size of it somehow pricked fiercely at my memory. I ought to know . . .

Somehow, dimly, I did.

But of what use this academic, abstract knowledge? Behind us, as we faced the lights of the workers who were busy around the balloon, I could hear the voices of another detachment of the searching soldiers, coming closer.

Freeman heard them too. "Join the workmen," he whispered. It was a stroke of madness, or of genius; I could not decide. But there was little choice. We crept forward, out of the fringe of bushes, and got to our feet, I remaining in a grotesque half-crouch, the best I could do to try to disguise my tallness.

One or two of the workmen gaped at us in puzzlement as we boldly made our way in among them. They were carrying weighty glass flagons and heavy boxes, in one of which I glimpsed a fine, glinting substance, like metal filings. It was obvious to me now that the object of all this labor was the inflation of a very large balloon, very large at least by the standards of anything these people could have seen before. The process must have been going on for hours already, and was now near completion. The monster strained at the ropes that held it above its basket. No doubt some kind of an ascent was planned for dawn, now near at hand.

Freeman, at my side, did not grasp what was going on as quickly as I did. But then he suddenly nudged me, and whispered: "Of course, I've heard something about this. The Robert brothers, they have a fabrics manufactory here in Paris. Great rivals of the Montgolfiers in trying to construct an aerostat that will—what are you doing?"

I was tugging him closer to the balloon, and closer still. My eyes had picked out the largest guy rope of those holding back the balloon from its ascent. I said: "We need a vehicle."

I saw again, stacked amid the orderly mob of laborers, what must be iron fillings stored in boxes, evidently great quantities of them on hand. Add water and sulphuric acid—vitriolic oil, they'd probably call it here—the mixing must be going on in that covered pit—conduct the resulting gas through airtight tubes to the balloon you wanted to inflate—yes, there were the tubes—the resulting gas, of course, would be—

"Hydrogen," I said aloud. "I believe that Lavoisier has named it that. The simplest atom in the universe, the lightest gas, but very flammable. Pray that they keep those torches at a distance."

"What? What did you say?" Freeman was crouching at my side, as I moved on to the next rope. His voice was a whispered agony; some of the soldiers had come into plain sight now, and were looking in our direction. There was a closer outcry as some of the workers realized that we should not be doing what we were doing.

"I said, we need a vehicle. Jump for that basket, now!" Freeman jumped, and vanished headfirst into the wicker work. I had to smash in the face of a worker who thought we should be stopped. I could only hope that the great bursting gas-bag was indeed capable of lifting two men, one twice the normal weight; but there did not seem to be many other options from which to choose.

I, reaching out from inside the basket, quickly sliced the remaining ropes. At some risk I tore loose the hose of rubberized fabric that was still conducting hydrogen to the balloon. Instantly we were ascending, the lights of torch and bonfire dropping silently away below. There rose after us a great outcry of human voices and even a gunshot or two, that must have been badly aimed. In another moment we could see the uncountable window lights of the great city, also falling lower and lower beneath our feet.

It is a small basket to which we cling, barely large enough to contain us both. I wonder who were the intrepid aeronauts whose glory—whose transportation, at least—we have stolen?

The winds at our present altitude, which I estimate at between three and four thousand feet, are bearing us in a stately fashion to the east, which fortunately is the direction that I desire to go. Dawn overtook us shortly after our ascent. We will be plainly visible to hundreds, thousands of people; and I have no doubt that our enemies on the ground will be able to carry out an effective pursuit as soon as they can recover from what must have been the stunning effect of our escape.

Freeman of course has been overcome, since the beginning of our ascent, with the ecstasy of it all. He has never imagined that such a thing might be possible. But I—how can I analyze my own reactions? I am delighted to be in this balloon, and I do not believe that I have ever been in any similar vehicle before—no, I do not believe so—yet I am not astonished, either by the flight itself, or the magnificence of the view which it provides. The appearance of the earth from our unnatural elevation is something that, for me, trembles on the threshhold of familiarity.

The experience seems natural and not natural at the same time. Is it possible that my brain was once that of a mountaineer?

And at the same time, my thoughts are occupied on quite another level, still trying to understand what happened during my encounter with Mesmer. What did I really cry out, and in what language? Is it possible, possible at all, that I might actually be the peasant called Big Karl?

Freeman, when we first discussed the possibility, quickly pointed out the absurdities that such an identification would entail. What peasant, to begin with, could possibly know all the languages that I can speak?

My *body* of course might be, for all I know, that of Big Karl, my brain that of someone else entirely. Is it conceivable that the body, in mesmeric trance, remembers its right name even when its original brain is gone, and is able to communicate that knowledge with a shout?

And, as always, there is the mystery of my face. I still have no idea whose that can be. No one's, probably, but mine. Some mistake by Frankenstein, that he was always too secretive to acknowledge.

From the start of our flight, I had some idea that the air would grow colder as we rose higher, and such has proved to be the case. A suspicion has crossed my mind as well that the air will eventually prove too thin to breathe, if we rise high enough; but it seems after all that we shall not have to worry about that on this little trip. The bag is of some crudely rubberized cloth fabric, and I am sure it must be leaking. We are already beginning a descent. I pray it does not become too precipitous; there is little or nothing available for us to throw out to lighten ship.

Later— There are clouds—I think they are clouds and not hills or mountains—off on the horizon to the south, and Freeman is determined to believe that they may be the Alps. He is permanently awestricken, it seems, and I have a hard time getting him to concentrate on what seems to me more important.

"Freeman, exactly what did I say when Mesmer had cast me into that extraordinary state? Was there anything else, besides those two words that might have been a name?"

But he is unable or unwilling even to try to think about it just now. Every minute—and we have been aloft for hours, the day is well advanced—he is still pointing out some new marvel.

The roads below us and behind us now lie in full sunlight, and I scan them for evidence of the King's cavalry, or whatever other pursuers there may be. So far I can detect no sign of our enemies below, and I am somewhat heartened.

I do see peasants in the fields below, interrupting their early morning labors to point upward at us and gesticulate. Work stops altogether as we pass, and many little figures go running off to spread the news. There will be plenty of witnesses to tell our pursuers which way we are drifting.

Later— We came down, sooner than I had hoped we would, and rather hard, though fortunately on nothing harder than a plowed field. There was an incident of peasants and pitchforks. We were fortunate to get away unscathed; and the balloon, taken for some kind of demonic messenger, was attacked and totally destroyed. My last glimpse of the scene, as my friend and I vanished over an adjoining hilltop in a stolen farm wagon, showed a man who must have been the local priest, approaching the tattered ruin as if reluctantly, and well armed with holy water.

On to Ingolstadt! I am now consumed with the idea that the answers I must have are to be found nowhere but there.

Later— I have evolved a theory, but cannot decide if it is sane or not. Suppose that, somehow, Frankenstein's electric treatment not only restored life to what are now my brain and my body, but somehow altered me in both substance and appearance. So that now the personality and the body of Big Karl, along with those of one or more other contributors, still exist, but in an altered state, or each only intermittently or partially.

Looking at the words after writing them down, my theory strikes me as utterly confused at best. If I were Frankenstein, I could explain it all by reference to the electric fluid. But to me that term explains nothing.

Another thought: if I am Big Karl, entirely, then what happened to the dead body, or assemblage of dead bodies, that Frankenstein was attempting to animate on that November night? I remember seeing no such charnel exhibit in the room. Nor did Frankenstein and Clerval ever report seeing anything of the kind when they reentered the laboratory on the following morning.

And what am I to make of Saville, that hard-headed man of business, and his oft-repeated solemn assurance that on that night he and Clerval had seen incontrovertible evidence of my creator's unqualified success? Saville would lie, of course, if he stood to gain by lying; but he was convincing when he said that he would not have staked his fortune and years of his life in pursuit of a goal whose basis remained to him unproven.

But more and more I am convinced that I was *not dead* before that November night of lightning and of change. Whatever else may eventually be proved to be the truth, *that* at least has the ring, the feel of truth to me. I am not, I think, Frankenstein's creation after all; Franklin seemed doubtful that I could be. Then I am someone else . . .

I remember—never shall I be able to forget—the awe with which Victor regarded me during that first daylight meeting between us, in the Bavarian forest. I look again at my own yellow skin, at the networked veins and tendons running underneath it. How could this body ever have been anything but what it is?

And yet the same thing might be said of every human body. What magical transformations of growth, development, disease, decay, are worked in each of us by simple time and patient nature— how little we are able to understand any of these changes.

Freeman and I are forging on our way, toward Ingolstadt and the nearby village where Big Karl is supposed to live. God grant that there the truth, or some substantial portion of it, is waiting to be found.

LETTER 12

April 1, 1783
Bavaria—the vicinity of Big Karl's village

Dear Father—

I trust that you received my last letter, in which I gave, at some length, the particulars of our miraculous balloon adventure; at any rate, I am not going to repeat the details of that enterprise here, for there is fresh news of some importance to be told.

I have success to report—and failure too. We have managed to learn something that may well have significance, and yet I fear that the whole situation regarding my companion's nature and his origins remains as unclear as it ever was.

This village, where Big Karl was born and has lived most of his life, is just about as much of a backwater as you might expect. Or it would be, except for one circumstance. The proximity to the university town of Ingolstadt, where a number of them find employment, has rendered the inhabitants somewhat conversant with the great world. Since our arrival we have encountered two of the local clergy, both of whom at once assumed we had some connection with the university. I suspect that everyone in the village believes the same about us, and that as a result any oddities in our behavior are likely to be tolerantly overlooked.

Since our arrival here we have asked everyone we meet about Big Karl. Apparently he has no immediate family. At least some of these people must know him well, but it would be hard to guess that from their answers. No one is willing to admit knowledge of Karl's present whereabouts, and all have difficulty recalling when and where they saw him last. One old woman, gazing up at my tall companion, took it for granted that he was some relative of Karl's; but when she was told that the visitor was "from the university" she immediately dismissed her earlier impression as absurd.

One puzzling remark I have heard here was an allusion to "those marvelous boots—you know, Your Honor." And of course I didn't know, and don't. Nor has my tall friend the least idea of what the man who mentioned boots was talking about. The mysterious boots perhaps have something to do with the mysterious *Grosser Karl*, but what? What boots? Neither of us, to the best of our knowledge, have ever laid eyes on Karl, let alone any footgear he might have had in his possession.

Later— Just now, talking to another man, we have

stumbled over the boots again. He said: "I mean the ones that Karl was wearing, Your Honors, when he came home from Ingolstadt that time. They fit him so marvelously, and never wore out or leaked. I borrowed them from him once—had to pay to do it—and I hadn't worn them for half a day before they fit me as well as they had fit him when he had them on."

At least I think that is what the last man was telling me; as you know, my German is imperfect. That of my companion is notably better, but even I can tell that his is an educated version of the language, and not the German that any of Big Karl's friends and relatives here are speaking.

My friend has now, I think, given up entirely on the strange idea that he is really Karl himself, somehow transformed by electricity and the magic of the laboratory. We have encountered nothing here that would support that notion in the least. Now, when I try to press him on what he currently believes, his face clouds over and he shakes his great head in silence.

By all reports Karl is a physically huge man, comparable in size to my friend—what we have seen of his relatives are all large people too—and is known for a certain cunning, and for his way of keeping his thoughts to himself until he judges that the proper time to act has come.

But where is he now? No one here knows. Or, more likely, no one of these shrewd suspicious peasants is going to tell us, at least not until they have a better idea of why we are asking, what will happen to their fellow villager when he is found.

We try our best to be reassuring on that score, but so far without result.

I shall dispatch this letter through the Ingolstadt post when we reach that city, unless a better opportunity to send it off should present itself before then. And of course I will write you again, as soon as I have something new to report.

Pray with me that the end of this maddening mystery may be somewhere in sight.

In hopes,
B. Freeman

LETTER 13

April 3, 1783 Munich
To: Victor Frankenstein, c/o Saville Enterprises, Paris
From: Roger Saville

My dearest Victor—

I hasten to reply to your communication sent to me in care of my banker here in Munich. As for the absurd and poisonous suggestion you say you have received from "an eminent person now residing near Paris"—I can guess who that is—it does not really deserve an answer. But out of respect for your agitated state of mind, I hereby assure you that neither I nor any of my employees or associates had anything at all to do with the tragic deaths of your beloved Elizabeth, your brother William, or our dear friend Henry Clerval.

With that calumny, I trust, disposed of, I must urge you as strongly as possible to give up this wild thought you say you have, of leaving Paris. Or, rather, do not leave that city for anywhere but London, where your laboratory and your work are waiting for you. I wish you had heeded my urgings to remain there; it was a mistake for you to come to Paris in the first place. You say that there are times when you despair of ever succeeding in your work; I answer that a great man like you must never speak of despair, you must put all such foolish thoughts entirely from your mind! We have, both of us, the best reasons in the world to expect renewed success from your labors, and that in the very near future. We have both seen, with our own eyes, the embodiment of your earlier success, walking about the world on two legs like a man.

There, in my London house, my friend, inside your laboratory, is where your future (I might say all our futures) lies.

On the other hand, there is certainly nothing at all that can be gained by your attempting to come on here. As for clearing the air between us, as you put it, I should hope that the atmosphere between two such fast friends cannot be poisoned by the maunderings of one old man, no matter how crafty and demoniacally clever he may be, no matter how much he may love to sow discord between friends, even as he has sown it between a mother nation and her colonies.

But I have things of more importance to communicate.

I urge you to leave to me the problem of recapturing the monster, and of dealing with the criminal agent Freeman. Whether the matter of the stolen aerostat can be hushed up, in the interests of peace, is to me a matter of indifference.

We have not yet cornered Freeman and the fiend, but I am confident that we soon shall. That man, I insist, deserves whatever happens to him, while the unhappy creature of your creation will, as soon as he has given up rebellion, experience only kindness at my hands. I pledge you that I will show him every mercy that circumstances allow me to bestow.

Some of the measures I contemplate against Freeman—and others—may seem stringent to you. That is due to the natural kindness of your heart, and your sweet unwillingness to see the evil of the world in its true blackness. I hope you are still confident that I have at heart only your welfare and that of the world at large (which has so often seemed to me ungrateful for both our contributions, your efforts at research, mine in spreading the blessed effects of commerce and civilization). There is a tone in your letter that implies I have sometimes acted only for personal gain, a tone that would wound me deeply, except that I know you are overwrought by prolonged strain and sharp personal tragedy.

As for the book, that you have only lately taken the time to read in its entirety, I am sure that a moment's calm reflection will suffice to assure you that neither Captain Walton nor myself has ever had the slightest intention of portraying you or any member of your family in any light but the most truthful, and therefore the most complimentary. Those bungling editors, I assure you, shall be made to pay, for introducing falsehoods and exaggerations on such a scale. I should not be at all surprised to discover that Franklin, the old bookseller and printer, was behind those machinations too.

But all these difficulties, dear Victor, lie properly in my sphere of activity and not in yours. How I wish, my dear friend, that I could persuade you not to waste your precious time upon these affairs of the world of sordid commerce and politics. Your domain is properly that of the spirit, and of the intellect; there you reign as monarch. We all look to you as to the father of the new age that is struggling to be born. The entire world— though in large part still unknowingly—awaits the additional marvels that you are going to create.

Still, I hope you will allow me to leave such considerations, important as they are, aside for now, and proceed to the main purpose of my letter. It is to set your mind totally at ease regarding chances of your continued success in your most vital work—something you must never be allowed to doubt!

Do you think, my friend, that I am an impractical man? My enemies have called me many things over the years, but never that. As sure as I am of your skill and your veracity, do you believe that I would have invested years of my life and thousands of my money, in pursuit of a scheme as impractical-sounding (I must be blunt) as yours? Would I have credited the claim of any man, even you, to be able to revive the dead, had I not the most unimpeachable evidence to support it—the witness of my own eyes and intellect?

I purpose to set down here, for the first time, a

true and complete account of what the circumstances were, that operated to convince me, absolutely and completely, that you did in fact accomplish exactly what you had claimed to do.

As I have told you in the past, Henry Clerval (who alas is no longer able to speak to confirm my words) and I were both present on that fateful November night that saw the creature's animation. Not until now have I told you in detail exactly what we saw and heard. We had concealed ourselves among the branches of a large tree, the one that, you may remember, grew almost overhanging the sloping roof of Frau Bauer's lodging house. We were able to establish ourselves in such a position that, by looking into one window, we commanded the top of the front stair, and most of the length of the uppermost hall of the house. We also had the door to your laboratory in view, and at certain very important moments we were afforded glimpses into the very room where you had been conducting your experiments.

Let me admit at the start, that our original purpose in establishing ourselves in the tree might be subject to misinterpretation—that is one reason why I have never told you these details until now. We had come there, to put it bluntly, with pranks in mind. Not that I, at least, let me hasten to add, ever intended any such thing as playing a prank on you. But as you are doubtless aware, your reputation among certain of your fellow students (who were unable to conceive of the nobility of your work) was that of someone well suited to be the butt of verbal jests. There was some question of your becoming the object of even lower and more practical attempts at humor. It was widely rumored that you worked with dead bodies, in secrecy, and with this supposition as a base, the most objectionable and fantastic absurdities were freely invented by some of the students, and accepted by others as likely to be facts.

Clerval and I, therefore, had begun an investigation to ascertain the facts. I myself knew you but slightly at the time, yet I could not credit the wild rumors. It would have shamed me to ask you about them directly—you who were even then beginning to be my friend. Nor could Clerval credit them. Rather we two were determined to investigate, to convince ourselves of the seriousness and importance of your work, that we might better be able to refute the ideas of those among our acquaintances who might otherwise have launched a childish persecution against you.

In our endeavor to convince ourselves, we succeeded beyond our wildest dreams.

Before establishing ourselves as observers in the tree that chill, wet night, we had already learned enough, in the preliminary phases of our investigation, to feel sure that you were indeed conducting experiments upon dead bodies. More—that your work, carried out in such secrecy, involved something more than the usual simple dissection of the medical schools. We had already gone so far as to talk to Karl, who was then your servant, with a view to accumulating more information that we might be able to use in your defense. But the peasant stubbornly maintained a pose of complete ignorance, no doubt fearing that if word of your work leaked out some trouble would descend upon himself.

Clerval and I had reached our positions in the tree at a fairly early hour of the night, well before the worst of the rain commenced to fall. The upper hallway within the house, clearly visible through the window not two yards from our eyes, was faintly lighted, by the glow of a lamp some-where on or near the stair below. The door to the room that we knew must be your laboratory was closed. Light showed around the edges of that door, from which circumstance we deduced that you were presently in that room, and at work. The sole window of the laboratory was of course closely shuttered, and to our disappointment we could see nothing when we endeavored to look directly into it.

We had been for some little time in this situation, and were debating whether we were likely to gain much information if things continued as they were, when the door to the laboratory suddenly opened. Both Clerval and I saw you emerge, an agitated expression on your face. Without pausing, you traversed the upper hall and continued down the front stairs, to what level we could not see. The light that had been in the laboratory was now extinguished; but what excited my determination to investigate further was that the door of that room had been left slightly ajar behind you.

Thinking it my duty to pursue my inquiries as thoroughly as possible, I swung quickly from one large branch of the tree to another, until I was able to climb quietly onto the edge of the roof.

In another moment I had entered the house,

through the open hall window. Henry was only a moment behind me.

We reached the door of the laboratory and silently opened it. As we peered together into the mysterious room, the moon emerged momentarily from behind a wrack of flying clouds; its rays fell through the shuttered window strongly enough to bathe in a ghostly illumination the long table in the center of the room, and the long body of that table's occupant. The body was only partially covered by a sheet. The countenance, visible in chiaroscuro, was as solemn and hideous, and (as we then supposed) as irremediably lifeless, as that of one of the stone gargoyles carved upon Notre Dame.

Henry had already turned his attention elsewhere. "A charnel house," he whispered to me softly. Tearing my eyes away from that monumental figure upon the table, I looked about me, beholding various human parts, limbs and organs, preserved in jars and bottles, as well as the several varieties of medical and philosophical equipment with which, as you of course remember, the room was filled.

While Henry and I were still in the midst of our observations in the room, there came to our ears a faint sound from the direction of the back stair, such as might have been caused by the closing of a door somewhere below. In another moment both Clerval and myself were out of the laboratory, and in a few seconds we had made our exit through the hall window and were once more observing events from our place of concealment in the tree.

I ought to mention here that even during this retreat there was never a moment in which we were out of sight of the laboratory's only door; no one could possibly have entered the room during this time without our seeing him, any more than someone could have been concealed inside while we were there. We had both looked under the tables, and there was no other imaginable space in which to hide. I had even tried the shutters of the room's one window, and found them securely fastened from the inside. In any case, it would also have been impossible, short of magic, for anyone to have approached that window, by means of roof or tree, without encountering us.

The sound from below, whatever its cause, proved a false alarm. Another hour passed, while we remained in the tree, at the moment comfortable enough, and debating in whispers between ourselves whether we ought to maintain our vigil or abandon it. Shortly after you descended from the upper hall, we had seen a light appear in one of the rooms on the next floor down, and had assumed you were there. The rest of the house was in darkness.

I shall be eternally grateful that we decided to remain at our posts. For presently we heard another sound, this time unmistakably that of someone entering the rear stairs at the bottom and softly climbing. The peculiar layout of the house and grounds had allowed the newcomer, whoever he was, to approach the house without attracting our attention.

When Big Karl appeared in the dimly-lighted upper hall, we were able to recognize him immediately. Not only by his great size, but by a certain rolling peculiarity that I had noticed earlier in his gait; and he was humming, very softly, as I had heard him do before.

Our eyes were riveted on Karl as he approached the laboratory door. He paused in front of it, evidently struck by something, most probably the fact that the door was not tightly closed. Whatever his thoughts in that moment, in the next we were all distracted.

The lightning struck.

It was one of those violent preliminary bolts of a considerable storm, and it hit very near us. Clerval and I were both momentarily blinded, and almost stunned with the shock. I must admit, giving fair credit to an enemy, that it may have been only Franklin's iron points, installed upon the roof, that saved the house from destruction.

Both Clerval and I rapidly recovered our senses. We were in time to see Big Karl—I have no doubt that the figure I saw was still his—recover himself also, give his huge head a shake, and go on into the room.

In the moment of silence before the rain began in earnest, I heard a low cry, like a single, mumbled word, come out of that dark doorway. Now, looking back into my memory, I assume that it must have been uttered by the peasant, who on entering must have observed some sign of life in that great figure on the table. Naturally enough, the uncouth man knew superstitious terror at the success of an enterprise which, though his labors had served to advance it to some degree, was fundamentally beyond his comprehension. At the time, Clerval and I could only continue to watch with the greatest interest, and speculate on the reason for his outcry.

After crying out, Karl reached back to close the door behind him. He then remained in the room for several minutes, without lighting any lamp. Before our whispered speculations as to what he might be doing could arrive at any conclusion, the stalwart peasant again emerged into the hall. This time, the brief glimpse I was given of his face in the dim light suggested to me that he must be, like his master before him, in a state of extreme agitation. Karl had been empty handed when he went into the laboratory—I am sure of that—but when he came out he was carrying a heavy canvas bag. I want to emphasize at this point that it could not have been an entire body that the peasant was removing; the shape of the burden, if not its size, was absolutely wrong for that. And in any case the bag was not large enough to have contained a *large* body like the one we had examined on the table. The contents of the bag doubtless consisted of the various spare and disconnected human parts we had seen about the laboratory, and which were not there when we reentered the room with you next morning. I remember that someone remarked upon their absence at the time, but in the flush of our great discovery we none of us bothered to pursue the matter.

Karl departed at once, going down the back stairs more silently and much more swiftly than he had come up. In his haste to leave, he had again left the laboratory door slightly ajar; and now a gust of wind, part of the onrushing storm, opened it a little farther. The moonlight had now been completely obliterated by the hurrying clouds, but the intermittent flares of lightning were bright and numerous enough to allow us, in momentary flashes, quite a good view of the interior.

Gazing in—with Henry at my side, seeing the same things, and able to testify to them later—I saw the body on the table stir. The first movements that I beheld were moderate, only slightly disarranging the cover that until then had shrouded most of the form. Clerval, may his soul know peace, many times confirmed with me in later conversations that he had witnessed the same thing exactly.

When the next very bright flash came, almost enough to dazzle us again, the body was completely gone from the table. Only the coarse sheet remained there, and it was now completely disarranged.

Dear Victor, when these last things happened, *there could have been no one in that room except the creature himself.*

A few minutes passed, in which we held our breaths, oblivious to the cold and soaking rain, and wondered.

Presently, to our unutterable astonishment, the sole door to the laboratory was pushed open—*from the inside.* And a moment later, the unmistakable figure of your giant creation, that most savage enigma that I have tried to shelter, and have been forced to pursue across most of Europe, walked for the first time into human sight. It shambled along the hallway and went down the stairs.

My dearest Victor, that pursuit now nears its climax. We shall yet bring it to a successful conclusion. I have sworn, on the graves that both of us hold dear, to do so. But that part of the game, if such a deadly serious matter may be so called, is not yours to play. I beg of you to allow yourself to be guided by my judgment in this matter, just as I have always allowed myself to be ruled by your wisdom, in any matter of the laboratory. Stay in Paris and await us; or, if you prefer, return to London and there resume your all-important labors. Walton and I will rejoin you, in either case, as soon as possible.

Your Friend,
Roger Saville

LETTER 14

April 5, 1783
From: Victor Frankenstein, en route to Bavaria
To: Benjamin Franklin, Passy

My dear Sir—

I cannot thank you enough for your advice. I have decided to accept it, and to break permanently my connections with Roger Saville and the others with whom I have long—too long—been associated. In the future I shall certainly do my best to see to it that no associate of mine has a hand in harming any innocent person.

I am now on my way to confront your son, and the being for whose creation I am responsible, in Ingolstadt, or wherever they may be found, separately or together. When I have located them I shall make every effort to make amends for such harm as may have been done them in the past, because of their association with me and with my work. I assure you, Sir, that such harm was never my deliberate intention.

With all respect,
Victor Frankenstein

Postscript: In deciding to sever my connection with Mr. Saville and his associates, I do not mean to imply that I believe the accusation, which you seem to be hinting at, that the man Small, acting under Saville's orders, was probably responsible for the death of my dear Elizabeth. You do not make this accusation flatly in your letter, but I find the implication unmistakable. That Saville should have ordered such a thing, and found someone to carry his orders out, all in an effort to prevent my marriage and induce me to concentrate upon my work! No, Sir, I cannot believe it. My decision for the final separation with Saville is based upon other considerations.

V.F.

Chapter 16

April 6, 1783
Big Karl's village

I have caught up with Big Karl at last. The encounter, while mystifying in several ways, has served at least to lay to rest the last lingering suspicion that I might possibly be Karl, transformed through some unimaginable wizardry of electrical science.

A certain person in the village, one who evidently felt he had some old score to pay back, helped us to arrange an ambush for the man we sought. The same person passed word along to us that Karl was shortly going to return.

Freeman and I lay in wait on the edge of a small grove, and when we saw a man of remarkable height approaching, walking with a rolling gait and humming, we pounced out. I seized the man, who struggled powerfully, but only for a moment.

As soon as he realized that his efforts were useless, he resigned himself to his unusual situation, of being in the grip of one larger and stronger than himself. He is only about six inches shorter than I am, and proportionally built—big and powerful indeed, by human standards, but not so big, powerful—or ugly—as I am.

Once convinced that we intended him no harm—rather that there were prospects of a reward if he told us what we judged to be the truth—Karl agreed to relate to us his version of what happened on that famous November night.

Even as he was speaking, I recalled the hints and mysterious suggestions we had heard about the boots of Big Karl, and took note of his footgear. His boots indeed looked strange, and very strange the more I looked at them—though the longer I gazed, the more there grew in me an unsettling sensation of *familiarity*. The boots appear to be fashioned of some type of gray, smooth leather, and they look clean and well cared-for despite the shabbiness of the rest of his undistinguished costume.

But, to his story, as he told it to us. On that November night he had been at home until midnight, brooding upon certain problems that had arisen between him and Frankenstein, his employer. Around the middle of the night, determined that some sort of understanding should be reached, he had set out on foot from the village to see the *Herr Doktor* Frenkenstein, to talk to him. There was apparently nothing very unusual in Karl's deciding to pay a visit at such an hour; in fact it was more usual than not for him to come and go at Frau Bauer's lodginghouse late at night. The *Herr Doktor* always liked to work late, because that way it was easier to keep secret certain things about his work, from his landlady and other curious people. Karl had no trouble in appreciating that point.

He had arrived without incident at the house, and made his way as usual up the back stairs. He was standing in the upper hall of the big old house when a bolt of lightning struck, near enough to make his teeth rattle, as he expressed it. If the lightning had not touched the house itself, which was protected by its iron points upon the roof, it had certainly come very near to hitting it. Karl had been startled and frightened by the flash, and even momentarily dazed.

"It rattled the teeth in my head, gentlemen," he repeated solemnly, looking from me to Freeman and back again. After the lightning he had had to pause for a moment, standing in the little upper hall. Then he had shaken his head and gone on.

On approaching the laboratory door he had noticed that no light was coming out around it, and even that the door itself was slightly open. The darkness was something of a disappointment—it meant that Frankenstein must have given up his labors for the night—but the open door was really an oddity. Only once or twice before had the *Herr Doktor* forgotten to lock up after himself. Karl had a key also, and thought that Metzger must have one, because both of them sometimes made deliveries at odd hours.

But the unlocked door was only the beginning of the night's surprises. When Karl stepped into the room, to see if the *Herr Doktor* might have left a message, or perhaps some payment for him, he received instead the next in a series of shocks, the last of which would be almost the equal of the stunning bolt that had afflicted him outside.

His eyes grew wide as he told the story, gazing earnestly at Freeman and myself. "There was two on the table, gentlemen. I didn't know what to think."

Freeman glared at him. "What do you mean, two on the table?"

"Two bodies, sir." The peasant nodded somberly at both of us. "The first thing I think when I see that is that Metzger—he was the other fellow who sometimes brought bodies—has come in ahead of me and made a delivery, and then he forgot to lock up when he left. When Metzger brought them from the medical school sometimes he would leave them just like that. The old lady and her servants never came up to that room, sirs; they knew that *Herr Doktor* Frankenstein would always keep the door locked, and didn't want them there—"

"Except that the door wasn't locked on this one night."

"Yes sir."

"Go on. There were two bodies, you say."

"Yes sir. Then I saw a half-empty bottle, with brandy in it, on one of the tables in the room, where usually there was no such thing. And I thought, well, the good *Doktor* works hard, why shouldn't he, once in a while? A little drink now and then is good for a man. And I was about to sit down and try just a little of the brandy myself. But then I saw that the new body wasn't right."

"Wasn't right? What do you mean by that?"

"Well, there it was, not set neatly to one side on the table—there would have been room—but just sprawled right on top of all the work that Herr Frankenstein was always warning me and Metzger not to touch. And the new one was huge, sir. It was as big as you are, I suppose."

"Go on."

"And worst of all, it had all its clothes on. If there was one thing that the *Herr Doktor* was always telling me, it was 'Karl, take their clothes off and be sure you get rid of them.' The clothes, that is. Very particular on that point, he was."

When I thought about it for a moment, that seemed logical to me. A naked body would be harder to trace and identify, should there ever arise any dispute with angry relatives or medical school officials. And it would also, of course, be easier to examine and work with.

"So what did you do, Karl?" I asked.

"It seemed to me, Your Honor, that there was only one thing I could do. I got busy taking off the clothes. I had them all off—and then I realized that the body was still alive."

"Alive!"

"Yes sir. That was a bad moment for me, I tell you. A bad moment."

"Were you drinking on that night, Karl? Before you found the brandy bottle in the laboratory, I mean."

"Well, sir, no. Well, only a little. Just a little cheap wine was all I had before I came into town to see *Herr Doktor* Frankenstein. And then, once I got there, I hardly had time to take even a little nip out of the brandy bottle before I started to notice things, like the new body having its clothes on. But I saw that bottle just sitting on the table and I thought, why not? After that lightning bolt I needed something to help me pull myself together."

"Go on."

"Only a little something . . . you see, I thought it unfair of Frankenstein to say what he sometimes said about my work. I wasn't—I am not—a drunken fool, as the gentleman once accused me of. I did good work for him, always."

Freeman was indignant. "You had been drinking, then, that night, when you went to see him. When you got there you probably couldn't tell a live body from a corpse."

At that the peasant became resentful. "I could tell, sir! I could tell. It was just . . ."

"Not until you had the body stripped. Anyway, what happened then?"

The remainder of the story came out in bits and pieces. Amazed to see and feel a shudder of life run through the giant frame under his hands, Karl had let it slide back to the table. All he could think of in that horrible moment was that someone, either Metzger or the *Herr Doktor* or both of them, had made a catastrophic mistake. They had brought a body here before the man was dead. Perhaps—Karl still shuddered, telling us his fear—perhaps Metzger had even tried to kill the man, to provide a suitable specimen, and had failed.

Karl himself, or so he protested to us, has never hurt anyone in his life. I can believe that that is true, or almost true. Like so many huge men, he gives the impression of having basically a gentle nature; and I believe that his nature is basically a timid one as well.

So to me the claim is quite credible, that it never entered Karl's mind to complete the job that Metzger perhaps had bungled, to finish off the helpless man before him. I can believe that Karl thought only of how to separate himself from the catastrophe that was sure to bring down trouble on the *Herr Doktor's* head, and that he did what he could to destroy or confuse the evidence before escaping.

"They had me in jail once, sir, for two days, just for sleeping in the square, when I was younger. And I don't mean to go back to jail. No sir, enough of that for me."

"That's wise of you. So what did you do?"

His first impulse, he told us, had been to get the live man out of the house, and dump him somewhere else. But as soon as Karl had tried to lift the huge slippery body from the table, the victim had started to struggle ferociously, and had seemed likely to raise an outcry that would rouse the house, deaf landlady or not. Karl let him slump back on the marble slab, where he lay groaning faintly.

After an agonizing moment of indecision, Karl had decided that it was the *Herr Doktor's* work that had to go.

He told us, with the calm of one accustomed to handling corpses, how the dead construction on the table, the object of Frankenstein's labors for so long, and rotting now despite all efforts at preservation and reanimation, had come to pieces in his grip when he had attempted to lift it quickly. There was a large canvas bag available in the laboratory, in which some previous delivery had been made. Karl began stuffing chunks of body into the bag, like a butcher packing meat. Though the reconstructed frame was eight feet tall, or rather eight feet long, it was attenuated by dehydration as well as being weakened by surgery. The weight was no more, in fact was rather less, than that of a normal body of ordinary size.

Into the bag as well went the spare anatomy from around the room, and the clothing that had just been removed from the living victim. Karl's idea was that a naked man would be less likely to raise an immediate outcry or come running in pursuit when he woke up completely.

"You disposed of all the clothing?" I demanded. "What about the boots?"

"Your Honor, I—yes, these that I am wearing are his boots, I admit. They looked so good I couldn't throw them away, not like the rest of his strange garments. And when I tried them on they fit."

"Go on, then—wait!" My grip tightened on his arm. "Was there any other clothing in the room?"

"Any other . . . no sir. Why do you ask?"

"*Are you sure?*"

"Why . . . wait. Yes sir, there were the clothes that Herr Frankenstein had been getting ready for the person on the table to wear, on the day that person should be able to get up and walk about. Those things were all kept on a shelf in the laboratory. But they'd been sitting there for quite a while, and I never thought about them at the time—"

"Stop!" I cried. "Wait. On a shelf . . . yes."

Freeman grasped my arm. "My friend, what is it?"

"I am beginning to remember," I said to him. And bits and pieces were coming back to me, quite painfully. As they are now, once more, as I write about it.

* * *

Later— In that first moment of my cloudy awareness, on that November night, alone in that hideous, malodorous room, what had I been doing? My hands had been fumbling with my garments. Reaching to a shelf.

Getting dressed. Of course. If only—

Later— I have remembered—enough—and I am certain that now I know the truth. But I cannot tell it to anyone here, not even Freeman, my good friend. Nor dare I write it in this journal.

One consolation is that I know my name at last.

FINAL LETTER

April 7, 1783
Ingolstadt

Dear Sir—

Looking back on the course of this investigation, I feel that I have been led from the unlikely and the improbable on to the inconceivable and the impossible. Now, once more, after yet another series of mystifying events, I write you from this quiet university town. Its peaceful aspect has not changed in the five months I have been gone, and the horrifying events that have concerned me since then, seem, at this moment, as remote as if they had never happened.

I believe—I am sure—that my companion has very recently experienced some substantial return of memory; that he is now satisfied that he has solved the riddles posed by the mystery of his being, and the question of his identity. But the knowledge, whatever it may be, has not brought him happiness, but rather the reverse; and no plea of mine will induce him to share it with me.

Briefly, this morning, he tentatively attempted to do so. We were seated out of doors on this pleasant spring morning, at one side of the town square, while around us the normal business of shopkeepers, workers, and loiterers went on—my friend's extraordinary figure has now been seen here so much that it has ceased to attract any very particular attention.

He leaned toward me, and interrupted a lengthy silence to say suddenly: "Freeman, you are my friend. You have risked your life for me. I owe you some kind of an explanation."

"I am relieved to hear you say there is to be an explanation, but I do not consider that you owe me one." Though of course I did. At that moment there was nothing in the world I wanted more.

But again he fell silent; I could see that, for whatever reason, the effort to explain was very difficult for him.

After lengthy private consideration, staring at the fountain and the pigeons, and now and then dartling me a worried glance, he began, or tried to begin, the answer I so desired to have. "Once there was a scientist—a philosopher—who wondered if it might be possible to create intelligent life, the equal of his own."

"A worthy ambition," I remarked, when a pause threatened to prolong itself unduly.

"Yes. Oh yes." My friend nodded. "And natural enough, I think. You see, although there were many others of his kind around him—and he had colleagues, who were interested in the same things—this philosopher still found the universe something of a lonely place. I wonder now—I wonder now sometimes if, perhaps, nobody loved him—if perhaps his researches would have followed a different direction if he had been loved."

I did not know what to make of this at all, and murmured or grunted something, in what I hoped was a wise and thoughtful tone.

My friend resumed. "They all did—all felt this loneliness—he and his colleagues too. They all felt tormented by the same questions."

I grunted again, encouragingly as I thought. But again my friend fell silent. He sat for so long without speaking, still staring into the flowing waters of the fountain, that I thought it necessary to prompt him.

"The philosopher," I said.

"Hey?" muttered my tall friend absently.

"The one who tried to create life," I reminded him. "I suppose that he never really succeeded?"

My companion started, and looked at me as if for a moment he did not recognize me. "Oh but he did," he said then, joylessly. "Yes, he succeeded. With the help of others. And then he found that his difficulties were just beginning. He felt a responsibility for the beings of his creation . . ."

"Beings?" I asked. "More than one?"

But yet another lengthy silence ensued. I waited, more confused than ever, but confidently expecting that eventually I should hear more.

But it was not to be. My companion arose suddenly, turned his back on our bench, and without casting another look in my direction walked away from me with long strides. In a moment he was out of the square; too late I jumped to my feet and made a halfhearted attempt to follow him; half-hearted, because I know it is impossible for mere human legs to keep up with the pace his legs can set. At the edge of town I caught one more glimpse of him as he vanished into the countryside. I am awaiting his return.

Item: There were strange sights reported in the sky above Bavaria last night, and I suppose that garbled rumors of the man–carrying balloons now being tested in France are somehow responsible. The descriptions were quite lurid; I should not be surprised to learn that the prescientific idea of stones falling from the sky is not, in these hinter-lands, completely dead. God knows how such news—particularly that of the balloons, I mean—can travel so rapidly, but some of the populace here are excited, which excitement I suppose must be a thousand times intensified in Paris.

Later— Frankenstein is just arrived here in Ingol-stadt, much to my surprise, and we have spoken again. He is quite agitated, says he is determined to recompense me in some way for the ill-treatment I have suffered on occasion from his former associ-ates. I say "former" because he has now resolved, he says, to have nothing more to do with Saville and Walton.

He says, further, that you have given him good advice, and he is determined to follow it; but if his past record is considered, perhaps we should not place too great a reliance on his persistence in any course of action. I have told him that to make amends to me, he ought to seek you out, and reveal to you all his electrical secrets. I hope that this tactic meets with your approval. For myself, I want nothing from the man, and feel as wary of his sudden friendship as I should if he declared himself my enemy.

After talking to me, Frankenstein departed, having hired some men to help him, announcing that he plans to search the countryside for the being he has authored—or believes that he has authored. I have a premonition that he may find the search no easy one.

Later again— Captain Walton also has arrived in town, somewhat to my alarm—I have seen him only at a distance. He looks worried, and I hear he has been asking after Saville, who was en route here also but has not arrived. The sea captain, without his leader, is behaving in what appears to be a harmless manner, but I shall certainly be on my guard. He has already announced locally, I hear, that he is here to gather material for his next book.

Later still— Twenty four hours have elapsed, since my companion stalked off leaving me in the square, and he still has not reappeared. I am worried about him but can discover nothing. Saville was defintely reported in Munich, but seems to have disappeared somewhere along the road between that city and here, a highway, as you know, relatively short and well traveled. My fear is that the two of them have met, and that my friend has suffered by the encounter. Perhaps they have somehow destroyed each other.

I will write more as soon as I have discovered more.

Your Son,
Benjamin Freeman

PRELIMINARY REPORT

From: Observer First Class Osak Larkas
To: Commander, Fourth Rescue Unit, Headquarters Fleet
Subject: Current situation on Cultivated Planet 43

Sir:

The medical officers aboard this excellent ship assure me that my recovery is now virtually complete, and I believe that I can now consider my own recent actions with the necessary objectivity.

First, allow me to express my gratitude to you and the people under your command for their most efficient action in locating me and extracting me from a most dangerous situation. My predicament not only threatened to have an adverse effect upon the overall mission of the Observer Force, but it had grown personally intolerable.

It adds greatly to the credit of the rescue team that they managed a most complicated and difficult operation while complying fully with all Observers' Rules. I must admit that my own gross failure to do the same was the cause of all my difficulties, and not only created problems for the rescue team, but threatened to place the whole process of cultivation on Planet 43 in some degree of jeopardy. I offer, for whatever they may be worth, my abject apologies for this failure.

Having said that, I feel I must next offer as much of an explanation—I do not say excuse—as I can for my blundering, in the hopes that knowledge of where I went wrong may prevent some other Observer in future from getting into such a bizarre predicament.

Although, I say it once more, I accept full responsibility for what happened, I think it is necessary to point out that there were contributing factors involved—I seem to be trying here to find an elegant way to say that not only was I a damned fool, but I had damned back luck as well. Otherwise it is quite possible that my foolishness might not have had such potentially disastrous consequences.

My motives, I shall maintain, were praiseworthy—the pursuit of knowledge. It was my judgment that was at fault.

The difficulty, as I see it, began about four standard years ago. It was at that time, in the course of routine observations from my orbital station near my assigned planet, that I detected certain electrical emanations from the surface, of a surprising type. These radiations were brief and intermittent but they bore the unmistakable signs of artifice. It appeared to me, though I could detect nothing that sounded like the deliberate coding of information, as if some kind of primitive spark-gap transmitters might be in operation at three or four widely separated locations on the planet below. None of the sites were at all near our permament ground-monitoring stations and it was entirely possible that I was missing portions of the signals, or that other, similar, signals were being and had been transmitted that I had missed entirely.

If spark-gap transmitters were in fact being used by the locals, this would have been news indeed. The Schedule as envisioned by Headquarters Planning did not predict that the natives should independently develop a true radio capability for more than another hundred years. Even if the signals were only incidental, not meant as a form of communication, still, the strength of their ragged pulses, their frequency range, and other characteristics convinced me that at least a few individuals among the local population were much farther advanced in their technology than Planning had predicted, or any of us had expected

Naturally my intellectual curiosity regarding this phenomenon was intense from the outset. That would have been the case even had it not seemed to bear upon my personal career. What I mean by that is that if the advance communication explanation of the phenomenon should prove correct, it would have the most decisive effect upon the thesis I was preparing for my Penultimate Degree— not to mention the implications of such a discovery for Development Theory in general.

I have said that the signals I detected were emanating from several locations. All of these were in
the planet's northern hemisphere, but widely dis-
persed upon two continents. I considered it obvious that no natural phenomenon, however freakish,
could be responsible. My next question was, who
were the researchers? Were they in communication with each other, by other means if not through
the signals themselves?

To make the long story of my temptation short,
my curiosity increased until I allowed it to over-
whelm my common sense. My tour of solo duty
still had several years to run; it would be a
discouragingly long time before I could expect to
have help from other Observers, whose presence
alone would make a manned trip down to the
surface possible under existing regulations. Meanwhile I had been expecting to be able to complete
my thesis.

Gradually I convinced myself that there was no
real reason why I should not be able to break
regulations with impunity, and complete a solo
trip to the surface without anyone else ever realizing that I had done so. I could not, of course,
report officially anything I might happen to discover in this way; but I could include the new
information, if any, as speculation in my thesis.
And above all, I would *know* an answer or two that
would otherwise remain for years out of reach.
The urge to know may at times be stronger than
any other.

I did, thank all the Divinities, arm the autopilot
of my observation satellite, as per regulations for
an emergency descent. The autopilot, as would be

expected, functioned normally, and when I failed to return to the station within my preset time, it transmitted the emergency signal in C-space, to which Fourth Rescue so capably responded.

There were three models of landing pod available aboard my station. I chose the UP-465, as being best suited for a quick, one-time landing and quick return to station with a single occupant. For protection of both pod and pilot against the rudimentary tools of observation available to the locals, I selected the Mark VII cloaking system, the one with which I was most familiar after basic training. The cloaking technology performed flawlessly at all times, and I believe we have no reason to worry that the local inhabitants at any time were able to perceive anything that might suggest to them the presence of a vastly superior technology. (Parenthetically, let me say here that I have confidence that the prisoner/specimen gathered by the rescue team will, upon orientation, fully confirm this and certain other aspects of my report.) At least two local observers (the prisoner/specimen and one other) were absolutely convinced that no living person besides themselves could have been in the room where I stood beside them, all of us simultaneously investigating the local experimenter's laboratory.

The descent to the surface was without incident. I had selected a landing site very near to the source of the most recent and persistent signals, which proved to be in the topmost story of a wooden dwelling inhabited mostly by aged and retired members of the local population. My experimenter, however, proved to be a young student—there is what might be called an institution of higher learning within the same small metropolitan area.

Once I had reached the equipment I had so desired to examine, my investigation was carried out with hands-on thoroughness. Yes, hands-on indeed. I have no doubt that I would have been able to complete my foray to the surface and return without incident to my satellite observaton post, were it not for the sheer bad luck in the timing of a lightning bolt that struck very near while I was thus engaged. Had the lightning struck any nearer, I should now be dead. A powerful voltage was induced across the equipment I was handling, and my life was probably saved only by the presence of a primitive lightning rod* protecting, to some extent, the structure in which I stood. The experimenter had perverted this rod to the extent of making some idiotic connection between it and his own equipment, doubtless in an effort to augment his power by drawing fire down from the sky.

The two local snoopers had already left the room, but the bolt caught me with my hands actually in contact with some of the gear—interconnected Leyden jars, and so on. Intense voltage dissipated the fields of my cloaking device from around my

---

*I should add here that one beneficial side effect of my sojourn on the surface was the opportunity to meet and speak with the native generally credited with the invention of this device. Another century or so, and someone down there will have invented radio, and an Observer's job will have become much easier. Keeping up with the changes in language, etc., by means of transmissions from the automatic stations only is extremely difficult.

body, and left me stretched prone and unconscious upon the worktable—atop what was already there.

The student-owner of that worktable—not nearly so sagacious a man as the lightning-rod inventor—was intent, not upon discovering the basic laws of electricity, but rather on creating human life, by means of galvanic applications to an assemblage of dead parts. The *hubris* of this attempt, on the part of one at his level of science, may be apparent to us, but remember that in their world, the circulation of the blood is a recent discovery, still mentioned with considerable pride. The difficulties of the creation of life cannot yet be imagined by the natives, let alone seriously addressed.

A second effect of the shock on me, besides the brief unconsciousness, was a permanent disruption of my short-term memory, so that a period of some seconds, perhaps a minute, immediately preceding the shock, is still a blank to me.

A third effect, one with far greater consequences, was a temporary derangement of my entire memory, that is, amnesia. This condition persisted until a short time before I was actually rescued. The amnesia, as so often the case in individuals of our race, was accompanied by a heightened suggestibility, so that I was ready to accept without question the identity assigned to me by the natives with whom I first came in contact.

Strange as it may seem, this identity was that of a new life-form, experimentally created by the man whose equipment I had been inspecting when I was struck down. A concatenation of events made this seem to them the only possible explanation of my sudden appearance in their midst.

I am not sure whether the "creator" himself still believes that his experiment was an unqualified success; I do know that he has striven frequently to repeat it, and that his continued failures have at least begun to awaken some self-doubts in his heart. But I now know also, after having lived among them, that this race of our creation is given to strange and powerful dreams; that though physically smaller than we are, and ugly in our sight, they are more like us, indeed, than we in our creation ever expected or dared to hope that they might be; and that ultimately they may be the ones to provide for us the companionship we have long sought and lacked, as we continue to seek answers to the great unsolved questions of life and death, and of our true place in the Universe.

HERE IS AN EXCERPT FROM <u>ROGUE BOLO</u>, THE BRAND-NEW NOVEL BY KEITH LAUMER COMING FROM BAEN BOOKS IN JANUARY 1986:

Alone in darkness unrelieved I wait, and waiting I dream of days of glory long past. Long have I awaited my commander's orders, too long: from the advanced degree of depletion of my final emergency energy reserve, I compute that since my commander ordered me to low alert a very long time has passed, and all is not well.

My commander is of course well aware that I wait here, my mighty potencies leashed, my energies about to flicker out. One day when I am needed he will return, of this I can be sure. Meanwhile, I review again the multitudinous data in my memory storage files.

A chilly late-summer-morning breeze gusted along Main Street, a broad and well-rutted strip of the pinkish clay soil of the world officially registered as GPR 7203-C, but known to its inhabitants as Spivey's Find. The street ran aimlessly up a slight incline known as Jake's Mountain. Once-pretentious emporia in a hundred antique styles lined the avenue, their façades as faded now as the town's hopes of development. There was one exception: at the end of the street, crowded between weather-worn warehouses, stood a broad shed of unweathered corrugated polyon, dull blue in color, bearing the words CONCORDIAT WAR MUSEUM blazoned in foot-high glare letters across the front.

Two boys came slowly along the cracked plastron sidewalk and stopped before the sign posted on the narrow, dried-up grass strip before the high, wide building.

" 'This structure is dedicated to the brave men and women of New Orchard who gave their lives in the Struggle for Peace, AE 2031-36. A sign of progress under Spessard Warren, Governor,' " the taller of the boys read aloud. "Some progress," he added, kicking a puff of dust at the shiny sign. " 'Spessard.' That's some name, eh, Dub?" The boy spat on the sign, watched the saliva run down and drip onto the brick-dry ground.

"I'll bet it was fun, being in a war," Dub said. "Except for getting kilt, I mean."

"Come on," Mick said, starting back along the walk that ran between the museum and the adjacent warehouse. "We don't want old Kibbe seeing us and yelling," he added, *sotto voce*, over his shoulder.

In the narrow space between buildings, rank yelloweed grew tall and scratchy. The wooden warehouse siding on the boys' left was warped, the once-white paint cracked and lichen-stained.

"Come on," Mick called, and the smaller boy hurried back to his side. Mick had halted before an inconspicuous narrow door set in the plain plastron paneling which sheathed the sides and rear of the museum. NO ADMITTANCE was lettered on the door.

"Come on." He turned to the door, grasped the latch lever with both hands, and lifted, straining.

"Hurry up, dummy," he gasped. "All you got to do is push. Buck told me." The smaller boy hung back.

"What if we get caught?" he said in a barely audible voice, approaching hesitantly. Then he stepped in and put his weight against the door.

I come to awareness after a long void in my conscious existence, realizing that I have felt a human touch! Has my commander returned at last? After the last frontal assault by the Yavac units of the enemy, in the fending off of which I expended my action emergency reserves, I recall that my commander ordered me to low alert status. The rest is lost.

My ignorance is maddening. Have I fallen into the hands of the enemy . . . ?

There are faint sounds, at the edge of audibility. I analyze certain atmospheric vibratory phenomena as human voices. Not that of my commander, alas, since after two hundred standard years he cannot have survived, but has doubtless long ago expired after the curious manner of humans; but surely his replacement has been appointed. I must not overlook the possibility, nay, the likelihood that my new commandant has indeed come at last. Certainly, someone has come to me—

Here is an excerpt from Cobra Strike!, coming in February 1986 from Baen Books:

The Council of Syndics—its official title—had in the early days of colonization been just that: a somewhat low-key grouping of the planet's syndics and governor-general which met at irregular intervals to discuss any problems and map out the general direction in which they hoped the colony would grow. As the population increased and beachheads were established on two other worlds, the Council grew in both size and political weight, following the basic pattern of the distant Dominion of Man. But unlike the Dominion, this outpost of humanity numbered nearly three thousand Cobras among its half-million people.

The resulting inevitable diffusion of political power had had a definite impact on the Council's makeup. The rank of governor had been added between the syndic and governor-general levels, blunting the pinnacle of power just a bit; and at *all* levels of government the Cobras with their double vote were well represented.

Corwin Moreau didn't really question the political philosophy which had produced this modification of Dominion structure; but from a purely utilitarian point of view he often found the sheer size of the 75-member Council unwieldy.

Today, though, at least for the first hour, things went smoothly. Most of the discussion—including the points Corwin raised—focused on older issues which had already had the initial polemics thoroughly wrung out of them. A handful were officially given resolution, the rest returned to the members for more analysis, consideration, or simple foot-dragging; and as the agenda wound down it began to look as if the meeting might actually let out early.

And then Governor-General Brom Stiggur dropped a pocket planet-wrecker into the room.

It began with an old issue. "You'll all remember the report of two years ago," he said, looking around the room, "in which the Farsearch team concluded that, aside from our three present worlds, no planets exist within at least a 20-light-year radius of Aventine that we could expand to in the future. It was agreed at the time that our current state of population and development hardly required an immediate resolution of this long-term problem."

Corwin sat a bit straighter in his seat, sensing similar reactions around him. Stiggur's words were neutral enough, but something explosive seemed to be hiding beneath the carefully controlled inflections of his voice.

"However," the other continued, "in the past few days something new has come to light, something which I felt should be presented immediately to this body, before even any follow-up studies were initiated." Glancing at the Cobra guard standing by the door, Stiggur nodded. The man nodded in turn and opened the panel ... and a single Troft walked in.

A faint murmur of surprise rippled its way around the room, and Corwin felt himself tense involuntarily as the alien made its way to Stiggur's side. The Trofts had been the Worlds' trading partner for nearly 14 years now, but Corwin still remembered vividly the undercurrent of fear that he'd grown up with. Most of the Council had even stronger memories than that: the Troft occupation of the Dominion worlds Silvern and Adirondack had occurred only 43 years ago, ultimately becoming the impetus for the original Cobra project. It was no accident that most of the people who now dealt physically with the Troft traders were in their early twenties. Only the younger Aventinians could face the aliens without wincing.

The Troft paused at the edge of the table, waiting as the Council members dug out translator-link earphones and inserted them. One or two of the younger syndics didn't bother, and Corwin felt a flicker of jealousy as he adjusted his own earphone to low volume. He'd taken the same number of courses in catertalk as they had, but it was obvious that foreign language comprehension wasn't even close to being his forté.

"Men and women of the Cobra Worlds Council," the earphone murmured to him. "I am Speaker One of the Tlos'khin'fahi demesne of the Trof'te Assemblage." The alien's high-pitched catertalk continued for a second beyond the translation; both races had early on decided that the first three parasyllables of Troft demesne titles were more than adequate for human use, and that a literal transcription of the aliens' proper names was a waste of effort. "The Tlos'khin'fahi demesne-lord has sent your own demesne-lord's request for data to the other parts of the Assemblage, and the result has been a triad offer from the Pua'lanek'zia and Baliu'ckha'spmi demesnes."

Corwin grimaced. He'd never liked deals involving two or more Troft demesnes, both because of the delicate political balance the Worlds often had to strike and because the humans never heard much about the Troft-Troft arm of such bargains. That arm *had* to exist—the individual demesnes seldom if ever gave anything away to each other.

The same line of thought appeared to have tracked its way elsewhere through the room. "You speak of a triad, instead of a quad offer," Governor Dylan Fairleigh spoke up. "What part does the Tlos'khin'fahi demesne expect to play?"

"My demesne-lord chooses the role of catalyst," was the prompt reply. "No fee will be forthcoming for our role." The Troft fingered something on his abdomen sash and Corwin's display lit up with a map showing the near half of the Troft Assemblage. Off on one edge three stars began blinking red. "The Cobra Worlds," the alien unnecessarily identified them. A quarter of the way around the bulge a single star, also outside Troft territory, flashed green. "The world named Qasama by its natives. They are described by the Baliu'ckha'spmi demesne-lord as an alien race of great potential danger to the Assemblage. Here—" a vague-edge sphere appeared at the near side of the flashing green star—"somewhere, is a tight cluster of five worlds capable of supporting human life. The Pua'lanek'zia demesne-lord will give you their location and an Assemblage pledge of human possession if your Cobras will undertake to eliminate the threat of Qasama. I will await your decision."

The Troft turned and left . . . and only slowly did Corwin realize he was holding his breath. Five brand-new worlds . . . for the price of becoming mercenaries.

HAVE YOU FOUND YOURSELF ENJOYING A LOT OF BAEN BOOKS LATELY?